Praise for *Sisters in Arms*

"This is not just another World War II story; this is a stirring and timely novel about the only all-Black battalion of the Women's Army Auxiliary Corps, a group of women who had to fight resolutely against countless obstacles in order to be permitted to serve their country. . . . Poignant and powerful; an untold story that you simply must read."

—Natasha Lester, *New York Times* bestselling author of *The Paris Secret*

"A thrilling anthem to the courageous sisterhood of the Six Triple Eight as they faced down racism at home and war abroad. . . . A powerful debut!"

—Stephanie Marie Thornton, *USA Today* bestselling author of *A Most Clever Girl*

"A poignant story about perseverance in the face of difficulties set against the uncertainty and danger of World War II. . . . Readers will cheer and cry with these trailblazing women as they break free of their sheltered and restricted lives to overcome individual and societal prejudices and succeed in a world rocked by war."

—Georgie Blalock, author of *The Last Debutantes*

"Heartwarming but fierce, a novel brimming with camaraderie and fire, starring women you'd love to make your friends. . . . Kaia Alderson's debut is a triumph!"

—Kate Quinn, *New York Times* bestselling author of *The Rose Code*

T0146001

"Unflinching, at times brutal, this novel pulls no punches while delivering a richly textured and unforgettable story of determination, courage, and friendship."

—Janie Chang, author of *The Library of Legends*

"What an exciting new voice in historical fiction! I couldn't put down Alderson's novel of two young Black women testing their mettle and finding friendship and purpose during World War II. With fascinating historical detail and complex characters, *Sisters in Arms* casts a brilliant light on a group of women too long kept in the shadows."

—Kerri Maher, author of *The Girl in White Gloves*

"A triumph of immersive storytelling about heroic Black women who served their country despite discrimination. An untold story finally getting its due."

—Denny S. Bryce, author of *Wild Women and the Blues*

"Eliza and Grace come alive on the pages of this gripping and inspiring novel of friendship, sisterhood, and the bravery of the women of the Six Triple Eight during World War II. . . . An incredible debut not to be missed!"

—Eliza Knight, *USA Today* bestselling author

"Alderson beautifully describes the lead protagonists, Grace and Eliza, with care and complexity to showcase the rich diversity that exists in Black womanhood. . . . Grace and Eliza, as well as the life choices they make, lingered with me for a long time after I finished their engrossing story."

—Piper Huguley, author of *By Her Own Design*

In a LEAGUE of HER OWN

Also by Kaia Alderson

Sisters in Arms

In a LEAGUE *of* HER OWN

A Novel

KAIA ALDERSON

wm

WILLIAM MORROW
An Imprint of HarperCollinsPublishers

This book is a work of fiction. References to real people, events, establishments, organizations, or locales are intended only to provide a sense of authenticity, and are used fictitiously. All other characters, and all incidents and dialogue, are drawn from the author's imagination and are not to be construed as real.

IN A LEAGUE OF HER OWN. Copyright © 2024 by Kaia Alderson. All rights reserved. Printed in the United States of America. No part of this book may be used or reproduced in any manner whatsoever without written permission except in the case of brief quotations embodied in critical articles and reviews. For information, address HarperCollins Publishers, 195 Broadway, New York, NY 10007.

HarperCollins books may be purchased for educational, business, or sales promotional use. For information, please email the Special Markets Department at SPsales@harpercollins.com.

FIRST EDITION

Interior text designed by Diahann Sturge-Campbell

Baseball image © Daniel Thornberg/Adobe.Stock.com

Library of Congress Cataloging-in-Publication Data has been applied for.

ISBN 978-0-06-322838-2

24 25 26 27 28 LBC 6 5 4 3 2

For Effa—"Flowers"

In a LEAGUE of HER OWN

Prologue

Philadelphia, Pennsylvania
1923

I left my husband."

Effa Bush snatched a side glance at her mother as she waited for the woman's reaction. But Bertha Brooks did not give her twenty-six-year-old daughter the satisfaction of an immediate response. Effa thought she saw Bertha's mouth bend into a frown. But it was so fleeting, she might well have imagined it.

"Aren't you going to say anything?"

Bertha leaned back onto the bleacher bench behind them and sighed. "What would you like me to say? That I told you not to get married in the first place to a stranger you met on the beach? That you got lucky that he was a good man so now you're a fool all over again for leaving him?"

Bertha took a long look at her daughter. This was it. Effa held her breath. This would be the moment that her mother would really see her. Would finally understand her.

Bertha rolled her eyes and redirected her gaze forward. "No, I am not going to do any of that. What I am going to do is enjoy this game."

The game she was referring to was the one being played in the field before them. The Hilldale Daisies, the local Negro baseball team, was hosting the visiting Atlantic City Bacharach Giants that afternoon. Both teams had been around since 1916, not that Effa cared much.

"Stupid game," Effa muttered under her breath. She kicked at a crumpled candy wrapper that had blown over to her shoe. Even in this rare moment of one-on-one time, her mother could still easily ignore her—the one thing that Effa hated more than anything.

"What was that?"

"Nothing, Mother."

"That's what I thought." Bertha leaned forward as the next hitter went up to the plate. She clapped her hands, calling out, "C'mon, Biz. You've got this."

Biz. Of all the things to call a grown man. Effa didn't get the point of baseball. It was just a bunch of guys scratching themselves in inappropriate places, giving each other weird nicknames, tossing a ball around, and waiting for something to happen. From their seats way behind the outfield, she could barely see what was going on.

Everyone in America was infatuated with the game. But not Effa. She wasn't one to wait around for something exciting to magically happen. She was a woman of action. Or at least, she hoped to be. That's why she had left her soon-to-be ex-husband.

Effa had come to the game because, with six children in the family, it was the only way for her to have some time alone with her mother. Time alone to share that she was about to engage in the biggest social taboo—divorce—and that she was scared as hell.

A loud crack rang out as Biz Mackey's bat connected with the ball over home plate. The crowd erupted in cheers. The ball disappeared into the blue of the sky, then reappeared like a bullet headed straight for them. Everyone around Effa stood. If Bertha had had any thoughts about Effa's revelation, they were gone now.

Effa jumped to her feet too. The red stitches on the ball's seams became more pronounced with each passing second. Effa reached out, her marital problems and her mother's indifference about them forgotten. While she was aware of the pain that exploded in the palm of her hand, what had her entranced was the awe that she felt as she snatched the ball out of the air.

"You just caught a home run!" the man next to her screamed as he patted her back. "You're a mighty lucky girl. I've come to every game here for the last five years and that's never happened to me!"

Now the cheers were all for Effa. All the spectators in their section were directing their smiles at her. Her mother squashed her in an embrace. "My daughter caught the ball! My child!" Bertha's words were bursting with pride.

Effa clutched the ball to her chest, in awe of the amount of adoration that the small white leather sphere could inspire.

This was the moment that Effa Bush fell in love with baseball.

Chapter 1

Garment District, New York City
Summer 1932

"Try this one instead." Effa Bush removed the dated straw cloche from Mrs. Everson's head and replaced it with a more daring deep purple fedora. Effa fiddled with it until she achieved the desired effect. "See, isn't that better?"

Mrs. Everson admired her reflection, which revealed the high angle of the fedora's brim as it swooped over one eye. A netted veil cascaded over the edge to add to the hat's mystique. Effa had to admit that it was one of her more dramatic designs.

Effa Bush discreetly checked the clock just beyond her customer's shoulder as Mrs. Everson studied herself in the countertop mirror, turning her head to and fro. Ten minutes until the store closed. Good, still plenty of time to make it to her evening rendezvous.

"Effa, my girl, you are a genius! I would have never picked out anything like this for myself."

Normally, such praise for her work would have Effa beaming from ear to ear. She had been employed at Fleisher's Millinery Shop for almost a decade. Half those years had been spent on the sales floor while she learned the art of hat-making. It had been only recently that Mr. Fleisher thought her creations good enough to display in the front window of the store. But today was different. Effa's mind went back to the newspaper headline that had left her stunned that morning: "Aubrey Lyles Dead."

"It's amazing how much one step outside your comfort zone changes everything." Mrs. Everson chattered on, oblivious to the shopgirl's distraction. Effa nodded absently. "You're right, as always."

Mrs. Everson removed the hat from her head and thrust it back in Effa's hands. "I'll take it!"

Effa retrieved a hatbox from behind the counter while Missy, the newest shop apprentice, rang up the sale. Mrs. Everson was one of the sweeter customers who frequented the shop. She was also one of the younger patrons. Effa wouldn't be surprised if Mrs. Everson was around the same age as her—thirty-five. Effa was grateful that today of all days, she was waiting on her and not one of their more obnoxious customers. The shock and grief over Aubrey's death had sapped the otherwise never-ending patience she needed to deal with some of these people.

Effa finished padding the side of the circular hatbox to protect Mrs. Everson's new purchase and handed the box to her by the string. "There you go. Please come back with pictures when you go out and wear it."

Mrs. Everson was a bit of a socialite around Manhattan, so there were always pictures of her at one event or another in the newspapers. The girls in the shop constantly clamored to see which one of their designs had made it onto the society pages. To Effa's surprise, her innocent comment caused Mrs. Everson's lip to curl.

"I should hope not. You see, Sawyer and I have been wanting to check out one of those Negro clubs up in Harlem. You know, to change up our routine for a bit of fun. But my mother would faint dead where she stood if anyone even hinted that I had been in one of those places, much less had a picture documenting the fact."

"Oh." The showroom chilled despite the summer heat outside. Effa took an instinctive small step back from her now former favorite client. The venom with which Mrs. Everson had spit out her horror had been subtle but clear. Effa took a moment to purse her lips, trying to keep back the words that had almost come out of her mouth. The pay at Fleisher's wasn't great, but with the economy nose-diving, she needed this job. "In that case, your secret is safe with me."

She doubted her own secret would be treated with such care were it to become known. Except was it really a secret if no one had ever asked Effa about her race?

Of course not. Effa smiled to herself. If she had been asked about her race, Effa would have had no problem letting people know that, despite her pale skin, she was in fact a Negro. She had suffered enough careless slights from her customers about those of her race who were of a darker hue that the verbal arrows didn't sting as much anymore.

Well, they didn't sting so much that she would risk losing a job she loved. The majority of unmarried Negro women didn't have the luxury of earning a decent wage while doing something they enjoyed. They were lucky if they made enough to support themselves and keep their dignity. Even her coworkers, all of whom were white—as far as Effa could tell, anyway—couldn't always support themselves. Millinery wages were so poor that many women who worked in the industry were forced to prostitute themselves at night to make ends meet. Fortunately, the Harlem community created safety nets to save Effa and other Negro women from such desperate measures. It was a hustle, but by modeling in fashion shows, throwing rent parties, and selling the occasional hat of her own outside the shop, Effa had built a comfortable little life for herself.

Effa escorted Mrs. Everson to the door and was thankful when the woman was finally out of the shop. In that moment, Effa wished she possessed the funds to purchase a camera and a roll of film. Effa grinned at the mischievous thought, then quickly forgot about Mrs. Everson and her hate-filled words. Times were getting harder and harder for everyone around here, rich, poor, and in between. For a variety of reasons, she was lucky to have this job. Mrs. Everson and her foul attitude were not worth her sacrificing her livelihood. Besides, Effa was in no position to say anything about the right- or wrongness of someone else's double life.

However, Effa never went out of her way to hide who she was. People made assumptions about her and she no longer had the energy to correct them.

She turned the lock on the front door and pulled down the shade.

"Finally." She sighed. Effa could feel the weight of the mask she wore while she was at work ease. But only a little. Her thoughts drifted back to that headline announcing Aubrey's death. She still couldn't believe it. A decade ago, she had been on the fringe of his circle of vaudeville comedians and performers, courtesy of her then husband, a chauffeur for the theater owners on Broadway. Effa had taken advantage of the party invitations that her spouse had declined. In hindsight, she had been no more than a young woman basking in the residual glow of Aubrey's success as cocreator of *Shuffle Along*, the first Broadway show written and produced by Negroes.

But that was a long time ago. Those fun times ended when she left her husband and she no longer had the luxury of a childless housewife's lifestyle. Rent had to be paid, and money was needed for food. A working girl couldn't afford to stay out on the town all night.

Effa shook off the memories of her past and brought herself back to her present. She slipped into the back workroom, where Missy and the two other girls who worked in the shop were gathering their coats and bags.

"Effa, we're getting together at my place tonight before we hit the town. Maybe sip on a little something my brother brought back from his last trip up to Canada." Sally, who was forever hosting little get-togethers after work as an excuse to drink smuggled-in alcohol, waggled her eyebrows mischievously.

"Thank you, but I already have plans." Effa always declined these invitations, but that didn't stop them from coming. It wasn't that Effa was a prude or a teetotaler. She liked her drink just as much as the next person. But she just wasn't comfortable with having a drink—or two, or three—with *them*; the women she worked with were at least a decade younger than she.

"What about tomorrow night, then?" Missy countered.

Effa's good-natured smile fell. She wasn't sure when Aubrey's funeral would be, and she didn't want to miss it. "I'm busy then too."

"You *always* have plans, Effa," Missy whined, then poked out her bottom lip. Effa raised an eyebrow at Missy's childish behavior. The outburst was further evidence that Effa's instinctive reaction to decline was a good one. Even on one of her quiet days, the girl was a chatterbox who barely let anyone else get a word in edgewise.

"That is because I have goals. Goals that do not include working in this hat shop for the rest of my life."

"Humph. Well, whoever your 'goal' is, I hope he's a looker and good in bed." That got a laugh out of the rest of the girls. Effa forced herself to chuckle along with them, although the "he" she would be seeing tonight—her neighbor "Smokey" Joe Williams—was more interested in cork balls wrapped in yarn and leather than in making moves on her. Her melancholy lightened a little. Effa wanted to thank them for that but couldn't. The girls had no idea that her plans for the next night included attending Aubrey's funeral. And she had no intention of telling them.

"We'll see," Effa responded cryptically. It was always about men and sex with that one. Effa had been just like her when she'd first struck out on her own. Effa debated whether to tell Missy to take it easy on the giggle juice before she ruined her life.

But what did Effa know? It had been about a decade since her divorce from George, and she had managed to escape her young-dumb-and-in-love mistakes just fine. And she knew enough never to do *that* again.

"Okay. But next time, I'm not letting you get out of it so easily." Missy nudged Effa with her shoulder.

"Maybe," Effa said. She pulled on her dated straw cloche

hat, her fingers brushing the threadbare spot on the brim that her expert needlework hid. Expert or not, her skills still didn't keep the sun from beating down on her head, despite the shade that the Garment District's buildings provided.

The heat made her long for the coming autumn. It would bring a cool reprieve and, she hoped, a chance for her adopted hometown's baseball team to play in the World Series. Not that Effa deluded herself that she might score tickets to one of those games. She would need a miracle for that to happen. Or, more realistically, she would need to hit the numbers. The Harlem numbers racket was a godsend for her neighborhood whether you were rich or poor. Thinking of this, Effa picked up her pace as she trotted down the stairs into the Twenty-Third Street subway station. She needed to hurry up if she hoped to catch her numbers man today.

The 1 train was rumbling into the station just as Effa reached the platform. The car she entered wasn't particularly full, thankfully. She dropped onto the seat nearest the door and leaned her head back against the window. When she exhaled, the weight of the mask she had been wearing all day began to fade.

Effa never felt comfortable hiding her true self at work. But who would? If there was anything she'd learned from Mother, it was that there needed to be a clear separation between one's home life and one's work life. The blurring of the two could only lead to disaster. In Mother's case, she wound up with a baby in her belly—that baby being Effa—who had been sired by her white employer, not her Negro husband.

Not that Effa would ever consider herself a disaster. More like a complication that had worked out for the best.

For the next few stops, Effa swung her head from side to side to work out the tension in her neck. When she finally looked straight ahead again, she caught the white man sitting across from her staring. He turned away, then quickly sneaked another glance at her. And then he smiled.

It took a moment for Effa to realize that he was smiling at *her.*

"Hello." He flashed all his teeth at her. Effa blinked, confused as to why this white man was directing his charms at her.

"Hi," she replied. Now it was her turn to look away. She caught the eye of a Negro woman sitting a few seats from her. She was wearing the white-trimmed black uniform of a domestic. The woman was looking at her too. Effa mouthed, *What is wrong with him?* Effa gave her a quick nod. The woman responded by cutting her eyes in the white man's direction. Effa watched her lips press together into a weary frown. Then she shrugged as if she wanted no part of the shenanigans that were unfolding before her. The woman muttered, "I don't know. Figure it out."

She got up, gathered her bag, and moved to the opposite end of the subway car. *He wants you,* she mouthed.

Me? Effa mouthed back. The woman coughed a laugh behind her hand, then looked away.

The man swooped into the empty seat next to Effa. Effa, confused, scooted as far away from him as she could so their thighs wouldn't touch.

Then it dawned on Effa what was happening here. This man was interested in her. He had mistaken Effa for a white woman. And now it was up to Effa to find a way to make him uninterested without pointing out his error. If he figured it out, there was no telling how he would react.

Couldn't these Midtown people give her peace for just one train ride?

"I haven't seen you on this train before. Are you new in town?" He slid closer to Effa.

Effa shifted farther away. "No. Just happened to get out of work a few minutes later than usual is all."

"Is that so?" He held out his hand. "The name's James."

She took it reluctantly. "Okay."

"Aren't you going to tell me yours?" He held on to her hand a beat longer than was required by polite society. His thumb lingered on the back of her hand as she pulled it away.

"I don't think that would be a good idea."

He arched an eyebrow. "You're playing hard to get. I like that. Fine. I'm game. Where do you work?"

"You've probably never heard of it."

He nudged her arm with his shoulder. "Try me."

Why wasn't this James person getting the hint? All Effa wanted to do was close her eyes and let the sway of the subway rock her into a light doze until it stopped at her station.

"I would prefer not to. One, because I'm on my way to the funeral of a dear friend." She hoped Aubrey's spirit would forgive that small lie. "And two, because you probably have a sweetheart already and I am not a home-wrecker."

He grinned like he had just hit it big with the numbers man. "I don't have a sweetheart, sweetheart. I was kinda hoping that you might want to be mine."

The woman on the other end of the subway car rolled her eyes. She shot Effa a look of pity, and Effa bit her lip to keep it from curling in disgust. The man had completely ignored her mention of the funeral. Had he no shame?

Effa scoffed. Her mother encouraged Effa to take advantage of her looks and try passing as a white woman while she, in Bertha's words, "still had a chance." A chance at what? To subject herself to James's ridiculous behavior for the rest of her life?

Maybe a normal girl dreamed of snagging a man like James. From the way he was dressed, she could tell he had a good job despite the hard times almost everyone else had fallen on. Effa probably wouldn't have to work another day in her life if she just kept her mouth shut. But . . .

He was white. And she was not a normal girl. She had long grown out of the simple goal of becoming a well-to-do man's wife. She wanted more than just money. She wanted power. She wanted respect. She wanted to walk into a room and be impossible to ignore.

With him, Effa would never be able to achieve her ambitions. She would always have to hide who she really was.

"You flatter me. But I have other plans."

"I'd clear my schedule for the rest of my life for a girl like you."

Effa gave him a small smile. She felt the apples of her cheeks warm. They were no doubt blooming into a faint dusky-rose color. *Cute.*

The train's brakes screeched as they approached the 110th Street station. When the doors opened, the man stood and began to make his way off the car. He took one last look at her from the platform. His eyebrows creased with surprise when he found Effa still in her seat. "Aren't you getting off?"

"This isn't my stop."

He placed his hand on the doorjamb as if that could keep the train from leaving the station. "But this is the last stop."

"No, it isn't." Effa stopped herself from adding that 110th was only the last stop if you weren't going to Harlem.

He frowned as if he were having trouble putting two and two together. "Oh, you must be one of the holdovers in East Harlem."

Effa shook her head at him.

"You're one of those Jews who live in the Bronx?" He lowered his hand. The horrified expression on his face made her stomach drop.

Effa squirmed in her seat. She didn't like the way that his lip curled up at the word *Jews*. What made it even more surprising was that, if he was getting off at the Upper West Side, he most likely lived in a predominantly Jewish neighborhood.

The hairs on the back of her neck began to prickle. She did not like the turn this conversation was taking.

"No. I live in Harlem. Just like the rest of the Negroes." Effa smiled.

The subway doors slid shut in the man's face as it bloomed into an unnatural shade of crimson.

The woman in the maid uniform started chuckling as the train jerked back into motion. "You shouldn't have crushed that man's fantasy of you like that. He looked like he was ready to propose."

"Living a lie for the rest of my life is no fantasy of mine."

"True. But you could've strung him along for a time. At least long enough for him to make it worth your while—a mink coat or something."

The corners of Effa's mouth turned up in a sad smile. "That's the thing. Eventually, the stress of changing how you talk, of walking past your friends and family on the street as if they were strangers, of making sure each hair on your head is perfectly straight . . . it'll never be worth it. I'll just have to figure out how to get that mink on my own terms. Then no one will have cause to take it away."

The older woman chuckled again. "You pretty young thangs always think you'll take on the world in some way or another. But you'll learn. It's not your ambition that's the problem. It's that those kind of men will never give women like us a chance to act on our ambitions. Because when we succeed, they think it makes them look bad."

Effa nodded her head sadly, her thoughts drifting back to her former husband, George. He had claimed to love her at first. But over time, the word *No* had replaced *I love you*.

No, Effa couldn't get a job. Not even if it meant that they could afford to buy their own brownstone.

No, they couldn't go to the parties that would have elevated their social connections in the community.

No, he would not pay for millinery classes so Effa wouldn't be bored out of her mind twiddling her thumbs at home. That had been the final straw. Effa started stashing away the spare change from their grocery money. When she had enough, she paid for those classes, got the job at Fleisher's, and left her husband—and his *Nos*—for good.

George was Colored and she could damn near pass for white, but the reason he had blocked her every attempt to make a better life for them had nothing to do with race. It had everything to do with the fact that she had been born into a gender that was told it looked good in a skirt. That, and George's main goal in life was to be the wet blanket thrown over her.

Effa sighed. It had been almost ten years since she left George. And where had all of that gotten her? She was making a living on her own. Her life was no different than the one that George had provided for her back then, but it was hers and she alone called the shots. There was plenty of room to grow despite the increasing poverty and breadlines that had popped up everywhere on the streets of Harlem in the past three years.

If she believed her mother, Effa would think she was a living, breathing, walking disappointment. Bertha Brooks was always going on about how Effa had no children and no man. What she didn't understand was that Effa didn't want children. She never had. Growing up in a house with six children had killed any maternal desires she might have had. And she was okay with having no man at her side as well. As far as Effa was concerned, it was better to have no man than be dragged down by one who insisted on holding her back. It didn't matter what color his skin was—a drag was a drag.

The subway screeched to a stop at the 155th Street station. Effa nodded at the other woman. "This is me."

The woman took note of the station sign before sizing up Effa one last time. "I guess it is, honey. You keep being exactly who you are."

"Yes, ma'am. I will."

LATER, ALTHOUGH MUCH more relaxed, Effa still found it hard to show her true self to her neighbors at their roof party atop their apartment building. That was because she was trying to minimize her presence there as a boarder among the group of more legitimate residents. She figured most of them already knew that, though, and most likely didn't care.

What was important to them was that she fit the mold of the respectable middle-class community they cultivated. She hoped she did, but that was a hard order to fill when her neighbors included well-known poets, writers, and . . .

"Matthew Henson!" boomed one man in a linen suit with a cravat loosened at the collar. Effa recognized the stylishly dressed older man as her neighbor Dr. Du Bois, who was said to be the first Negro to receive a PhD from Harvard. He gave Mr. Henson a hearty pat on the back. "I bet you wish you were at the North Pole today."

Mr. Henson held a sweating glass of lemonade to his forehead. "I was not only the first man to reach the North Pole, I was also the first one to leave it. That place was too damn cold. This cool drink will do just fine."

Effa smiled as everyone else laughed. She made her way over to the less populated far corner of the roof. There sat a middle-aged gentleman with his back to the gathering. His attention was focused on Yankee Stadium, which was located right across the Harlem River from them.

She touched his shoulder lightly. "Are the Yankees winning, Smokey Joe?"

Joe didn't respond. From the way he was leaning forward with his elbows on his knees, Effa hadn't expected him to. The view inside the stadium wasn't great from their rooftop, but it was good enough that they could see the ant-size players on the field react every time the pitcher on the mound released the ball.

Effa settled into the canvas folding chair next to him. A breeze off the river brought a much needed reprieve from the day's heat. That meant that dusk would be upon them soon, and the game had to be nearing its end.

She knew better than to attempt further conversation. Joe had had a disappointing summer. Effa knew that he played baseball and that he had come home a few weeks earlier when the East-West League he was in folded. Since then, Joe could always be found right in this spot, watching the games at the stadium.

From Effa's viewpoint, it looked like one team was leaving the field as the other ran onto it. That's when Joe finally spoke.

"The Yanks ain't playing tonight. They're on a three-week road trip."

"Oh." Effa felt stupid. She supposed she would have known that if she'd paid more attention to the sports columns. "I didn't realize other big-league teams played at the stadium too."

"They don't," Joe said flatly. "Negro teams rent it out for exhibition games when the Yanks are on the road. Like tonight." He gestured toward the stadium. "The Pittsburgh Crawfords are playing against the Pennsylvania Red Caps."

"Really? I didn't know that." Effa knew that Negro teams passed through the city and the surrounding areas, but she'd never paid attention to where they played. She just assumed their games were held in schoolyards or in neighborhood parks. "Have you ever played at Yankee Stadium, Joe?"

Joe leaned back in his seat. His eyes held a gleam that she had not seen in them since he had come home from his interrupted season. "I've pitched on that mound a time or two."

"Wow. I'm impressed. But tell me, why are two Pennsylvania

teams playing in the Bronx tonight? I've never heard of the Red Caps before."

Joe spared a moment to turn and smile at her, then the crack of a bat against a ball yanked him back to the game. "They're the Pennsylvania Red Caps because the team is made up of redcap porters out of Penn Station in Midtown."

"Oh, that makes more sense." Effa leaned forward, mirroring Joe.

Joe, taking notice of Effa's interest, pointed into the distance. "You see there? How the outfielders are coming in closer and the infielders are almost on top of the plate? That means they think the batter is about to bunt."

"A bunt?" Effa barely had time to get the question out before cheers came from the stadium. Joe jumped to his feet as the little ant men scrambled around the field.

"My word. Look at that ball go." Joe went still as he took in the action. Effa stood up too and tried to follow what was going on, but she was too far away. She had lost sight of the ball as soon as the batter hit it.

Joe let out a long whistle. "I can't believe it. He hit that ball clean out of the park. I betcha that was that young fella Josh Gibson who whacked the ball like that."

"Josh Gibson?"

"I don't care what those white newspaper writers say, Josh Gibson is the greatest hitter to ever play the game. You mark my words, young lady."

The mention of newspapers and Joe calling her "young lady" brought Effa back to the sad headlines from that morning. Someone not too much older than her had died much too soon. Streetlights began to dot the landscape below. Another cooling breeze off the river swirled around them. Effa blinked back the tears forming in her eyes.

Joe's wife broke away from the rest of the gathering and waved him over. "Come here, honey, before you fall off the roof. I need you healthy and in playing shape for next year."

That was the out Effa needed; she could leave before the tears threatening to fall made her embarrass herself. "Oh my, that breeze. I think that's my cue to go back downstairs. Thank you for letting me sit with you."

Joe placed his hand on Effa's shoulder, stopping her. "You are here because you belong. You are part of our community. Don't let all their impressive résumés intimidate you. Those accomplishments were but one season in the long stretch of their lives. I might look like I'm past my prime, but I still have some gas left in my tank. You do too, Effa. A lot of it. So what if you're not where you wanted to be in life right now? Keep going. You never know what you might find around the corner."

Joe joined his wife at the refreshment table. Effa turned her back to give herself some privacy, no longer able to keep her tears at bay. She'd need the rest of the night to process Joe's encouraging words.

All it would take was one season for her to become "somebody" for the rest of her life. She was determined to make the next season of her life the one that counted.

Chapter 2

Harlem

The new season of Effa's life began a few days later as she stood at the end of a long line on 131st Street. She had worked through lunch so she could leave the shop early to pay her respects to Aubrey Lyles, but when she saw the line of mourners stretching between her and the funeral parlor, she realized it hadn't been early enough.

Effa tapped the shoulder of the woman in front of her. The woman shifted the infant she was holding from one arm to the other as she turned around. The baby's eyes fluttered open from the movement. Effa immediately felt bad for causing the child to wake up. "Excuse me, do you have any idea how fast this line is moving?"

"Oh, it's not that bad. Based on what I've heard from the people coming out, maybe a half an hour." The baby cooed. Most people would have found that adorable. But Effa wasn't most people. Yes, the baby and her big round eyes were adorable. But . . .

Effa hugged herself to hide her shudder despite the heat of the day. As one of her mother's middle children, she'd had a hand in raising two of her five half-siblings. She had had her fill of babies—no matter how cute they were—and their crying and their spit-up and their dirty diaper rags a long time ago.

"A half an hour. Are you sure?" Effa sighed. "It looks like all of Harlem is in front of us."

Shuffle Along, the Broadway show that had made Aubrey Lyles famous, had debuted in 1921. The musical had an all-Negro cast and was one of the first shows on the Great White Way to be written and produced by an all-Negro team. Aubrey, along with his comedy partner Flournoy Miller, composer Eubie Blake, and lyricist Noble Sissle, had made untold fortunes from their production. Effa had been right there to witness their rise from struggling vaudeville performers to bona fide stars. As a chauffeur for the Strand Theater, her husband, George, could have ridden their coattails and taken Effa along for that ride to the top. But her now ex-husband had lacked the ambition to do so.

In the eleven years since, the foursome had failed to recapture the magic of their first show. For that reason, Effa had assumed that maybe Harlem would not show up for its latest fallen star. But seeing the line that stretched down the length of the residential block, she realized she had underestimated her adopted hometown. Harlem had indeed shown up to give Aubrey Lyles a proper homegoing service today.

A brown and tan Lincoln K series car rolled past them and stopped in front of the funeral home. Excitement buzzed down the line. Someone farther up the street let out a long whistle. Yes, the vehicle was impressive. But Effa noted that it was in need of a good polish, and its tires, while not worn down completely, had definitely seen better days.

The woman in front of Effa patted the baby's back as a hopeful smile spread across her face. "I wonder who that could be."

Effa mentally scrolled through a list of possibilities. The struggling actors, dancers, and writers who had been a part of their circle back when she rubbed elbows with the theater crowd were now the most famous Negro entertainers in the country. It could be Andy Razaf, who had hit it big in '29 with "Ain't Misbehavin'," a song he cowrote with another friend, Fats Waller. Even Josephine Baker was a possibility. That is, if she was in the country. Baker had made her New York debut as a *Shuffle Along* chorus girl before becoming a sensation in Europe with her scandalous banana costume and dance routine.

The sound of a baby's burp yanked Effa back to the present. Effa took an instinctive step away as the child spit up on her mother's shoulder. She returned her attention to the car, trying to see who was inside it. She wasn't the only curious onlooker. She frowned at the crowd of people who had begun to surround the vehicle, blocking her view. The crowd moved as the car's door opened. The unmistakable egg-shaped dome of Eubie Blake's head emerged, distinguishable above all the people. Behind the famous pianist and Broadway producer was a shorter and less recognizable head covered by a netted beret that Effa would have known even if she had been a mile away. That was because, years ago, she had molded the shape of that beret with her own hands.

Maybe Effa didn't have to wait in this line after all. She was just about to leave when the woman shoved the baby into her arms.

"Here, hold her for a second, would ya?" The woman pulled

a balled-up rag out of her pocket and dabbed at the spit-up. She put the rag away and took the baby back. "There, there, baby girl. Everything's all better before you can bat an eye. All you gotta do is be patient."

Even though the woman was looking at the baby as she spoke, Effa felt like the words were intended for her. She gave the woman a smile as she watched a fashionable couple making their way up the stairs of the funeral home. *Unfortunately,* Effa thought, *I am not a patient woman.* Remembering what her neighbor Joe had said the other night, she told herself, *I am an ambitious one.* Then Effa Bush stepped out of the line and hurried to catch up to her old friends as they greeted the mourners closest to the entrance.

"Avis? Avis Blake, is that you?" Effa touched the back of the mink wrap her old friend wore. Her fingers sank into fur that felt like softened butter. The woman Effa remembered never missed a chance to show off the fine things her husband gifted her. It looked like not much had changed since Effa had last seen her, almost a decade ago—she wore her fur even though the day's heat was clinging to everyone like a damp winter blanket.

Avis turned around. Her eyes sparkled with recognition the second they landed on Effa's face. "Oh my word. Effa Bush, look at you!"

Effa's knees almost buckled, she was so relieved. She couldn't imagine how she would have recovered from the humiliation if Avis had failed to recognize her in front of all these people.

Avis wrapped Effa in an embrace. The scent of Avis's perfume teased her nose. Effa stepped back and crossed her arms. Her heart began to race for reasons that had nothing to do with the day's heat and everything to do with envy. Effa had no doubt that Avis has sprayed herself with Chanel No. 5.

Effa shook off the feeling and reached for her old friend's hand. It wasn't that she was jealous of Avis. True, she wanted all the things that Avis had. Correction—the things that her husband, Eubie, had bought for her. But Effa wanted to get those things for herself, without having to endure the drama and heartache Eubie had put his wife through.

"It's good to see you too, Avis. I can't believe that Aubrey is gone. He was so young!"

"Tuberculosis." Avis shuddered as if the Grim Reaper himself had set foot on her grave. "Such a nasty disease."

Whatever strain of envy left in Effa evaporated. A sense of despair took its place. "That's terrible. It kills me to think how he spent his last days on this earth locked up in that sanatorium."

Eubie came back down the stairs of the brownstone to collect his wife. "Come now, Avis. Time to go in."

Avis gave Effa a friendly shove and sandwiched her between herself and her husband. The gesture ensured that Effa would not get lost in the shuffle when they proceeded into the building. There was no question that Effa belonged with the Blakes. Now Effa was warmed by the sense of her own triumph.

When they entered the funeral home, the jovial air of renewed friendship thickened with the sad occasion that had reunited them. Electric fans were set up throughout the viewing parlor, but they provided little relief from the somber reality laid out before them. Their friend was dead.

As she approached the body, Effa couldn't get over how peaceful Aubrey looked in the casket. Clichéd or not, he really did look like he was sleeping. But he didn't look like himself. The Aubrey she knew had been vibrant and full of jokes, not this withered shell.

"I can't get over how much he looks like an old man." A sob caught in her throat.

Avis nodded. "He was only forty-eight." Effa clutched her handbag to her chest. Now it was her turn to feel Death's breath upon her neck.

Little more than a decade separated Aubrey's age from Effa's. He had achieved his greatest success in his thirties. And here Effa was at age thirty-five—divorced, working a dead-end job, and still figuring out how to make her mark on the world. What if she wound up where Aubrey was in thirteen years but with less to show for her time here on earth?

What if she died still a nobody?

The thought stopped Effa in her tracks. This time, the sob succeeded in escaping her lips.

"Are you all right, honey?" Avis reached out to touch her arm. A chill went through Effa. Had Death wrapped its icy grasp around her wrist? She pulled away, clutched her hand to her chest.

"I'm fine." But that was a lie. Effa's feelings were all over the place. It bothered her that she couldn't tell if the barrage of emotions overwhelming her came from the heartbreak of losing a friend too soon or from the shame of her own personal failure.

Avis patted Effa's shoulder and dabbed at her eye with a

linen handkerchief. Effa could see the monogrammed initials in the corner of the fine fabric. "There ain't no shame in getting emotional. This *is* the place for it, honey."

Effa agreed with Avis, except for one thing—they weren't the only ones in the viewing parlor. From nationally syndicated social columnist Gerri Dismond to New York City school board member Bessye Bearden, the highest echelons of Harlem society had shown up to give Aubrey Lyles a proper send-off. Effa took a deep breath, straightened her spine, and blinked back the waterworks that had threatened to spill out of her eyes a few moments ago. A crowd of this caliber didn't "do" falling out over the casket. And she wouldn't do it either. The last thing she needed was to have her name splashed in the *New York Age,* the *Chicago Defender,* and the *Pittsburgh Courier* for making a fool of herself. Effa would reserve those sobs for the privacy of her own bedroom. She'd rather save her debut in the Negro press for something more worthy of her ambitions.

But right now, Effa was determined to maintain a dignified appearance. These people would one day be the customers supporting her entrepreneurial endeavors. She needed them to believe that she belonged there among them. Because she did.

"Thank you. But I *am* fine. Let's have a seat. It looks like the reverend is ready to start the service."

Effa followed the Blakes to the sectioned-off reserved seats right behind Aubrey's family. But since she had not been a recently known business associate or friend, there was no reserved seat for her. Avis gave her an apologetic look as she attempted to scoot over in her chair to make room for Effa.

"We both know that little chair can't handle both of our

hips." Effa laughed awkwardly. "It's fine. I'll find something in the back."

Avis tugged on her arm before she got too far. When Effa looked at her, Avis placed a white rectangle in her hand. "This is my calling card," Avis whispered. "Keep in touch, okay?"

Effa nodded and made a beeline for the exit, her head held high. For a brief moment, she'd been one of them. She would not embarrass herself and give the eyes she felt on her back a reason to keep her out again. But then, despite herself, Effa turned around. When she did, she made eye contact with Mrs. Bearden. The woman smiled and said, "It'll be all right, baby."

Effa quickly turned away from her and scanned the room for an open seat. She managed to grab one near the exit where she felt the hint of a breeze coming from the front entrance. Good. It was already getting stuffy in the room. There were so many people there. Effa looked around. Even with the service starting and everyone facing forward, she couldn't shake the feeling that someone was staring at her.

She looked around again. And then she found the eyes that were indeed directed her way. Henry.

Effa felt her face grow warm. She should have kept facing forward. Her former lover—and the other reason her marriage fell apart, if she was honest with herself—was the last person she wanted to see. As far as Effa could tell, Henry paid not one lick of attention to the service.

He only had eyes for her.

When Reverend Garner finished the closing prayer, Effa hid amid the throng of people exiting the funeral home.

"Effa, wait!"

Effa couldn't tell if the voice calling her name was male or female. With her emotions all over the place, she was lucky she still remembered where the subway station was and which train was the right one to take her home.

She looked back only when the doors of the subway closed behind her. To her relief, Effa did not see any faces she knew among the people still waiting on the platform.

Effa told Avis she would keep in contact. That she would do, even though she knew Avis would read her the riot act for leaving the funeral parlor so abruptly. Effa could withstand that. Avis's wrath wasn't what caused her bottom lip to tremble.

What Effa did fear was that she didn't have the strength to resist Henry Clinton's charms. Not on a day like today. Not now, not ever again.

New York City
September 1932

As Effa had expected, it didn't take long to resume her friendship with Avis. Effa had sent her a short note apologizing for leaving the funeral without a proper goodbye. She dropped the note in the mail the day after, then forgot about it.

That is, until Effa woke up to a thunderous knocking on her apartment door a few weeks later. "Effa, are you in there? Get up! Let me in!"

"There had better be a fire." Effa groaned into her pillow at the interruption to her sleep. She fumbled for the wristwatch that she had placed on the side table. It was half past nine. Half past nine in the morning on one of her rare weekdays off, to be more precise.

The heavy beating on her apartment door started up again.

"Who is it?" Effa yelled. She grabbed her throat. Yelling like that was uncharacteristic for her. It was downright unladylike.

"Effa, darling, it's me, Avis."

Effa crawled out of bed and let the woman in before her landlord woke up and found reason to put her out. Avis barreled her way into the flat as soon as Effa opened the door a crack.

"Put on something decent and get yourself together."

"Why?"

"Because we are going to the World Series, darling. The Yankees are playing and I have tickets!"

"How?"

"It doesn't matter how. All you need to know is that we're going. Now, git!"

Once Effa was a little bit more awake, she quickly got herself together. She had planned to watch that afternoon's game, but from the roof of her apartment building.

"Avis, I think we'd have a better time watching the game from my roof than at the stadium," Effa called from the wash-room. "My neighbor will be there. He used to pitch for one of the Negro teams. He gives the best play-by-play explanations. He and his wife are such a hoot."

Avis scoffed. "Darling, you don't forfeit tickets to the World Series to watch the same game on a tar-slicked roof a half a mile away in Harlem with a married couple. Girl, listen, it's the World Series. That means there will be men there. Unmarried men. Sheesh, no wonder a pretty girl like you is still single."

Effa hopped around as she pulled her dress over her hips. "I'm still single because a man would only hold me back. I have goals I'm working on."

"Fine, you have goals. That doesn't mean you can't have a little fun now and again."

It wasn't the fun that Effa was worried about. She had had boyfriends here and there since her divorce. Being with them was like playing the same old scratched-up record over and over again. They would wine her and dine her at first, then those men would start demanding more and more of her time or complaining about her working all the way downtown while hitting her up for a loan every Friday night. Loans that were never repaid and left Effa in a worse spot than she had been in before she had met the man.

"In my opinion, the kind of fun you're talking about is overrated." Effa smoothed the skirt of her dress. "How do I look?"

"Perfect. Now, c'mon. I don't want to miss the first pitch."

LATER, WHEN THEY arrived at Yankee Stadium, an awed Effa followed Avis into a lower-level box along the third-base line. She ran her fingers along the wooden seat backs as she took in the view of the field. The men who normally looked like little ants from her rooftop now had faces Effa could see. She did a double take when she got a good look at that Babe Ruth everyone was talking about. She stared at his sun-kissed skin and round nose. If she didn't know any better, she'd think he was . . .

Effa held her gloved hand up to her mouth to hide her shock. Avis took a playful jab at Effa's ribs. "That Babe Ruth is a looker, isn't he?"

"He's all right, I suppose." Effa glanced down, scared that if she looked at him again, she would do something to give away his secret. That was silly. She was just projecting her own concerns about her job situation onto a stranger. As far as she or anyone knew, Babe Ruth's skin was that shade of tan because he was out in the sun every day. Time to think about something else. Anything other than the politics of racial passing. "I definitely wasn't expecting to be this close to the field. How in the world did you get these seats?"

"Oh, some new guy in town wanting to impress Eubie. Sounds like he has a lot of money. I'm still not sure how he got them. He's a little bit older but might be your cup of tea. Quiet but personable. I didn't get the sense that he was married. He seems like the type who's looking for someone to spend all his money on. He'll be here soon."

Effa frowned. She didn't like where this conversation was headed. "Sounds like a setup to me." Effa looked back onto the field. She couldn't believe how good these seats were. All of the action would be right there, right in front of her face. The players continued with their warmups. She was close enough to see their smiles and hear them rib each other playfully.

"It's not a setup," Avis assured her. "I promise you, I only invited you because Eubie is out of town and I didn't want these tickets to go to waste."

Effa eyed her friend with suspicion. "Okay, if that's all it is. But I swear to you, if this turns out to be something else . . . well, let's just say it's a good thing that I live close enough to see my window from here!"

Avis just laughed. The Harlem River was behind them, and Effa couldn't spot her window, much less her apartment building, from where they were seated. They both knew that Effa would be going nowhere.

"Girl, please. Relax and enjoy the game."

"Hello, ladies. Avis, I'm so glad you came."

The man who greeted them wasn't the tallest man in the stadium. But he definitely wasn't the shortest either. An easy smile spread across his face as he strolled into their section. He was good-looking without the annoyance of being devastatingly handsome. Effa had to admit he looked nice.

Still, she probably wouldn't have given this nice man another thought if not for two things. The first was that his shoes looked like they were made of the softest leather. She wouldn't have been surprised if they were lambskin. And the second was that, when he put his hand on Avis's back and began introducing her to the other men who arrived with him, Effa saw that his left thumb was shorter than it should be. The entire last segment of the digit was just . . . gone.

The quality of his shoes told her that this man had more money than the average Joe around Harlem. That made him interesting. But the partially amputated finger? That meant that there was something dangerous about this otherwise harmless-looking man. That made him intriguing.

She kept her eyes on him as he made the rounds, introducing Avis to his friends. She noted how he did not shrink away from individuals there who *did* look like they were, in fact, dangerous. And also how they deferred to him with the respect of a peer. *Interesting*, she thought for the second time in less than a minute. *Very interesting*.

Effa watched and waited for her opportunity to turn on her charm.

Finally, he turned and took a good look at her. "And this is Mrs. Blake's friend . . ." He paused. "I'm sorry, I didn't catch your name."

"That's because you never asked for it." Effa hoped that her voice gave an air of uninterest with none of the budding curiosity she had about the man.

He straightened his spine like a schoolboy who had been scolded for not minding his manners. But Effa didn't miss the gleam in his eye. A gleam that made her insides quiver.

"My apologies, ma'am. Let me correct my mistake now." He turned to Avis. "Mrs. Blake, who is this gorgeous, sassy creature you have with you today?"

"She's an old friend of mine. Mr. Abraham Manley, may I introduce you to Effa Bush. *Ms.* Effa Bush."

Effa gave Avis a look. "*Mrs.* Effa Bush will do just fine." Effa didn't appreciate Avis's obvious attempt at matchmaking, especially as she had not yet decided if Mr. Manley was worth her time.

"Oh." Mr. Manley's smile had widened just a smidge at Avis's not-funny joke but then lost its luster upon Effa's correction. *Very interesting.* Or it would have been if Effa were interested.

"I'm so sorry to hear that." He uttered niceties as he took hold of her hand and brought it to his lips.

"Don't listen to her, Abe," Avis said, butting in. "Effa can call herself whatever she wants, but that doesn't change the fact that she is divorced and has been for some time."

"Is that so?" Mr. Manley leaned back to study Effa with new eyes.

Effa whispered to Avis, "What are you doing?"

"Helping you out," Avis whispered back. "You'll thank me later." She winked.

"Having been divorced twice myself," Mr. Manley said, "I'm sorry that you had to go through the painful circumstances that must have led to you and your husband—excuse me, your ex-husband—parting ways. But I'm hoping I'll be lucky enough to turn his loss into my gain."

He did not stutter over one word. His easy smile remained unaltered. He continued to exude quiet confidence.

He had put the ball in her court. Now it was up to her to decide if she wanted to play.

She smiled as she pulled her fingers out of his grasp. "I guess we'll have to see about that."

"I guess we will, *Ms.* Bush."

She inclined her head in his direction. "Mr. Manley." She turned away from him and gave her friend a pointed glare: *Now look what you did.* She glanced back over her shoulder to sneak another peek at Mr. Manley. She found him seated a few spots away, watching her. He flashed her another smile, then returned to his conversation with one of the spectators nearby.

Avis nudged her in the side with her elbow. "Calm down, girl! Try not to be so obvious."

"Ow!" Effa shifted and faced forward. She rubbed her side. "Your elbow is pointier than the creases in these men's pants. And anyway, I'm not being obvious."

"Yes, you are."

"No, I'm just being . . . curious. Yes, that's it. Now spill—tell me everything you know about this Mr. Manley."

Avis never got the chance to respond. The crackle of the stadium announcer's voice filled the bowl of Yankee Stadium. He began to read off the opening lineup of both teams, first the Chicago Cubs, the visiting team, followed by the home team, the New York Yankees. Effa stood up and cheered at the top of her lungs along with the rest of what must have been fifty thousand other people when Babe Ruth's name was called.

Effa decided to set aside her earlier suspicions and become the biggest Babe Ruth fan in attendance. Yes, anything to keep her from turning around and getting ensnared in the net of the man sitting behind her. Effa stood and leaned forward with feigned enthusiasm as the player with the charismatic smile wearing the baggy pin-striped uniform with the number three embroidered on its back jogged out to the first-base line. She remained on her feet and continued to cheer as Lou Gehrig, number four, was called next. The crowd's collective excitement was contagious. It didn't take long for Effa to get swept up in the jubilant atmosphere. For once, she didn't have to worry about whether she belonged or stuck out like a sore thumb. She was just . . . Effa.

Her eyes stayed on the Babe as the home team took the field. She could see his face but couldn't quite make out his expression. Still, the view here was a heap of a lot better than it was from the other side of the Harlem River on the roof of her apartment building with Joe and the rest of her neighbors. If she were in the upper-tier seats and not along the field, would she have been able to see the silhouette of her neighbor sitting on his old milk crate?

She looked behind her in that general direction and found herself staring into the eyes of Mr. Abraham Manley. The depths of his eyes appeared to smolder as the moment sparking between them drew out longer than an accidental glance.

Effa was torn between wanting this connection with him to last forever and wanting to turn around and focus on the historic event playing out on the field.

From behind home plate, the lead umpire yelled, "Play ball!"

Effa's curiosity about Mr. Manley disappeared as the game began. It was the second one of this year's World Series and the Yanks had won the first. Effa found herself fully emotionally invested in the game from the start. When the Cubs scored off a sacrifice fly, she jeered with the best of them. "Oh, come on!" she yelled while the Yankees players scrambled to minimize the damage. Thankfully, pitcher Lefty Gomez held them to just that one run by the third out.

Effa loosened up when it was time for the home team to bat. "I can't believe I'm finally going to see Babe Ruth bat up close." She turned to Avis excitedly. "Do you think he'll hit a home run?"

One of the men seated behind them leaned between the two women. "Well, he is third in the batting order. You won't have to wait long to find out."

Effa gave him a funny look. "I know that. I'm not a total rube. Can't a girl just be excited?"

Abe placed his hand on the man's shoulder and pulled the interloper back into his seat. "My apologies for my friend here. Can I get you a cola to make up for his rudeness?"

Avis nodded and said, "We'll take two, thank you," before Effa had a chance to say no. Avis was meddling and Effa didn't like it. Then the umpire called, "Batter up," which put an end to further conversation. Effa made a mental note to address the issue with Avis later.

The Cubs pitcher walked the first two batters. The Babe was up now. Effa watched him stroll out of the on-deck circle. She and everyone else in the stadium went wild.

"Let's go, Babe!" Effa clapped her hands. "Looking good, Babe!"

Ruth took one practice swing before stepping into the batter's box. The stands were electric with anticipation. Effa held her breath. With just one swing of the Bambino's bat, the Yankees could easily take the lead.

Effa cupped her hands around her mouth and yelled, "Knock it out of the park!"

The roar of the crowd almost drowned out the deep chuckle coming from behind her. "Is it safe to assume that you're a Yankees fan, Ms. Bush?"

Effa turned her head just enough to give Mr. Manley a glance. It was her first time seeing Babe Ruth at the plate this close. She didn't want to miss a second of it, but she also didn't want to be rude. "I think it's more accurate to say that I'm a fan of Babe Ruth." Effa turned her attention back to the game. Yes, it might have seemed rude, but come on, who had time for small talk when Babe Ruth was at the plate?

The Cubs pitcher began to wind up. Effa couldn't tear her eyes away from the action. She prayed that Mr. Manley wouldn't say anything else to her. Her eyes widened as the ball sailed low across the plate. Ruth's body twisted into the big trademark swing she had seen so many times in the newspapers . . .

And she watched his bat fly right over the ball.

"Strike one!" the umpire growled in a gruff voice. The entire stadium groaned.

Effa watched Babe step out of the box. It was only then she noticed that his gait had a slight hobble to it, as if his knees were bothering him. Her heart went out to him. Even if he wasn't in his prime today, in her mind, he was still the greatest player who had ever played. Especially since she was convinced that he was carrying around a secret. One that she knew well, because she had the same Achilles' heel. Like when she went to her job downtown and pretended to be someone she wasn't.

Effa knew the slump in Ruth's shoulders as well as she knew her own. Sure, it would be easy to say it came from the weight of superstardom on such an iconic team. But maybe, like her, he suffered under the weight of a mask he never wanted to wear.

Effa thought back to Smokey Joe. A talented pitcher, maybe even one of the best to ever step on the mound. But he would never know for sure, simply because his skin was what some would call too brown. So he was forced to watch the World Series from a faraway rooftop rather than play in it himself.

Effa dipped her head in a small nod as Ruth stepped back into the batter's box. Yes, just maybe George Herman Ruth had donned the mask of the Babe—perhaps he was wearing it even now—because it was the only way he could demonstrate his talents at the highest levels.

Ruth leaned into his batting stance and gripped the bat tighter.

"Strike two!"

The next pitch produced the same result—a swing and a miss. "You're out!"

The entire stadium erupted in a chorus of boos: "Umpire, you suck!" "You're a bum!"

Effa was tempted to join in the chorus of insults being hurled at the umpire. But she couldn't get over the irony of it, given that Babe Ruth struck out from swinging. Not one strike had been the result of a bad call on the umpire's part.

Maybe you can't ever really be at the top of your game while you're under the burden of living a double life. This realization made Effa shiver. It was another reason that she would never intentionally cross the color line. She was a woman who wanted the world to know who she was.

"Now that that's over, you were saying that you were a fan of the Babe. Doesn't that mean you're a Yankees fan too?" Once again, Mr. Manley was leaning forward in his seat and smiling at Effa. It was a nice smile too. The kind that made Effa flip-flop on the inside. Just the kind of distraction she did not need in her life right now. She forced her eyes back to the game.

Lou Gehrig was at the plate. According to Smokey Joe, he was another player who was a sight to see. But Mr. Manley had asked her a question and she didn't want to be rude.

Wasn't it just like a man to keep her from the good stuff.

Effa sighed. "Yes, but I can't say I have a lifelong allegiance to them. I was born and raised in Philadelphia. In my heart, Philly will always be home, despite my living most of my adult life here in New York City." The crack of a bat hitting the ball stopped her short. "Look at me, just babbling away."

Mr. Manley leaned back with a thought-filled look on his face. "You're a Philly girl, eh? Interesting. I recently moved here from Camden, just across the Delaware River from you."

Effa paused. She had never been to Camden, but she had heard it was crawling with gangsters and ruffians. She eyed him suspiciously. "I wouldn't have guessed you were from New Jersey. Not with that hint of a Southern drawl to your voice."

"That's because I was born and raised in North Carolina." He played up his drawl as he pronounced the name of his home state. Effa thought he sounded . . . charming. "I've lived up north only since I was grown."

Effa had to find a way to end this conversation. If it went on any longer, she might start finding this Mr. Manley attractive. "I've heard Camden is a dangerous place."

Mr. Manley shrugged. "New York City is a dangerous place. Philadelphia is too—especially for pretty young girls on their own, like you."

"I'm a divorced woman, remember? I haven't been a girl in quite some time. I'm not saying I'm old. Not yet, anyway. I just have way more experience under my belt than you seem to be insinuating, sir."

There—her feigned indignation had surely been enough to run him off. But there was one thing Effa couldn't let slide, and that was a good compliment. So despite herself, she followed up with "But I thank you for saying that I'm pretty."

Mr. Manley smiled at her again. That doggone smile was going to get her into trouble. He opened his mouth to respond, but the cheers of everyone in the stands stopped whatever he had been about to say. Lou Gehrig had just hit a single, driving in the Yankees' first run of the game.

"Oh, darn! You made me miss Gehrig's at bat." Effa felt bad as soon as she said it. Her distraction was as much her own fault as his. What was she doing? She was too old to be playing these kinds of games with him. She should just tell him flat out that she wasn't interested.

And she would have, if only they didn't have eight more innings of play. If things got any more awkward, Effa might just have to make good on her earlier threat to walk home alone.

Mr. Manley looked sheepish. "I beg your pardon. You won't hear another peep from me, Ms. Bush."

THE YANKEES WON the game, five to two. Effa was thrilled that she had been able to see Babe Ruth get a hit in his last at bat of the game. With the umpire's final call of "You're out!," everyone in the box stood up and cheered. The Yankees had won again. They were now leading the series by two games.

Effa turned to Avis while they were waiting to file out of the stands. "I can't believe it! They won and I got to see it up close. Thank you for making me come today." After this, those rooftop viewing parties would pale in comparison. "Do you think they could sweep the whole thing?"

Some of the other spectators near them stopped and stared. One man shot Effa a dirty look. Avis held up her hand just short of covering Effa's mouth. "Shh, don't say things like that out loud. You'll jinx the whole thing!"

"Oh no! You're right of course. I'm sorry. I'll just have to think of a way to unjinx it. Maybe if I go out by the players' exit and shake all of the Cubs' hands . . . Do you think that will work?"

Avis shrugged. "Maybe."

The line in front of them started moving again. Effa noticed that Mr. Manley wasn't right in front of them. Which was odd, given that his seat had been so close to theirs. She looked around, but he was nowhere to be seen. Effa frowned. "I should ask the West Indian lady who lives downstairs from me about unjinxing it. She has all these superstitions and rituals she brought from the islands. I bet she'd do something like sacrifice a goat and cook it up in the delicious yellow stew she makes."

Avis said, "I don't see how a goat could make the Cubs' luck any worse. But it's worth a shot."

"Did you enjoy the game, Ms. Bush?" Mr. Manley appeared out of nowhere.

Effa thought about asking where he had disappeared to, but that would make it seem like she cared. "Yes, it was quite a thrilling thing to watch. My first time at the stadium, and the Yankees win. During the World Series, no less. Maybe I'm their good-luck charm."

"You say it's your first time at the stadium? How is that possible when you live so close?"

Effa arched an eyebrow at Mr. Manley. She did not recall their previous conversation going beyond greetings and pleasantries. "What made you think I lived nearby?"

A mischievous smile spread across his face. "I made some discreet inquiries about you while you were focused on the game."

"Is that so?" Effa paused. She didn't know how she felt about his asking around about her. "I can't imagine you being so shy that you couldn't have asked me directly yourself."

"I'm not shy. I just didn't want to interrupt you and your friend again."

He tripped over one of the stairs. His hands flew out, and he caught himself on the back of a stadium chair. Effa enjoyed watching him stumble over his feet as well as his words. The act took some of the polish off his smooth veneer. It made him more . . . down-to-earth.

"Oh. Well, that was thoughtful. Thank you." The line had stopped again. She took advantage of the lull to slip on her coat. Effa hugged herself. Dusk was starting to creep over them. A crisp breeze coming off the Harlem River swirled around the bowl of the stadium. The temperature had dropped a few degrees.

He inclined his head. "You're welcome. I learned from my mama that a woman needs her space in the few moments she can find to enjoy herself. I don't think I've seen any woman as enraptured by a baseball game as you were this afternoon."

"Then maybe you haven't been around the right women. I can think of at least ten of my friends who are just like me when it comes to competition." That last bit was an embellishment on her part. But he didn't need to know that she was driven by engaging in competition, not just watching it.

"I'd have to disagree with you there, Ms. Bush. I don't think I have ever met another woman quite like you. I'd even go so far as to say that you're in a league of your own."

Effa felt her cheeks warm at the compliment; a blush was no doubt beginning to spread across her face. It was at times like these that she yearned for a darker complexion. Even a tinge of brown would have helped conceal her embarrassment at his flattery. Her first inclination was to wave away the notion that she was special.

As she began to open her mouth to do just that, she paused. On one hand, she *was* just like any other girl trying to make her way in the world. Effa couldn't think of many women she had encountered who didn't have fires in their bellies, a yearning to make something of themselves, to make their dreams come true. The only reason more didn't do it was that society locked them in a box filled with expectations of propriety and silly social graces and kept them focused on mundane things that had nothing to do with changing the world. Too few had the opportunity to walk away from marriages that left them unfulfilled and do something more stimulating with their lives. In that, Effa had been lucky. But she didn't plan to rely on luck alone.

Effa cleared her throat and started again. "I do believe that I agree with you there, Mr. Manley. I'm nothing like what most men expect a woman to be."

Mr. Manley took a step back. His eyes darted up and down as he studied her. She could almost see the clockwork gears in his mind spinning around as he tried to make heads or tails of her. She could tell that she had impressed him when he broke out into a grin.

"I think I like you, Ms. Bush."

"Thank you." They finally made it through the exit and found themselves on the plaza just outside the stadium. "I guess we'll get going. It has been a pleasure." As she began to move past him with a nod, he reached for her arm. "Forgive me, but I must see you again. That is, if you would allow it. So may I?"

"May you what?"

"May I call on you? Tell me how I can reach you."

Effa smiled at him faintly as she racked her brain for the best way to turn him down.

"Thank you so much, Mr. Manley. I am flattered by your interest. I just don't think I have the time for a gentleman caller. You seem like a nice enough man. I just . . . I am so close to achieving my dream. You would only be a distraction from my reaching it. I do hope you understand." She gave him what she hoped was a kind smile.

"Let me know how I can reach you so we can discuss this dream over coffee. If it's that important to you, I'd like to know how I can help."

Effa laughed. His persistence added to his allure. "I doubt you'd be of much help with my interior-decorating and millinery business. That is, unless you have a lot of girlfriends."

He laughed at that. "I'm new in town so I don't have a girlfriend here. Yet. But I'm the kind of man who needs only one woman in his life. The *right* woman."

"And you think that one right woman is me?"

"I'm hoping. I'm a betting man, Ms. Bush. And my gut has yet to steer me wrong."

"Then we'll leave it to your gut to find me again, Mr. Manley." Effa offered him her hand. He took it and kissed it, letting his lips linger just a breath longer than was necessary. Her words caught in her throat. She quickly composed herself. "Again, it has been a pleasure."

"Likewise, Ms. Bush. I'll see you around. Soon."

As Avis and Effa walked away, Avis nudged her with her shoulder. "Woo, girl, are you in trouble. The way he said that . . . that wasn't just a pleasantry. That was a promise."

Effa walked faster and urged Avis to do the same. She had picked up on that. The thought made her knees wobbly. She had to get out of there before they gave out and made her look like a fool in front of all of the Bronx *and* Harlem.

It TOOK LESS than a week for Mr. Manley to track Effa down.

Effa was crammed into a corner backstage at the Manhattan Casino on West 155th Street and Eighth Avenue. The New York Mission Society was hosting yet another fashion show to fund their upstate summer camp for inner-city youth. The dressing room was a madhouse. Effa placed a deep blue fascinator atop a model's head. She secured the hat's combs in the model's hair. Next, she floofed the hat's delicate crinoline trim that had been smooshed in the chaos and straightened the pearl brooch she had attached earlier. The headpiece was one of Effa's own designs, so she had to make sure it was just right.

"There." Effa lifted her hands. "You're good to go."

"Thanks, hon." As soon as the model popped out of the chair, another seated herself in front of Effa. The new model was a young girl with her hair plaited in braids on either side of her head.

"Well, aren't you a cutie?" Effa studied the assortment of headpieces she had brought with her and ultimately decided on a pink headband with white polka dots. She had arranged the trimmings on this one into the shape of a sweet bow. Effa carefully placed it on the girl's head. "There. Don't you look precious?"

"You're not so bad-looking yourself, Ms. Bush." The unexpected baritone voice caused Effa to flinch. She looked up and there he was, leaning on the door frame with a wide grin on his face.

"Mr. Manley? You shouldn't be here." Effa rushed to him and pushed him out the door. "There are ladies getting changed back here!"

Thankfully, the little girl was fully dressed. But everyone else was a different story.

"Fine. Fine. I'll go." Effa caught a wicked gleam in his eye. Oh no. She had a feeling he was about to ask something outrageous of her. "But only on the condition that you let me take you out when you're done with the show."

Okay, it wasn't completely outrageous. Effa sighed her relief, then pushed him again. "A real gentleman wouldn't employ manipulation to get his way."

"It's only manipulation if you don't want to go out with me."

Effa did not have the time or the mental capacity for his banter. She had been up since before the crack of dawn to haul her hatboxes and emergency sewing kit across town. The only thing she wanted to do after the show was fall into her bed. Alone.

But on second thought, she decided it would be nice to have some help hauling those boxes back across town. "Okay, I'll go out with you. But you're paying for the cab."

"Now who's manipulating whom?"

"Take it or leave it." Effa wrung her hands while peering around Mr. Manley's back. If any of the matrons sponsoring the show saw her with a man backstage, she'd never be invited to another event. Her attempt to become an independent entrepreneur would go down the drain.

Mr. Manley grinned in triumph. "It's a date."

"Good." Effa pushed him one last time, sending him into the casino's main room.

When Effa returned to her station, a woman was hovering over the girl and adjusting Effa's headpiece. She had to be the girl's mother. The resemblance between the two was unmistakable.

"Hello, ma'am. I'm Effa Bush." Effa held out her hand. The woman took it. She was dressed to the nines. A row of pearl buttons held her jacket closed. The matching skirt was expertly tailored. There was no gaping at the waistline or anywhere else, for that matter.

The girl's mother nodded at Effa. "I'm Lillian Jones. I'm one of the organizers of this event. And this is my daughter Eliza."

Effa needed a second to recover upon hearing that this woman was indeed one of the Harlem socialites in charge of this event. If Mr. Manley had lingered a few seconds longer, Effa's reputation would have been ruined. Oh yes, she definitely would be waiting around for him after this. She couldn't wait to give him a piece of her mind.

Effa cleared her throat. "Very nice to meet you both."

The woman's gaze flickered over the worktable where Effa had laid out the rest of her hat collection for the show. To Effa she said, "Do you have anything there that would complement what I have on?"

"How about this one? It's one of my favorites." Effa selected a headband that she had blocked out of straw into a wider halo shape and accented with white pearl-like beads and a large ostrich feather. She placed it on the woman's head, and a few pins and a nudge just slight of center was all that was needed to secure it.

"Perfect!" the woman said.

"I'd love to show you more of my collection after—" But before Effa could say more, the stage manager yelled, "Lillian! Eliza! You're on next!" The mother and daughter hurried off to the wings, leaving Effa behind and forgotten. The two had been polite enough, but Effa smarted at the feeling that they hadn't regarded her as their equal. She was just the nameless woman who had given them some headbands to wear.

With a sigh, she began packing up her things. She could hear the band out front playing the big finale number. It would be easier to keep track of everything if she had it all tucked away before the models returned. She would just have to be content that a Harlem socialite on the level of Lillian Jones was seen wearing her designs.

"And next we have creations from the workshop of Ms. Effa Bush!"

A polite round of clapping followed. But to Effa's ears, it wasn't enough. Only a thunderous roar of applause would satisfy her. Anything less might as well have been crickets chirping.

That was fine for now. Still, she wanted more.

Effa relished the glamour of it all—the flutter of silk and satin gowns that draped the billboard beauties that had been rushing to and fro moments ago. And Effa loved that it was all for a good cause on top of getting the eyes of the finest women in Harlem on her hat designs.

Now, if only those women would support Camp Minisink *and* her handmade headwear with their wallets. Then, just then, she might have enough funds to make a go of a hat shop of her own here in the part of town she called home. Then there would be no more pretending about who she was or catering to the snooty clientele downtown. Effa would be on her way to truly becoming her own woman and earning the respect and power in this town that she rightfully deserved.

Then maybe, just maybe, she could begin to feel like she had accomplished something special with her life.

WHEN THE SHOW ended, the VIP guests and designers were whisked off to a reception off-site. Effa had not been invited. Which was fine, because she had a shopping cart full of hats and pins and combs and . . . a stray lock of hair fell into her face as she tried to wrestle it all into the cart. She let go of the cart to tuck the hair back behind her ear. The cart keeled over, spilling its contents onto the floor.

"Oh, bother." Effa blew the troublesome hair out of her face. Forget selling enough hats to buy her own shop; right now, she'd be happy to sell enough to pay for an assistant.

"It looks like you could use some help." Mr. Manley knelt down and retrieved a box of hairpins.

"Thank you, Mr. Manley." She took the box from him and stuffed it back into the cart. "I can't believe you waited for me. I promise I didn't forget about you. I was just"—she waved her hand over the mess she had made—"trying to put Humpty-Dumpty together again."

He stood up. "You're welcome. And I'd like it if you were to call me Abe."

Effa could protest on the grounds that it wouldn't be proper. "I don't know if I know you well enough yet to call you by your given name. But then again, you were just crawling around on the floor to help me out. I guess that's not much to ask for in return."

"Thank you." Abe brushed the dust off the crease of his pants.

"Then I insist that you call me Effa." She stood up too, this time keeping a firm grip on the unstable cart.

"Thank you. I do not enjoy calling you by your husband's name."

"Ex-husband," she corrected.

"Ex-husband." They smiled at each other. Effa could tell that the new friendship they had just forged was going to be one that was out of the ordinary. She couldn't tell yet in what way. She just had a feeling in her gut. Abe gestured for the shopping cart's handle. "May I?"

"Please. Just be careful."

Abe paid for a cab to take the two of them and all of her hatboxes back to her apartment. He even helped her carry the hatboxes to her walk-up. He lingered in her doorway as she stowed them all in her small sitting area. She would reorganize them later.

But first, Effa had to figure out how not to invite him in. It was bad enough that Abe now knew the building in which she lived and her apartment number. Under normal circumstances, a gentleman caller wouldn't have gotten past the sidewalk entrance. But this wasn't a typical visit. And, luckily, he had behaved like a gentleman so far.

"Thank you for the help. And the cab . . ." Effa grabbed her purse. Abe stopped her before she could open it.

"What about your promise to let me take you out?"

"That sounds lovely, Mr. Manley—"

He cut her off. "I asked you to call me Abe. We're friends now . . . Effa."

She blushed at his use of her first name. She liked how the North Carolina in his voice made it sound. "You know where I live now, so I guess you're right, Abe."

He smiled. "That's better. So what do you say to a cup of coffee at the diner downstairs?"

Effa smiled. "A coffee would be wonderful."

AT THE DINER, over coffee and scrambled eggs, she learned that Abe was a real estate investor with interests from Washington, DC, to Baltimore and as far west as Pennsylvania.

"So how did you get your start in the real estate business?" She knew the question bordered on rude. It was just short of asking him how he had found the money for such a venture. But times had been hard for everybody since the stock market crash of '29. Even longer for those of a duskier hue up in Harlem and around the country.

Abe waved away her comment and chuckled. "That story could cure a bad case of insomnia. I'd much rather hear about you and your hats."

His response set off a warning bell in her head. She had dealt with this before. When a man wouldn't answer basic questions about his livelihood, it meant he was involved in an illegal operation.

Effa took a slow sip of her coffee before responding. "Is it safe to assume that your nonanswer to my question tells me all I need to know about your business?"

Abe shifted in his seat, but his smile never wavered. "Would it be safe for me to assume that you're just like all the other hat-shop girls I've met, most of whom have had to transform themselves into ladies of the night to make ends meet?"

"Touché." Effa looked down at her coffee, embarrassed. Even though the assumptions he could have made about her would clearly have been wrong, her gut was telling her she was right. "However, I have had a boyfriend or two in the past who made their money illegally. I'm not naive. If you are involved in the same kind of businesses, there's no need to pursue your interest in me any further."

Abe dropped a cube of sugar in his coffee, then stirred it. "I will be pursuing my interest further. You can bet on that. As for whatever type of business you may or may not be refer-ring to, you can rest assured I have long since retired from anything associated with that. All my current affairs are one hundred percent legit."

What could it have been? Had he been a numbers man? An alcohol smuggler? A hit man? She knew better than to press him further—no matter how interested in her he was, he wasn't going to tell her today. They barely knew each other, and they were in a public place where anyone could be listening.

Effa narrowed her eyes at him. "I want to believe you. The more time I spend with you, the more I really, really want to believe you."

"Then why not spend more time with me and find out the truth for yourself?" She watched him shift in his seat. Abe glanced around at others nearby who might have overheard their conversation. His tight expression relaxed when his eyes confirmed that the closest patron was an old man dozing off in a booth in the far corner of the diner.

Abe leaned in closer. He spoke again, this time with his voice lowered: "Take a risk. Get to know me better. I promise, you can trust me."

Effa studied his face. His body language. The tone of his voice. All told her that this was a man who was not accustomed to begging for anything. Yet here he was, putting his pride on the line for her.

Effa locked eyes with him. When that connection was made, it was like a deal had been sealed between them. He needed her to have faith in the new man he was trying to become. In exchange, Abe would support her ambitions. But first, she had to trust him.

"Do I need to worry about becoming a target on the street because of something you did back in Camden?"

Abe shook his head. "It wasn't like that. No one is looking for me. No one will be looking for you." He pointed at her food. "I'm as harmless as the butter and eggs on your plate. You are safe with me." Abe gave her a long, hard look, like he was trying to convey an unspoken message.

She looked down at her plate, processing what he'd said. On the street, the butter-and-eggs man was the guy who bankrolled the numbers operations. She looked up. She wouldn't ask him to confirm her suspicions. If Abe had indeed been a numbers banker, he wouldn't do himself any favors by announcing that to the world.

They locked eyes. Abe shifted in his seat and tilted his head forward slightly. That was the only confirmation he would ever give her. She nodded in return, indicating that she understood. "Okay. From here on out, whatever is in our pasts stays in our pasts," she said. She held out her hand, and they shook on it. Effa prayed that she wouldn't regret this moment.

"I knew you were a smart one. Now, back to you. Tell me about your dreams."

Effa stilled. No one had ever asked her that before. Her mother had attempted to dictate how Effa should live her life through secrets and deception. Her ex-husband had tried to mold her into the housewife that he wanted.

Even Avis—bless her—spent the bulk of their renewed friendship trying to parade her around to every rich eligible bachelor she knew. Since dragging Effa to the World Series, Avis had insisted that Effa accompany her to Smalls Paradise and the Savoy, both times on work nights. She had planned to help Effa at the fashion show but had to cancel at the last minute because an out-of-town friend had come to town unexpectedly and invited her to lunch.

None of them had ever asked her what she dreamed of doing in this second act of her life.

"You want to know what my dream is? In a nutshell, I want to be my own woman."

Abe raised his eyebrows. "I wasn't expecting that. Tell me more."

Encouraged, Effa explained how she was scraping together the cash she needed to put a down payment on a brownstone. She would use the downstairs as her hat-making studio and shop and the upstairs as her living quarters.

"It's a modest dream." She shrugged. "But it's something I know I can manage on my own. Even if a man does come along in my life, it's something no one can take away from me."

Effa stopped and took a sip of her coffee. She cradled the warm mug in her hands. She had never told anybody about her ambitions in this much detail.

Abe rubbed his chin as he took it all in. "There's only one thing that bothers me about this plan you've described."

Effa put her coffee mug down. His comment made her chest grow tight. This man had been a stranger to her not even a week ago. How had she come to value his opinion so much in such a short time? "Oh, really? Which part?"

"The part about not needing a man—"

She held her hand up, shaking her head. "I never said that I didn't need a man or that I wouldn't welcome one who came along and wanted to help," she continued carefully. "What I meant was that I will not allow myself to be stuck in a position where the man in my life feels he can stop or block my dream."

"You say this because you used to be married."

"Yes, I was." Effa frowned. She did not like to think too much about that part of her life.

"Do you mind if I ask what happened?"

Of course she minded. She had made such terrible mistakes back then. She had graduated from high school, then married the first man to flirt with her the following summer. "Didn't we just agree to keep the past in the past? But you did pay for the cab and this coffee, so I'll humor you. In a nutshell, I had ambition. He did not."

"Ouch! You're not even talking about me and you just made me feel this small." Abe held two fingers about a quarter of an inch from each other.

Effa flinched. She had not meant for the summary of her marriage to sound so harsh. Especially when it had been her who had been unfaithful. "To his credit, he did provide adequately for me. And for his mother, who lived with us. The problem was that he thought an adequate life would keep me satisfied. But there's a difference between meeting the bare basics of life and being comfortable. I wasn't comfortable."

There—she had laid all her cards on the table. Effa knew that she sounded like she was only about what was in a man's pockets. But she didn't care. All the better if it sent Abe running away from her for good.

If you weren't able to live in a manner that you desired—that you were willing to work for—then what was the point?

But Abe stayed in his seat. His eyes remained focused on her. "Define *comfortable*."

Effa was baffled. She was beginning to think there was nothing she could say that would send this man running for the hills. Well, if he was that invested, she might as well go for broke. "A night on the town every once in a while. Maybe a fancy dinner once or twice a year. Having a little extra for when something luxurious caught my eye. That doesn't mean I wanted to be dripping in diamonds, although I definitely wouldn't try to dissuade anyone who wanted to do that for me."

"Nothing you've said so far sounds unreasonable, Effa. I can easily make all of that happen for you. If you'd let me."

Effa let out a short laugh. "Forgive me if I'm not that easily charmed by the promises of a man I just met. That's how I wound up in divorce court."

"Point taken. But everything you've just described is attainable. And I'd like to be by your side when you do it."

Effa bit her lip to stave off the tears that were threatening to form. It felt good to have someone encourage her ideas. She'd had to pretend that she didn't have any for so long. "We're just talking about dreams, right? Okay, here goes one more. Someday, somehow, I want to buy myself one of those black mink coats that I see those ladies in the society pages and fashion magazines wear."

"A mink, eh?" Abe whistled. "Something like that would set you back a pretty penny."

"I know. It's silly to wish for something like that. Especially with times being what they are right now. But like I said, I'm just a girl with a dream."

"There's nothing wrong with dreaming. I started out as a dirt-poor farm boy from North Carolina. If it can happen for me, it can happen for you. Anything is possible. Especially for a lady as pretty as you."

Effa felt her cheeks grow warm at Abe's compliment. No doubt splashes of red that did not match the shade of the blush she wore were coloring her cheeks. People were always commenting on her looks in one way or another. Abe's words made her feel genuinely pretty. Like he had meant them. She wouldn't mind giving him the opportunity to tell her something like that again, and again.

"Thank you. But if I am to make it in this world, it won't be from trading on my looks. Like I said, I want to make it on my own terms and in my own way."

"You have some fire there in your belly, Effa Bush. I just want to let you know that, no matter how you look, I like it."

"Well, when you put it that way, Abe Manley, I am inclined to come along for the ride to see whatever this thing brewing between us becomes."

"AND THEN HE tells me that"—Effa lowered her voice to imitate Abe's—"'I plan for this thing between us to last a very long time.'"

Both Effa and Avis broke out into laughter as they waited to cross Seventh Avenue. Effa had just finished recounting the conversation she had had with Abe the day before. The one that ended with him becoming her . . . not boyfriend. That would be a ridiculous thing to call him. Abe was in his fifties.

Effa wasn't sure what his official title should be. Calling Abe her man didn't feel right. Not yet, anyhow. Their relationship

felt too new for that. They had left the diner with the understanding that he was interested in her and she him. Maybe . . .

Her special gentleman friend. Yes, that felt right. But she
wasn't going to mention that to Avis. Effa could tell that the
woman was itching to I-told-you-so her to death.

Avis sniffed back her tears. "Oh, he's got it bad. It sounds
to me like you either slipped something in that man's mug or I
need to find this diner and fill my husband up on their coffee."

The light changed. They crossed Seventh Avenue and continued along 125th Street.

"I promise you, I was trying to discourage Abe's interest."
Effa was still awed by how quickly the casual relationship had
transformed into . . . a thing.

"Abe? So you two are going by your first names now. How
intimate."

Effa swatted Avis on the arm to keep her from gloating.
"Stop making it more than it is. The way we opened up to
each other at the diner . . . what we shared . . . well, it'd be
ridiculous to keep being so formal."

Avis's smile fell away. Her face morphed into a more serious expression. She grabbed Effa's coat sleeve and pulled her
to a stop. "Wait—just how much did you share with him?"
Avis stepped closer and lowered her voice. "Did you sleep with
him?"

Effa pulled away. "No. Of course not. He's a nice man. I enjoy
his company. That's it. He seems like a homebody type. Given
how much I go out with you, I wouldn't be surprised if he gets
fed up with me by Christmas."

Chapter 3

Valentine's Day 1933

When Effa arrived outside the Fifth Avenue Automat, she had a bone to pick with Abe. Her irritation began to ease—a little—the moment she spotted him. "Abe, I still don't understand why you insisted I meet you here. There are plenty of places we could have had lunch that are closer to my job than this one. As it is, I only have time to grab a sandwich before I head back to the Garment District."

But no place too close to work, of course, she thought. Everyone at the hat shop still assumed she was a white woman. While she wasn't ashamed of her blossoming relationship with the darker-skinned Abe, she had no plans to correct her coworkers' assumptions about her. She still needed her job.

"How many times have I told you that you don't need to work at that place anymore? I can take care of you. You just won't let me." Abe opened his arms. Effa stepped into his embrace. It had been a busy morning down at the shop. Yes, she might have made a fuss, but meeting Abe here was a nice break. Effa felt like she was worlds away from work.

She ended the hug with a sigh.

"And I've told you each and every time that I like making

my own money. I like knowing that I can take care of myself."
Most important, Effa liked her independence.

But . . . she also liked the way Abe took care of things when
they were together. He brought her to nice places like Smalls
Paradise and the Savoy, where, because she was with him, the
staff and other patrons treated her like she was somebody.
Like she was important. Like she mattered. And no one cared
that the two of them looked like an odd couple: Abe, the older
Negro man with a baby face, and her, the pretty, young, apparently white woman. She assumed that Abe got a kick out
of making a spectacle of wining and dining the "white" girl
on his arm. As long as they both knew the truth of who Effa
was, she let him have his fun. It hadn't gotten them into any
trouble yet.

Effa gave the lapels of her overcoat one last squeeze before following Abe into the Automat diner. She had brought
the garment back to life more times than she cared to count.
The fabric was of good quality and tailored to fit her perfectly.
But it was threadbare in some spots along the shoulder seams.
Abe had caught her admiring a newer and sturdier coat in the
newspaper, one with a beaver-fur-trimmed collar. He'd offered
to buy it for her, but Effa refused. It would have been too ex-
travagant an item for someone with her low wages. She would
have had to field questions from her coworkers that she didn't
feel like answering.

At least, that was the excuse she made to herself. Well,
according to Avis it was. "You just don't want to sleep with
him."

They were at the home Avis shared with her husband when

Effa told her about turning down the coat. Avis pointed to a line of furs in her closet. "How do you think I got Eubie to give me all these? Every time I give him some real good, he comes home with a new one the next day."

Effa didn't know what Abe wanted from her, but it definitely wasn't sex. So far, they'd done nothing more intimate than hold hands. He never tried to push her for more. No sliding his arm around her shoulders at the cinema. No invitations to come over to his place. Nothing more forward than a kiss on the cheek.

Christmas had come and gone. Despite Effa's prediction, Abe was still around, still asking her out. But that's all Abe ever wanted from her. Her interest and her time.

Besides, she wanted to be able to buy a fur for herself one day. But she wasn't going to explain that to Abe. What would be the point? They had a good thing blossoming between them. No sense in messing it up by offending his male pride over something like that. Effa had tried to explain what she wanted to her first husband and he hadn't understood, and look where that had landed them. Last she heard, he was still living with his mother in the same Washington Heights apartment they all had shared while he and Effa had been married.

Effa hadn't been to Abe's home yet. She didn't even know his address. But she was pretty sure that he didn't live in a cramped walk-up apartment with his mother.

Once they were inside the diner, Abe helped Effa take off her coat and hung it on the side of a booth. Such a gentleman. Effa sat down and slid over so he could sit beside her. But Abe sat on the opposite side and smiled. His smile made her insides flutter. But a ping of disappointment soured her mood.

"Abe, may I ask you an odd question?"

"You can ask me anything."

"Where do you live?"

"In Harlem, just like you. Down at the Theresa for the moment. The apartment is a little small but it was adequate until now . . ." He let his words drift off, reached for her hand, and gave it a squeeze. Effa felt her cheeks warm and knew they had most likely flushed a deep pink. She had not been to his home, and he had not been inside hers other than that one time after the fashion show. He always stayed just outside her front door. Abe had not shied away from innocent public displays of affection since they had started seeing each other. But he had yet to push for any kind of intimacies.

Like she had said, such a gentleman.

He squeezed her hand again. "And now I get to ask you a question."

"Okay . . ." She dragged the word out, uncertain what his question would entail. Whatever it was he wanted to ask her, she hoped it wouldn't take long. She had to get back to work.

"But I'm not going to ask it until *after* we eat. I'm starving. Aren't you?"

"Abraham Manley, you can't be serious. I barely have time to get something to go." She had polished off the apple that was her breakfast hours ago, and now she was hungry enough to devour a Thanksgiving feast.

"I won't take long, I promise. But I'm famished." He let go of her hand and stood up. "You sit here and relax. What can I get you?"

She glanced at the offerings on the menu overhead. Normally, her lunch consisted of an egg salad sandwich from the deli down the block from the shop. This place had a metal compartment labeled *Egg Salad* in the sandwich section, but she would not be ordering that today. That was partly because she had eaten enough egg salad sandwiches to last her a lifetime, but, more important, because she had no idea how long the sandwich had been sitting in its compartment. At least at Mr. Solomon's deli, they made the food fresh when you ordered it.

"I'll have a meat loaf sandwich, please." As hungry as she was, Effa didn't want to appear greedy. She was a lady, after all.

"That sounds good. I think I'll have one myself."

She watched him walk away to retrieve their meals from the vending wall. That's when she caught a glimpse of the clock overhead. Her breath caught in her throat. It was 12:45 p.m. She would never make it back to the shop on time. Effa began drumming her fingers on the linoleum table.

Shoot. She should have stood her ground when Abe insisted that she meet him here. She got up. Abe returned with their entrées. His face fell when he saw she was putting her coat on.

"Hey, where are you going?"

"I'm sorry. I have to go. I'll be late getting back to work as it is."

"But I haven't asked you my question yet."

"How about dinner tonight? You can ask me then."

Abe set the food down on the table and shook his head. "No, I can't wait that long. I have to ask you here, now."

"My boss isn't so forgiving of tardiness. Especially since it's Valentine's Day. The shop has been busy all day."

"Just hear me out. Then *you* can fire *him*."

An hour later, Effa was pretty sure she no longer had a job at the hat shop. But she didn't care because she and Abe were in the Tiffany and Company showroom shopping for diamond rings with what looked like every salesgirl on duty clamoring to assist them.

From the curious expressions on the girls' faces, Effa could guess what they were thinking: Why in the world was this old Colored man buying this young white girl an engagement ring? Effa bit the inside of her lip more than once to keep from bursting out laughing. The girls' expressions spanned from shocked to borderline horrified. And Abe wasn't helping with his insistence that she try on the most expensive rings with the largest stones.

"I want to see a diamond as big as a baseball," he bellowed. Effa felt her face bloom with heat.

Now, Effa liked the finest things her budget could buy. And she didn't want to be rude and ask Abe exactly what his budget for this purchase was. But the huge diamonds looked gaudy on her slender fingers. She was relieved when they moved on to the store's slightly more modest offerings.

When all was said and done, they agreed on a square-cut stone that satisfied Abe's urge to splurge but still looked elegant and balanced on Effa's hand. The ring needed to be sized, but Effa held it up to the light one last time before she returned it to the honey-blond salesgirl, the one who had triumphantly suggested it and thus earned herself a hefty commission. Effa liked that she was the one salesgirl who had not treated them like a freak show once she got over her initial shock. When Effa took a closer look at her, she was even more satisfied that she would be *their* girl. Clearly no one else had noticed the girl's brown freckles and rounded nose. As they were getting ready to leave, Effa made eye contact with her.

"What's your name?"

"Dottie."

Effa nodded at her. "Very nice to meet you, Dottie. And thank you for waiting on us so kindly and professionally." She gave Dottie a knowing look. Dottie glanced away and then busied herself with paperwork.

Effa didn't say anything to Abe when they left or when they returned a week later to pick up her ring. But she was pretty sure that Dottie was just like her: A Negro girl who passed as white, not because she wanted to but because it was the only way to make a decent living with dignity in this city. With economic times as they were, a girl did what she had to do to survive.

And Effa would not get in the way of another woman's hustle.

"HONEY, ARE YOU sure this isn't a mistake? It's not too late to back out." Effa watched her mother's reflection in the mirror before them. The woman's question soured whatever pre-wedding excitement Effa had had.

It wasn't the question itself that bothered Effa. Her mother had been expressing her doubts about Abe ever since she'd found out that he was fifteen years older than Effa. It was the fact that she had the nerve to say it while flashing a bright smile on her otherwise perfect June wedding day.

Effa reached up to stop her mother from fiddling with her ivory headpiece. "Please, Mother. I've already pinned it down just the way I like it."

"But let me just . . ." Bertha's hand hovered near Effa's ear, her fingers poised to pin up a stray lock.

Effa caught Bertha's hand just in time. "Mother, I know you

mean well. But I'm fine. My hair is fine. My new marriage will be *fine*."

Bertha sniffed, snatching her hand out of her daughter's grasp. "Well, then . . . fine. I know when I'm not wanted."

Effa rolled her eyes. "Of course you are wanted. It's my wedding. I just don't need you working on my nerves with advice I didn't ask for."

"I don't care if you asked for it or not. You need a talking-to. I mean, you don't have the best track record when it comes to men." Bertha knelt beside Effa and clutched her daughter's shoulder. "You should have listened to me before you married that last guy, and I wish you would listen to me now. You can still walk out of here, start over in another city, and find someone else, someone who can really take care of you."

"You mean someone who's white." Effa faked a laugh. "Maybe you should go take your seat."

"I'm not going anywhere until I have my say. At this point, I don't care what color the man's skin is. I just want you to wait more than nine months after meeting the guy before you say 'I do.' I don't see what the rush is. You have the rest of your life with the man. You are too old to be repeating the same mistake. At least this time you waited nine months instead of four, like you did with the last one."

Effa took a deep breath to steady herself before speaking again. "I appreciate your concerns. I know they come from a place of love. But I assure you, this time will be different." She had her own doubts about what she was about to do—what bride didn't?—but they weren't going to stop her from exchanging marriage vows with Abe in a few minutes.

Effa stared out of the dressing room's window. Outside, the

neighborhood kids were playing a pickup game of stickball. A girl ran into the batter's box, and the boys laughed when she began taking her practice swings.

The pitcher threw the ball tight over the inside corner of home plate, knocking the girl into the dirt. Effa clutched at the window frame. Convinced the girl had been hit, Effa opened her mouth to yell for help. But the girl was back on her feet before Effa could make a sound.

"Yes!" Effa pumped her fist. She leaned closer as the girl dusted herself off.

The pitcher, still laughing, threw a soft toss right over the plate. It was a money shot if ever Effa saw one. She held her breath as the girl swung . . .

And whooped for joy when the bat connected with the ball, sending the boys in the outfield scrambling. The ball sailed over the fence and into the street. The girl easily rounded the bases to score.

Effa's doubts about her choices disappeared the moment the girl's foot touched home plate. That was when the pitcher, the boy who had tried the hardest to put that girl in her place, loped off the mound and approached the girl. He patted her on the back and spoke to her. Effa imagined that it was something to the effect of "Good game" or "Well done."

Respect. That was all Effa had ever wanted from those who loved her and from the rest of the world. To have her voice and opinions valued. To be recognized as more than someone with a pretty face and a good work ethic. It was how Abe had ultimately won her over and gotten her to the altar today.

Effa took one last look at her headpiece, then picked up her small bouquet of white lilies. She strutted out of the dressing room, more confident than ever about proclaiming "I do." Now she just had to make her mother and the rest of the world see that she was worthy of their respect.

Chicago, Illinois
Two weeks later

Marrying Abe was, hands down, the smartest thing Effa had ever done. From the sleeping-car upgrade on their train ride out to Chicago to the respect shown to her by all the ladies she'd met so far, she was loving married life this go-round. For the most part, anyway. Abe took spoiling Effa to a new level. But at the same time, she was convinced that she had made a huge mistake.

Like their nine-month courtship, the ceremony and reception were a blur. Which was fine with Effa because she was more than ready to become one with Abe in more than just name. Looking back, Effa barely remembered holding Abe's hand and saying, "I do."

But when they reached the hotel after the wedding reception, Abe had gone straight to bed, claiming that he was tired and that they had to catch an early train the next morning for their honeymoon. It turned out that their train wasn't until noon. The next thing she knew, she was alone in a private Pullman car on a train speeding toward Chicago.

Abe had explained that the accommodations on the train were too small and the walls too thin for lovemaking, so he had booked them separate rooms. And once they reached Chicago, Abe used the excuse that since they were staying in the home of a friend's mother, Mrs. Cora Rollins of Champlain Avenue, he didn't want to disrespect her hospitality. It was just one excuse after another; Abe was exhausted or just not in the mood.

The problem was that Effa *was* in the mood. All the time. Which was why, halfway through their honeymoon, Abe had to flatten himself against the wall as Effa, getting ready for dinner, stormed through their room like a tornado.

"Calm down, honey. Everything's going to be fine."

"That's easy for you to say." Effa brushed past Abe to get to the mirror. She bent down just enough so she could see what she was doing as she pushed the pearl stud—another gorgeous wedding gift from Abe—into her earlobe. Her fingers trembled as she put on the back, but thankfully, she did not drop it. Her nerves were such that she would have become an emotional mess if she'd had to crawl around to look for it. "I've been trying for years to get an invitation to a dinner party like this. All you had to do was waltz into town and—boom—invitations are thrown at your feet."

"Yes, but I had you on my arm when I waltzed into town. You made it easy." He threw a hopeful smile at her.

She smiled back and kissed him on the cheek. In moments like this, Abe had the power to lull her back into a calmer state. Make her believe that this marriage would go the distance. "You always know the right thing to say, don't you?"

"That's because you are stunning." Abe offered her his arm. "Let's go downstairs so I can show you off to these fancy people."

Effa and Abe's first dinner-party appearance as a married couple was a success. Abe was his usual charming self. The ladies in the room perked up when Effa mentioned her plans to get her millinery business going with her husband's support.

Cora's neighbor Robert handed Effa his card with a promise to send her home with a letter of introduction to his contacts in New York.

After the other guests had left and Abe had gone outside to smoke a cigar with Robert, their hostess, Cora, waved her fingers at Effa, then patted the seat next to her. Effa sat down, wanting to wring her hands in her lap. But that kind of fidgeting wouldn't do, not in a setting like this. Not with someone like Cora watching her like a hawk.

Cora Rollins was a heavyweight in Chicago. A social worker by trade, she was a member of all the right civic organizations, temperance leagues, and bid whist clubs. It didn't hurt that she also lived on the right street, where she and her neighbors represented the height of Negro Chicago society.

Cora gave Effa a good looking-over. Her eyes lingered on Effa's hands, which were fingering the lettering on the business card she held. "Oh, good, Robert gave you his card."

"Yes, he said to contact him before we return to New York and he would connect me with his people there."

Cora raised an eyebrow. Effa could have been mistaken, but she got the feeling that the gesture meant that Cora was impressed. "Make sure you hold him to it. Your name will be in the paper for sure."

Effa looked at the man's card again. She could have fainted when she read his full name; it was the same one she had read on the masthead of the newspaper that morning. "Your neighbor is Robert Sengstacke Abbott, the man who owns the *Chicago Defender*?"

The *Chicago Defender* was a weekly Negro-owned newspaper, but its influence spanned far beyond the city limits.

Abbott was famous for his hard-hitting stances against Jim Crow laws in the South and urban racism in the North. The paper was so hated by Southern politicians that Negro Pullman porters smuggled copies into the Deep South like contraband. Some credited Robert Abbott with single-handedly sparking the mass migration of Negroes out of the South for the past twenty years.

"Yes, the one and the same. Gerri Major covers the Harlem society news for him. I assume you know her?"

The cogs in Effa's brain slowly began to catch. What had started as a typical honeymoon trip was beginning to turn into something else. Something crucial to the future Effa wanted to build for herself and Abe. "I've seen her around at a few events," Effa said carefully. There was no way she was going to say that the former Gerri Dismond—now Gerri Major, after her divorce and remarriage—had looked right through her at said events. "But I've never had the pleasure of an introduction."

"Really?" Cora scratched her chin. "Well, that ends today. Next time you see her, introduce yourself and send her my regards. Be sure to mention that you stayed here as my guest and that you had dinner with Robert."

Cora pulled a pad and pencil from a nearby table and started scribbling. "And while you're at it, do the same with reporters from the other papers out of Harlem. I'll give you their names. And I'm making a note to myself to send an announcement of your visit to the *Pittsburgh Courier.*" Cora continued to drop names of her New York friends in high places and write them down on her list. Names of people Effa had encountered in passing as a volunteer at their functions or as a friend of an acquaintance. None had ever let a single girl like her breach their inner circles.

But now she was a married woman. Married to a man of means. That changed everything.

Effa stared at Cora. She had had limited contact with the woman back when they both lived in Philadelphia. Effa had been a girl at the time and had only known her as the mother of her best girlfriend, Mauvolyene. The two girls had kept in touch once the Rollins family had moved to the Midwest. This trip to Chicago had been an opportunity for the friends to re-connect in person, but Mauvolyene's growing family kept her from hosting Effa and Abe. Cora, a widow, offered her home instead. An offer that was now transforming into something more than Effa could have ever imagined.

"I—I don't know what to say." Effa fought to keep her bottom lip from trembling. "Thank you."

"You did well tonight. Opening doors for you will be the easy part. The real work comes after. You have to give those Harlem people a reason to keep your name in the papers, to keep them inviting you back into their homes and inner circles."

Effa nodded up and down in understanding. "I'll find a way. I promise."

Chapter 4

Harlem
Summer 1933

Abe had to abandon his attempt to carry Effa across the threshold of their new apartment when they returned from their honeymoon. He had tried to bump open the door with his hip, but it wouldn't budge. The door was blocked by the many calling cards and invitations that had been shoved into the mail slot.

Once the couple had hauled their luggage into the apartment, Effa fell to her knees and gathered the notecard-size envelopes into a more manageable pile. They had been away for a few weeks, so Effa had been expecting to find a large stack of mail. Maybe even a handful of late wedding cards and greetings in addition to mail that had been forwarded from their previous addresses. But this was ridiculous!

"There's so many of them!" Her eyes grew round as she recognized more than a few of the senders' names. The Beardens, the Days, the Carters . . . these were names she had previously seen only on the society pages of the *New York Age*, the *Amsterdam News*, and other Negro newspapers. Effa had never imagined that these people would ever know who she was, much less send her handwritten notes.

Abe knelt on one knee beside her. "Didn't I promise you that life with me would be more than washing dishes and serving me dinner?"

"Yes, you did." Effa stood with the pile cradled to her chest. She felt giddy from moving too quickly and was overwhelmed by what all of this could mean for her new life with Abe. She placed the mail on a nearby table, then braced herself against it to keep her balance. "I also told you that I don't mind washing dishes. You still haven't tried my cooking yet. It's going to be more like you rushing home to get a taste of my goodies."

Effa gasped as soon as she realized how that sounded. Abe's good-natured smile fell away. She wanted to slap herself on the forehead. While she had been joking, she hadn't intended for it to come out as a sexual innuendo. "I—I meant that I've gotten special requests for my pound cake and fried chicken in the past . . ."

There was no way to take back her careless words. She'd kicked the elephant in the room between them. Today was their one-month anniversary, and they had yet to consummate their marriage.

Abe pulled their suitcases farther inside their apartment. "I'm sure you have."

Effa winced. She had no doubt that Abe thought she had been referring to previous boyfriends who enjoyed her cooking. "I was talking about my family, my brothers—"

Abe held up a hand. "You don't have to explain. We've been traveling all day. We're both exhausted. How about I take you for steak down at Smalls Paradise? And then *tomorrow* you can introduce me to your highly requested fried chicken and pound cake."

"I like the sound of that." Effa wrapped her arms around Abe's neck and planted a sweet kiss on his mouth. She teased his bottom lip with the tip of her tongue to show that all was well between them on her end. "Then after, maybe some dessert?"

"That sounds . . . sweet." Abe smiled, then gave her a squeeze before loosening his hold on her. She noticed, however, that his hands remained on her waist, like he was hesitant to let her go. "I sure am glad I went to that World Series game. I thought I loved baseball before. Now that it's brought you into my life, I absolutely adore it."

"Same. I admit that I had daydreamed that Babe Ruth would see me in the stands and whisk me off into a glamorous life of baseball, wine, and showbiz. But he led me to a cozy life with you. I'd much rather spend the rest of my life like this. I don't have to pretend to be something I'm not with you. And I have everything I could ever need and more right here at home."

"You say that now." Abe nodded toward the pile of mail Effa had set down beside her. "I don't see you being satisfied as a housewife for long."

"I wouldn't worry about that." Effa held up a handful of the calling cards and then nestled her face against Abe's arm.

"I hope so." Abe gave her a playful tap on her behind before returning his hands to her waist. While he continued to hold her close, Effa felt a shift had occurred, causing a kind of rift between them. Almost like he was pulling away from her. She hugged him again, then leaned her head higher into the crook of his neck. She inhaled deeply, drawing in his scent.

"Hold me just for a little bit longer. Everything between us has been such a whirlwind since the moment we met. I just want to enjoy 'us' alone together."

He squeezed her again. This time he let her go all the way and stepped back. "You have nothing to worry about, Mrs. Manley. From now on, it's you and me together against the world."

January 1934

Mrs. Lucy Richards was the epitome of Effa's ambitions: self-made, influential, and respected. Widowed at a young age, she put herself through the first class of Madam C. J. Walker's Beauty College and was now on the board of the school's New York branch. She owned her own business and sat on the boards of numerous social organizations and racial-uplift causes.

Mrs. Richards's business—a beauty salon that catered to both Negro and white clients—was so successful that she was the breadwinner in her home. Her profits gave her second husband, Adam, the freedom to cross the country spreading the racial-uplift message of Marcus Garvey and his Universal Negro Improvement Association.

Mrs. Richards was also a passionate social activist. When she hosted a fundraiser, the money came rolling in. Everyone wanted to be on her good side, including Effa.

Effa had yet to meet the woman formally, however. They

had crossed paths only once. Abe had taken her to the Polo Grounds for game two of the 1933 World Series to celebrate the one-year anniversary of when they'd first met. Effa had spotted Mrs. Richards as she and Abe made their way to their seats. They had locked eyes for just a second. Effa couldn't be sure, but it looked like Mrs. Richards had nodded in her direction. Effa convinced herself that she was imagining things. She looked away before she embarrassed herself by doing something silly like waving or smiling at her with a toothy grin.

The New York Giants had triumphed over the Washington Senators that afternoon, six to one. The excitement over the win overshadowed the brief encounter. Effa had forgotten about it until the invitation to Mrs. Richards's dinner party arrived.

It took Effa three days to send her response. She was sure the invitation had either been sent to her in error or was someone's idea of a cruel joke. Lucy Richards didn't invite just anybody to her social gatherings. Only the big-time somebodies and movers and shakers had the opportunity to grace her door, much less her dinner table. At least, that was what Avis told Effa. There had been no way for Effa to know for herself until now. The gatekeepers at the top tier of Harlem society had cracked the door open for her. Effa would have to make a good impression on Mrs. Richards at this dinner if she was going to shoulder her way in any further.

Which meant that Effa needed the perfect outfit to wear. Abe agreed and set up an account for her at Blumstein's department store.

Blumstein's, on 125th Street, was the heart of Harlem's

shopping district. Of all the stores that could be found there, Blumstein's was the most fashionable. A few daring women from the Upper East and West Sides still made the trek uptown to buy the latest styles there.

Effa loved to shop at Blumstein's because there was no threat of being recognized for who she really was. An ever-present tension gripped her whenever she set foot in Macy's or Gimbels in Midtown. With Blumstein's located right in the middle of Harlem, Negroes made up the majority of the customers. Despite being all white, store employees were accustomed to seeing Negroes of all shades, although they occasionally mistook her for one of the white women who still shopped there. She could even bring along a friend—a real one—to enjoy the experience with her.

Effa had visited Blumstein's many times to buy small accessories or have lunch in the basement. But it wasn't until she married Abe that she could actually afford to purchase their top-of-the-line couture. She felt like a woman reborn when she hit the sales floor.

Before, Effa Bush would mull over what her one purchase would be based on price and how much money she had. Today, she entered the store as Mrs. Abraham Manley, a woman who had been empowered to splurge.

When she asked Abe what her budget was for this outfit, he'd waved her off. "Don't worry about it. Get whatever you need," he'd said before returning his attention to the broadcast of the New York Renaissance basketball game on the radio. Those were the words every fashion-conscious woman longed to hear. Effa left the apartment before Abe had a chance to reconsider.

Effa was alone on this day. But she was enjoying the ambience of the store. The floral bouquet from the perfume department wafted around her as soon as she wandered through that part of the store. But Effa wasn't on the hunt for a new scent. Abe had given her a bottle of Tabu by Dana for Christmas. What she was prowling for now was the perfect evening wear.

An hour later, she rode the down elevator with a Blumstein's garment bag draped over her arm. The salesgirls had fallen all over themselves to help her find this lovely navy-blue bias-cut dress with a matching sheer detachable cover-up on the shoulders. True, it was impractical for the cold weather outside. But the hem had the most darling lift when she had twirled around while trying it on. Yes, it was childish, but for the past year of her life, she had felt like she was living in a fairy tale. She was determined to extend the magical ride for as long as she could.

Now Effa needed to find the right brooch to complement her new outfit. She used to have a pearl stickpin that would have been perfect. But Abe had made her get rid of it when he found out that a previous boyfriend had given it to her. She told Abe that he was being ridiculous since she hadn't spoken to Henry in almost ten years. But Abe insisted. So in the trash the pin went.

She pushed that memory aside as she entered the jewelry section of the store and immediately felt like she had stepped into a wonderland. It was January but it looked like this particular department had a head start on its Valentine's Day decorations.

Effa took her time looking over the display case. The lone

salesgirl behind the counter was helping another customer. And there was one other woman behind her waiting to be served. Her lovely dark brown face looked tense, like she was agitated and doing her best to keep her temper in check. She had on a lovely camel overcoat. Effa had been around the fashion world enough to know that a coat like that wasn't cheap. But after further scrutiny, she could see the uneven stitching under the arm where the sleeve attached to the bodice. The elbow of the sleeve was worn just shy of needing a patch. Effa could tell that coat had seen better days. Evidence of the hard times people in Harlem seemed to be facing could be seen everywhere if one knew where to look.

Effa continued to wander around the jewelry department. But she couldn't help looking back at the woman in the lovely camel coat. What could be going on in the life of someone like that to produce that kind of distress?

Maybe her maid quit on her with no notice?

Maybe she was late for the ladies' church luncheon?

Maybe . . .

"Hello, ma'am. How may I help you?" Effa glanced up and was surprised to see the salesgirl smiling at her.

"I'm still looking around, so I'm not quite ready yet. But she was here first." Effa pointed toward the camel-coat woman standing at the counter a foot or two away. "I'm pretty sure I'll have narrowed down which brooch I want by the time you finish with her." Effa nodded at the other customer in acknowledgment with a smile. The woman did not return the gesture. In fact, she directed her deepening frown at Effa.

Effa had never seen this woman before in her life. She didn't have any idea why this woman would have a problem with her.

"Well, I'm here now helping you. I'm sure she won't mind waiting until we're done."

"But—"

The salesgirl ignored Effa's protest and reached into the case for the most stunning brooch on display. It was a peacock with brilliant teardrop stones arranged to make the tail. "You said you were looking for a new brooch, right? You must see this one. It goes so well with your coloring."

The girl proceeded to make a fuss, more than was necessary, about removing the jewelry from the case and presenting it to her. The whole time Effa kept glancing back uncomfortably toward the other woman, whom the salesgirl continued to ignore. The woman's eyes darted back and forth between herself and the salesgirl, her gaze full of justified disgust. Effa didn't blame her. The optics of the situation sickened her too.

"Would you like to try it on?" The salesgirl pasted a bright smile on her face as she thrust the brooch at Effa. Too bright. Everything in the store had become too bright—the lights, the displays, this rude girl's smile. Effa blinked a few times to focus. Now Effa could see the girl more clearly than she had ever seen another person before. And the energy that radiated from this girl's being was as disgusting as it was false.

"No, I would not like to try it on. Not today. And not in any circumstance in which you would earn a commission."

Now it was the salesgirl's turn to blink rapidly. "Excuse me?"

Effa gestured at the other customer again. "It is obvious that this woman was here before I arrived. You should be waiting on her right now, not me. However, for some reason, you have gone out of your way—and rather rudely, I might add—to focus your attention on me. Would you care to explain why?"

The girl looked over at the darker woman. She made a big show of widening her eyes and rounding her mouth into an O as if she were noticing the other woman for the first time. "Was she here first? I didn't see her there."

Effa wanted to scream. That was a bunch of hooey and they both knew it. The other woman carried herself with such regal grace that Effa found it difficult to look away from her. She radiated beauty from within.

Effa took a step toward the counter and the girl behind it. "Are you really going to pretend you didn't see her when I pointed her out to you when you first approached me? Would you care to share with both of us why you're choosing to ignore her? Perhaps you would like to explain to your manager why your selective vision impairment caused the loss of not one but I suspect two sales today."

"No, ma'am. I don't. Does this mean that you don't want to see this item?" The salesgirl still held the box containing the brooch uselessly in her hands.

"I think my husband's money would be better spent in an establishment that respects customers who share his same shade of skin color."

The salesgirl gasped. Her eyes went wide with shock. She jerked the jewelry away as if Effa were the type to throw herself over the counter to snatch the item. "I see—you're one of *them*."

"What does that mean?"

"You know, the kind to turn her back on her own. On second thought, I'm glad you won't be spending your money with me today. I don't need it." The girl placed the jewelry back in the display and walked away, now ignoring both Effa and the other woman.

The other woman chose this moment to finally approach Effa. "You didn't have to do that. Not for me. You were getting along just fine."

"Of course I had to do that. It was the right thing to do. What a person looks like shouldn't determine what kind of service they receive in a store. It doesn't matter that she assumed I was a white woman. It wasn't like I was trying to pass myself off as one. Her mistake is not my problem. The only problem here was the unacceptable way she treated you."

Effa felt like the wind had been snatched out of her. This whole situation had exhausted her. She had entered Blumstein's feeling like a brand-new person. The reality was that nothing had changed. Only that she had come in off the street with a few more dollars in her pocket. Dollars that were more her husband's than hers, if she really thought about it. The true irony was that, even though it was Abe's money, he would never receive the level of service Effa had experienced here. Well, that she had experienced before challenging the jewelry salesgirl.

"Then let me thank you for sticking up for me," the woman continued. "I hate shopping at this store. Most of the other ones around here aren't much better. But where else am I to go? Blumstein's always has the best dresses at a reasonable price. It's our neighborhood's hard-earned money that keeps the Blumstein family in business. This should be the one place where we are treated with respect and dignity."

"I agree." Effa wanted to say more. She wanted to tell this

woman about her dream of opening her own shop right here in Harlem. A locally owned shop where she would guarantee that all customers would be respected. But it wasn't the right time for that. Not when the woman before her looked just as exhausted as Effa felt.

The woman nodded at her, pulling the lapels of her coat together. "I guess I'll just have to figure out someplace else to get my daughter a set of pearls. She's having a big piano recital at St. Philip's next week. I'm a seamstress and I just got the deposit for a big commission. I thought she should have something nice for once."

"St. Philip's, you say? I think the minister there will be attending the event I'm going to tonight. Talk about coincidence. I must let him know that I ran into you. And I will tell him the circumstances around our meeting."

The woman smiled and held out her hand. Effa took it and they shook. "Then be sure to tell Reverend Johnson I said hello. I'm Loreli Steele. My daughter's name is Grace. Mark my words, she will be a great concert pianist one day."

It was hard to miss the gleam in Loreli's eyes as she talked about her daughter. The force of this mother's pride made Effa feel warm inside. It's what Effa felt when she thought about her own ambitions. This was also how she knew that becoming a mother herself was not one of those ambitions. "I believe you. It sounds like your Grace's concert is something I shouldn't miss."

"Thank you. Please come to her concert if you can. You won't be disappointed."

"I'm sure I won't be." Effa paused for a second. She so badly wanted to give Loreli a hug, to somehow make up for the shameful way she had been treated. But Effa held back, not sure if that was the kind of gesture Loreli needed. "You know, up until fairly recently, I was in the millinery business. How about I make a piece for your daughter—and for you too, of course. Then that horrible salesgirl's behavior won't have been a total waste of your time."

Loreli beamed. "I think I'd like that. I'd like that very much. Thank you, Mrs.— I'm sorry, I don't know your name."

"That was my error. I got so caught up in the pride you have for your daughter that I forgot. My name is Effa Manley." Yes, Effa would have definitely made a fool of herself if she'd tried to wrap her arms around Loreli before she had properly introduced herself.

"A pleasure, Mrs. Manley."

Loreli found a scrap of paper and wrote down the name and address of her sewing shop. Effa took it. "We will definitely be seeing each other again."

Effa would make it to Grace's concert the next week. She found herself in awe at its conclusion. Loreli's daughter indeed possessed a talent that was something special.

Chapter 5

Harlem
January 1934

Reverend Johnson gently nudged Effa with his shoulder. He held up a platter with a puffed pastry on it. "Would you like some?"

The glazed dessert had a swirled pattern on top that intrigued her. Effa nodded. "Please."

Reverend Johnson cut a slice with a serving spatula and gently slid it onto her dessert plate. Effa took a moment to study the dessert before digging in. It had a creamy filling inside the pastry shell, but she couldn't figure out what it was.

She leaned over to Reverend Johnson and whispered, "I feel silly for asking, but what is this?"

"It's Mrs. Richards's version of a three kings cake." Reverend Johnson smiled.

Mrs. Richards's claim to fame in Harlem social circles was holding the first dinner party of the year. In this case, it was to celebrate the Epiphany feast that kicked off the calendar year in the Episcopal Church. Which explained why Reverend John H. Johnson, the rector of St. Philip's Episcopal church, was there. Some of the most influential Harlem residents worshipped at St. Philip's, including Mrs. Richards.

Effa nodded at the reverend's explanation. She'd enjoyed kings cakes back when she was a girl in the Catholic Church. She cut off a piece with her fork and tasted it. It was a mixture of buttery crunch and almond-flavored cream. "Oh my, I've never had a kings cake like this before."

"Neither had I until Mrs. Richards made one for our bake sale at the church. It's actually called a galette des rois. It's the French version of a three kings cake. Mrs. Richards had one during a visit to Paris and has been blessing us with it ever since."

"In that case, I should attend your events at St. Philip's more often." Effa had yet to attend a service at St. Philip's, mostly because she considered herself a "casual" Catholic. While she didn't attend Mass every Sunday the way she had as a little girl, she did still light a candle and pray every morning and evening. Her last confession had been . . . well, right after she divorced her first husband, George. She didn't feel quite as comfortable in the Catholic community after she committed that particular sin. As for Abe, who had been raised in the Quaker faith down in North Carolina, he had no interest in attending anybody's services no matter the denomination.

"Speaking of which, I met Mrs. Loreli Steele earlier today. She said her daughter Grace has an upcoming piano recital at your church."

Reverend Johnson smiled at the mention of the Steeles. "Yes, Grace is one very talented young lady."

"I hate to say it, but I met Mrs. Steele under the most unfortunate circumstances. It's been weighing on my mind ever since." Effa didn't want to ruin the festive mood by bringing up the Blumstein's incident tonight. Her goal in attending this dinner was to make the right impression. Coming off as someone who complained about service in a high-end store was not the look she was going for.

But she had given Loreli her word.

Reverend Johnson leaned back and studied her. "Uh-oh, I've seen that expression before. Everyone wears it when they're about to tell me about a new problem to tackle in the community. It's all right. Give it to me."

Effa bit her lip. She had a feeling that she was about to rip the lid off Pandora's box. She looked away and caught Mrs. Richards watching her. Was this how she or her dear friend and mentor Mrs. Rollins felt right before they took on a new cause for the good of their communities? Was there ever a situation where they opted to bow out and retreat to the comfortable lives their hard work had afforded them?

Effa knew the answers to those questions. She knew because she had pondered them herself time and again when she was a miserable young housewife. For a woman with ambitions such as hers, the answer was always to swing for the fences.

She told him it had to do with the big department stores on 125th Street. "They're more than happy to take our money," she said, "but they don't have the same enthusiasm when it comes to offering meaningful employment to those of us who live in the community. Other than cleaning up and working the elevators, I mean."

The volume of Effa's voice rose. Abe, who had been conversing with the man next to him, placed his hand on her arm and gave it a gentle squeeze to calm her.

She pulled her arm away. No. She'd had to hold back her rage when she was at the store. Now that she had found a receptive outlet, it was like when the sweet spot on Babe Ruth's bat connected with a pitch. There was no retrieving that baseball. It was out of there.

And just like when Babe Ruth hit a home run, the rest of the room went silent. Everyone, including Mrs. Richards, took notice of Effa.

Effa was so passionate about what she was saying that she didn't notice. "We have plenty of educated young people struggling to find work right now. Any one of them would be a fine addition to the Blumstein's sales force. But I have yet to see any of our own on their sales floors."

"Ah, yes. We've tried to do something about their hiring practices. I was a part of a community delegation that went down there to talk to management about that. It was led by that Muslim fellow, Sufi Abdul Hamid, who was known for shouting his particular gospel from Preachers' Corner. I'm afraid it never got any further than the talking." Reverend Johnson took a stab at the dessert on his plate.

"So what are you going to do about it?" Mrs. Richards asked. Her voice was gentle but heavy with challenge. "I don't see you having any problem getting hired based on your looks."

"I . . . I . . ." Effa looked around the table, finally noticing that everyone was listening to her conversation with Reverend Johnson. She felt like a rock had been dropped into the pit of her stomach. "Pardon me, Mrs. Richards. I didn't mean to disrupt everyone's meal."

"You haven't, Mrs. Manley. In fact, you've just made the

table conversation vastly more interesting." Everyone nodded in agreement. Mrs. Richards gestured in Effa's direction. "Enlighten us. Tell us why the solution isn't you going down there and working those retail counters yourself."

Effa hesitated. These people didn't know her. They didn't know her story. She did not want their first impression of her to be her whining about the hardships of living as a Negro woman in a light, bright, damn near white body. Nor did she want to sound like new money by bragging that she did not have to work now that she was married to a wealthy man.

The truth was, she wanted to make a difference with the blessings she now had. It wasn't just about flaunting and spending Abe's money. She also wanted the power to make life better for young women in the circumstances she had been in not too long ago. She also wanted the respect that women like Lucy Richards commanded for wielding their power. Power they had earned on their own merits, in their own names.

Effa took a deep breath. "Yes, I could get a position for myself. But that would only take away the opportunity for someone else to make a living." She sent Abe an appreciative glance. "Let's be honest—my husband is able to provide a comfortable life for me. Plenty of other women need those wages more than I do."

Effa looked around the table. A few people nodded in agreement. But not Mrs. Richards. Effa continued to press her case. "When I was working, the only way I could get a decent job was to go downtown and pretend to be someone I wasn't. I had to go far enough away that no one knew me, where no one knew that I was a Negro. Let's not pretend that that's a solution for the rest of Harlem. Not when the choice to pass is not available to the majority of our community. Only a few of us can get away with it. And I doubt that those of us who can find any joy in living that way."

Mrs. Richards remained unimpressed. "Okay, but now you have the resources to open your own business."

"I do," Effa agreed. "But only enough to hire two or three salesgirls at the most. There would still be hundreds of Harlemites in need of work. The Blumstein family has the resources to employ more people than I ever could. Enough to get a whole city block's worth of families off the breadlines. Besides, the way that salesgirl fawned all over me today while ignoring Mrs. Steele, who had been waiting ahead of me—well, it got under my skin. Her behavior was completely unacceptable, and I let her know it. If these girls behind the counter are making commissions off our purchases, then they need to show everyone who shops there the proper respect. No matter what the patron looks like." Effa stopped to take a sip of water.

"If you're willing to do something about it, Mrs. Manley"— Mrs. Richards paused to smile at Reverend Johnson—"*and* see it through to the end, then you have my full support."

Reverend Johnson nodded in agreement. "Get a group together to start the ball rolling and I can whip up my congregation to support you too."

It had been less than half a year since Effa and Abe had been welcomed into Harlem's more comfortable social circles. By the end of that dinner, the other guests treated her as if she and her husband had been in their mix longer than that. Effa had arrived thinking that she needed to observe the rules and customs of this particular group of friends. But she'd had it all wrong. These people were about action, and so was she. Effa was leaving Mrs. Richards's home more comfortable in her new world. Comfortable enough that she was ready to do something more than just talking to the women she'd been meeting via dinner parties and afternoon teas. Like Mrs. Richards said, it was time to *do* something.

Effa stopped Reverend Johnson as he was on his way out. "Thank you. Your support means a lot." And victory would mean a lot more to Effa. Why, something like that would be big enough to get her name in the newspaper. Effa smiled to herself. She wouldn't be an anonymous somebody who worked behind the scenes at neighborhood fashion shows here and there. She'd be making a difference for her people out in front.

Mrs. Richards was waiting for Effa when she and Abe went to retrieve their coats. Effa swallowed and braced herself for the epic scolding she knew she deserved.

Instead, Mrs. Richards said, "You did well tonight. You have spunk. I like that."

"Her spunk is why I married her." Abe grinned.

Mrs. Richards handed Effa a sheet of her personal stationery. On it was a handwritten list. "These are the ladies who have what it takes to get things done in this city. I think you all would work well together to hatch a plan that will get those store owners to listen."

Effa relaxed a little as she slid the list into the pocket of her overcoat. "Thank you. Our young people need those jobs. I won't let you down."

Once they were outside, Abe gave Effa's hand a squeeze. "You did good tonight, babe. I think Mrs. Richards likes you."

"We'll see." Effa beamed.

EFFA WENT TO bed that night satisfied that she would be able to do something useful in the community. Finally, another box she could check off.

Married to a man of influence: Check.

Social do-gooder: Check, because in her mind it was as good as done.

Run her own business: Now, that was still on the table. She was finishing up her first hat collection. The problem was that her social calendar had yet to slow down since she and Abe had returned from their honeymoon last summer.

Effa made a mental note to do something about that. She needed to be more intentional about carving out the time to transform the sketches on her notepad into actual wearable pieces. That is, if she was serious about making a go of it. She still had to set up her workspace. The apartment she shared with Abe had only two bedrooms. They slept in one, and Abe used the other as his office. But Abe had taken to sleeping in his office more and more, she noted grimly. There wasn't much room left to accommodate a full-blown hat-design studio.

Surely there had to be a way for her to find the space she needed. The YMCA on 135th Street, perhaps. The Y served the community as a boardinghouse, a meeting area, an athletics facility, and an overall supportive space for all. Community members could rent out offices for their organizations and fledgling businesses. That was it! Effa made a mental note to go down there within the week to check out what options the Y had available.

She closed her eyes, pleased. Her plan for phase two of her life was coming together nicely. She hoped Harlem was ready for the force that was about to hit its streets. A force by the name of Effa!

THE NEXT WEEK, Effa had the women recommended by Mrs. Richards seated snugly around her living room. She had not met most of them before. Thankfully, the two Effa had personally invited showed up. Avis Blake appeared to be acquainted with almost everyone else. But Loreli Steele—the Blumstein's customer who had inspired this gathering—sat in a chair off in the corner, a teacup and saucer balanced on her knee.

Effa had a sense that Loreli was uncomfortable. Everyone was as much of a stranger to her as they were to Effa. Effa went over to her with a plate of cucumber sandwiches.

"Would you like a sandwich? I can get you another cup of tea. I can't thank you enough for coming."

"I'm fine. Thank you for inviting me. I don't get a chance to socialize nearly as much as I would like anymore. All my free time is spent taking my daughter to her piano lessons and performances." Loreli made a face. "When I'm not chasing around my son, that is."

Effa smiled. Loreli's eyes sparkled with love when she talked about her children. Effa felt even better about putting this gathering together. Loreli and her daughter deserved better. "What was your daughter's name again, Loreli?"

"Grace. She's sixteen. Sometimes, I can't believe my baby is practically a grown woman."

Effa took in the look of maternal pride on Loreli's face. She was sure that look would make most women yearn for babies in their arms. But not Effa. Not in the same way. She imagined that the closest she could identify with such an emotion was when she thought about her business aspirations. That is, if she ever got them off the ground.

Effa reached for the cup and saucer in Loreli's hand. "I'll be right back with more tea."

Effa came back a few moments later with the tea, then she turned to the rest of the group and cleared her throat.

"I guess this is a good time to get started. I'm sure you all know that we have gathered here today to discuss the intolerable employment situation with the department stores in this neighborhood. Mrs. Lucy Richards suggested that each of you be included in this group."

Effa spent the next ten minutes providing the women with the details of the shopping trip where the salesgirl had ignored Loreli in favor of Effa. She told them that Reverend Johnson had said he would put the support of St. Philip's behind whatever they decided to do.

"Hear, hear!" one of the women cheered when Effa finished. "It's about time someone had the guts to tell these department stores about themselves. I think we have the manpower—excuse me, *woman*power—in this room to get the job done."

Effa grinned. "Now let's draft a statement of our goals. How about over pound cake?"

THE NEWLY FORMED Harlem Women's Association went into action the very next day. Each member got to work compiling her receipts to document purchases made from the stores on

125th Street. Next, they reached out to their friends and acquaintances to do the same. By the end of the week, the group members found that the women in their social circle collectively spent an admirable sum—five thousand dollars—in those white-owned establishments, with the bulk of their dollars going to Blumstein's, the largest department store on the street.

At the second meeting of the Harlem Women's Association, they agreed that the next step was to address the issue with Blumstein's management. The task of drafting a letter to the store's owner was assigned to Effa.

By the beginning of the next week, they had an appointment to speak with the management of Blumstein's. The women had decided that if they could get the largest department store on 125th Street to change its hiring policy about front-of-the-house positions, the rest of the stores around it would follow suit. It was in that store, after all, where the campaign had started. If Effa had anything to say about it, Blumstein's would be begging for customers like Loreli Steele to continue spending their money with them when this project was done.

On the day of the meeting, Effa donned her best suit and her royal-blue felt beret. She slid on her fur-lined gloves and beige ankle-length coat to complete the outfit. Despite the coat's thick wool, the chilly winds blowing down St. Nicholas Avenue found a way past the lapels she held close to her chin. She definitely wasn't waiting for the subway to Blumstein's today.

Effa stood on the curb and held up her hand. "Taxi!" One quickly pulled up beside her.

"Where ya going?" the cabbie said.

"Blumstein's on One Twenty-Fifth, please."

The cabbie grunted in response. Effa sat on her gloved hands to keep them warm. She was looking forward to warmer days in a few weeks. Maybe Abe would take her to a baseball game. Not too long ago, he had mentioned that some of the Negro teams on the East Coast were talking about attempting to put together another organized league this year. The economy had bottomed out a few years ago, and the tough times on top of the cold weather seemed to have everyone around here in the dumps. A new Negro baseball league would be a bright spot for Harlem.

Effa settled back in her seat as the cab pulled away from the curb. It wasn't that long ago that she would have considered taking a cab to a destination only a handful of blocks away a luxury. My, my, my, how her circumstances had changed.

For just one second, she wished that Henry could see her now as the cab whisked her down St. Nicholas Avenue. Or any of the other men who had underestimated or abandoned her over the years. The cool air from outside slipped into the cab like an unwanted slap back to reality. Effa frowned. She knew that would never happen. But the girl who still lived inside of her could dream, right?

It would be even better, she mused, if her ex-husband could see what she had made of herself through her own ambition and determination. George had thrown the words *too ambitious* at her as if they had been a curse.

"Ha!" The last Effa had heard, George was still chauffeuring around rich white folks downtown. He had not remarried. "No, George. My having too much ambition was not the root of our marital problems. It was that you had too little."

"What was that?" the cabbie said over his shoulder.

"Nothing," Effa responded. "Just talking to myself. But let me ask you something. Driving people all over Manhattan— are you satisfied with that? Or do you long for something else?"

"Driving this cab wasn't my first choice. But you don't really have a choice when your family is relying on you to put food on the table. I don't complain, though, because it's a job, ya know? And over time, it's grown on me. How else would I meet interesting people like you?"

"You make a fair point."

She mulled that over. Maybe George was satisfied with driving interesting people around. He had met a number of them during the time they were together. He had come home in the mornings with tales of the biggest stars and producers on Broadway and their back-seat antics.

Effa sniffed. Meeting interesting people had its place. It just wasn't enough for her. She would rather *be* the interesting person that everyone talked about.

"Now, do you mind if I ask you a question?"

She looked at him in the rearview mirror. "You can ask all you want. But that doesn't mean I have to answer."

The cabbie nodded. "I hear ya. I'm wondering what a pretty, well-dressed lady like yourself is doing this far uptown."

She gave him a faint smile. Effa knew where this was going. She looked out the window to give herself a moment to rein in her facial expression. "I live up here."

The cabbie stared at her in the rearview mirror. She could see him raise an eyebrow. "You live up here?" He chewed on that thought for a moment. "Oh, you must be one of those holdovers from back in the day. From one of them immigrant families."

Effa sighed. He was definitely going there with this conversation. "I'm not an immigrant anything. I'm an American. Born and raised in Philadelphia."

"Philly, eh? I'm surprised you're not farther down in Italian Harlem with the rest of 'em."

"Why do you say that?" Effa wasn't sure how he would respond if she blurted out that she was a Negro. Either he'd spend the rest of the trip trying to convince her that she was not or he would pull over and kick her out of the cab. As much as she wanted to end this torture, they weren't within walking distance of 125th Street yet.

"Well, if you're from Philly, you must be Italian. Italians are all I see when I'm there."

That comment warranted an eye roll. But the cab still wasn't close enough to Effa's destination. "There are all kinds of people in Philadelphia, just as we have here in New York." The words came out sounding more tense than she had intended.

"No need to take offense, lady. I'm just trying to look out for you here. It's not every day you see a lady like you alone in this part of town. It can get kind of dicey with the riffraff that's here in Harlem."

"Are you saying that there isn't any riffraff in Italian Harlem?" Effa caught a glimpse of her smile in the rearview. It looked fake. So, so fake. She coughed into her hand so she could rearrange her expression.

"No. But over here it's different. It's . . . you know."

"No, I don't know." Effa was officially bored by this conversation. Luckily, the cab was turning onto 125th Street. She saw the Blumstein's sign ahead of them. "Pull over, please. I'll get out here."

"But we're almost there."

"I can see that. But I'd rather walk among my people than spend another minute in this cab with you." Effa smiled when the cabbie's brow wrinkled with confusion.

"Your people?"

"Didn't you know? I'm one of the riffraff too." Effa yanked open the car door and got out. She threw a quarter back in, not bothering to check the meter. And if she wound up shorting him on the ride, she was not really concerned.

Chapter 6

Effa was not the first member of their group to arrive at the appointed meeting place; Lelia Howard was already standing beside the entrance to the store. She waved to Effa as she walked up. Lelia was a popular manicurist who owned her own shop and had grown up in Harlem with some of the other women in their group.

"Darn, I was hoping to be the first one here. That's what I get for taking too long to settle on the right hat."

"Well, it was time well spent. That one is stunning, Effa. Where did you get it?"

Effa reached up and ran her fingertips along the brim of her beret. It was not exactly one of her own creations. The beret itself had been purchased by Abe. But the handmade flower trimmings that had been stitched on later were her doing.

"I might have done a little something to it." Effa allowed a shy smile to play on her lips. Not that she felt an ounce of coyness on the inside, but she was still new to the social scene. She was still trying to see how much of herself she should reveal to the women of this world. It wouldn't do to let herself be seen as someone who was comfortable being "the help," even if her previous work had been with high-fashion items such as millinery and accessories. True, she would like their support in the future when she opened her own boutique. But she wanted them to view her as a fellow business owner, not a mere shop worker.

"Well, whatever you did, it is stunning. We should talk later about putting your work on display in my salon. You have such a talent."

"I'd love that. I've wanted to start my own business for a while now." Effa took a moment to admire Lelia's outfit. She couldn't tell for sure, but she was pretty confident that the woman's felted hat was made of rabbit fur.

"Your hat is . . . divine." Effa's gloved fingers twitched with the urge to touch the fur. She balled her hand into a fist before she could embarrass herself. Effa added *control impulses* to her mental checklist of personal improvements to work on. "It looks so soft and warm."

"Yes, it is."

Effa was in her mid-thirties now; she should have had her spur-of-the-moment urges in check. She had been doing well in curbing them, but then she had married Abe after knowing him for less than a year. But that had turned out to be a smart move, a strategic one, even if it hadn't started out that way. Look at how far she'd come in the past year by following Cora's and Mrs. Richards's advice. And she had farther to go. As long as she reined in her impulses during this meeting.

"Yoo-hoo! Effa! We're here!" Avis Blake and two other women from the Harlem Women's Association emerged from a cab that had just arrived. Effa pulled herself out of her reverie.

There was no mistaking the kind of fur that hung from Avis's shoulders. That was definitely a mink. It went all the way down to her knees.

"I feel like I know that coat," Effa said to Avis after hugging her. "But it looks brand-new."

"This old thing?" Avis slid her hands down the front of her coat. "Eubie got this for me after his first big show. I can't believe you remember that." Avis turned herself around in a circle, so she didn't see how her words made Effa's face fall. Effa remembered all too well how big a smash hit Eubie Blake's show had been. It was the reason why Effa wound up leaving her first husband, George.

Shuffle Along was already destined to be great. It was the first all-Negro musical on Broadway. The ball had started rolling on opening night in 1921, and for the next fourteen months, it seemed like it would never stop. A week after opening night, Avis had come over to Effa and George's crowded flat to show off her new prize—the mink. After she left, Effa finally voiced her frustration with their own living situation— a one-bedroom walk-up that they shared with his mother, a woman who constantly nagged Effa about when she would make her a grandmother. As if Effa and George could do what they needed to do to make her a grandmother with the woman busting into their bedroom whenever she felt like it.

Effa shuddered at the memory. No, that was her past. Her present was much more comfortable. And with the position she was in now, Effa was much more likely to get a mink of her own.

Effa didn't like how jealousy consumed her when she compared what another woman had to what she didn't. Especially when that other woman was her dear friend. She had her own coat now. At least, she was on her way to having it, or would be once Abe funded her hat shop. And when the shop became a success, Effa would get herself a mink. Then she would have everything she needed, really—a place in society, a coat to keep her warm, and her own little empire to watch over. Just a few more steps and Effa would be on her way.

You are the organizer of the newly formed Harlem Women's Association and you sit on its executive board as treasurer, she reminded herself. *You really did it, Effie. You got these society women to follow you!*

"Come on, ladies. Let's go show these Blumstein's people we mean business."

THEY RODE THE elevators to the top floor, where a secretary—a white woman—ushered them into what looked like the chief executive's office. They all glanced appreciatively at the wood-work and the dark furniture. Effa saw a few women share knowing looks as they took in the mess of papers on the desk. The most comfortable-looking seat in the room was behind the desk. This was definitely a man's office.

"I fancy myself to be a bit of an interior decorator. It wouldn't take much to give this room some spunk. Maybe curtains in a brighter color." Effa nodded toward the window that looked out onto the Apollo Theater on the opposite side of 125th Street. "Even a little pop of a contrast color here and there would do wonders."

The other women nodded in agreement.

"I don't know anything about that, honey." Avis sniffed. "Whoever has to clean up after this man, I just hope she's paid well."

That earned her a round of chuckles.

Effa wondered how many of these women knew that dynamic from experience. Had any of them come from a background where working as a domestic was a necessity? Had they cleaned up after this same kind of white man and then somehow attained the more comfortable lives they led now? Effa hadn't. But her mother had. That was the reason Effa even existed. Mother had worked in the home of a rich white stockbroker in Philadelphia. One thing had led to another and— poof—Effa had been born, with skin that was much too pale for her to have been fathered by the dark-skinned man her mother called her husband at the time. Effa didn't judge her mother for the circumstances surrounding her conception. Bertha Brooks had been doing her best in a world not designed for women of any shade to thrive. Still, Bertha had managed to enjoy the fruits of her labor. And Effa would too, one way or another.

Effa sat down. Another glance at the messy desk gave her a little bit more appreciation for her mother's insistence on maintaining an immaculate home. It was a practice that Effa continued to this day.

The door opened and a man walked in. "So sorry to make you ladies wait," he said to no one in particular. He didn't meet anyone's eyes as he strode toward the power seat behind his desk. Effa took in his smooth pomaded hair and the fine cut of his suit. Definitely tailored. Most likely fitted by his own employees in the basement of this very store. But it was the slight olive tinge of his skin that gave Effa pause.

Wait. Is he . . . just like me?

He removed his suit jacket, carefully folded it, and draped it over the back of his chair. He sat down and said, "Blumstein's the name. Just like the sign on this building."

Effa leaned back in her seat, the small flicker of hope in her gut gone. She could tell by the way Mr. Blumstein spoke that he was nothing like her.

"Which means that you are *the* Mr. Blumstein, the owner of this store, I presume." Effa kept her tone light but it was nonetheless clear that she meant business.

"One and the same. I represent my family's business concerns here. How can I help you fine ladies today?" Mr. Blumstein leaned back in his chair, stretched out his legs, placed his feet on the desk, and crossed them at the ankles. Effa was taken aback. This was not the posture of someone about to engage in a serious business discussion.

Effa cleared her throat. "We are the executive board of the Harlem Women's Association and we have come to you today because we are all frequent shoppers at this store—"

"Yes, you are," Mr. Blumstein interrupted. "As a matter of fact, seventy-five percent of our shoppers at this location are Negro. We're so glad that we are able to serve this community's needs."

"Yes, but . . ." Effa tapped her fingers on her knee to keep her focus. The man's interruption made her want to scream. "Yes, but as frequent shoppers in this store, we've noticed that the quality of customer service has been inconsistent. It's fine if we're recognized as regular patrons or mistaken for white people. But we've seen darker-skinned customers ignored or worse by the white sales staff. Quite frankly, we are concerned about the lack of, well, *color* on the sales floor here."

Mr. Blumstein leaned farther back in his chair and put his hands behind his head. To Effa's horror, the sweat stains under his arms were now on full display. One of the other ladies gasped. "I'm not clear on where you're going with this, uh, Miss . . ."

"*Mrs*. Manley," she supplied.

"Yes, Mrs. Manley. The fact is, we do employ Coloreds here. A good many of them."

"Yes, we are aware of your elevator operators, janitors, maids, and the like. But we see your Negro employees only in low-wage service positions. There are twelve of us in our organization. We've compiled our receipts and those of our acquaintances from your store, and they represent five thousand dollars in sales for this year alone. We can see that this store's clientele is mostly Negro. However, not one of us can recall ever seeing a darker-skinned employee in a commission-based position in your establishment."

The frozen smile on Mr. Blumstein's face made him look like the salesman that he was. Effa gripped the armrests of her chair and leaned back, mirroring Mr. Blumstein's posture in a more elegant fashion. Out of the corner of her eye, she saw others in her group steel themselves similarly, some with raised chins or harrumphs of indignation. They could tell that whatever was about to come out of this man's mouth would be nothing but bluster and steaming horse droppings.

"Ladies, am I to believe that you've wasted my time this morning to harangue me about giving you jobs? You all look well taken care of—very well taken care—by your husbands. Do they even know you are here bothering me with this? Let me guess: You're looking for a markdown or a sale so they won't know how quickly you blow through your monthly allotments—"

Effa felt her face warm as Blumstein continued to insult them with his smug paternalistic assumptions. She cursed her fair complexion as she prayed that her cheeks did not reveal the red-hot fire of her temper. "Mr. Blumstein," she interrupted with as much civility as she could muster. It was a struggle to speak without clenching her teeth. "We appreciate your concern, but none of our husbands are here, and therefore they and their ability to provide for their families are none of your business. What is your business is making sure that your customers are treated well so they continue patronizing your store every week. *We* are your customers. And *we* are not satisfied. Nor will we be until we see members of our own community earning commissions from our purchases on your sales floors."

Mr. Blumstein took his feet off his desk and shuffled papers around. Then he made a big show of checking his wristwatch. It was clear that he wanted to avoid making eye contact with them. "Ah, I am about to be late for another meeting. Thank you for coming down to share your concerns with me. As you can see, I'm a busy man. But I will see what I can do."

Effa's heart sank. It didn't take a genius to recognize that he was just bumping gums with them. Even worse, it was obvious he would not give the matter another thought once their group walked out of his office. "We expect to see changes for the better sooner rather than later, Mr. Blumstein. We won't let you sweep this under the rug."

"As I said, I will do my best. But it's out of my hands. The kind of changes you ladies want take time. And if you haven't noticed, the money ain't rolling into Harlem like it used to."

As Effa marched to the door, her balled-up fists were the only outward sign that she didn't believe that malarkey. But on the inside, she was screaming. "That sounds like an excuse, Mr. Blumstein. We didn't come here for excuses. We came here expecting results."

"Good day, ma'am."

Outside the store, the women agreed to hold an emergency follow-up meeting at the 135th Street Y the following night. Some of the group's members were teachers and office workers and had been unable to join them at today's meeting. Those who had attended would need to debrief the others. Then they would need to map out their next steps.

Avis nudged Effa as soon as the two of them were in a cab. "That . . . did not go well."

"All that man had for us were veiled insults and lazy excuses," Effa fumed. "What a waste of time." What Effa didn't say was that she had naively thought their group's respectability within the community would be enough to get that man to reconsider his hiring practices. Boy, talk about a big swing and a miss.

Avis patted her arm. "If it were that easy, the last attempt to integrate the Blumstein's sales staff would have been successful."

"I heard the previous group was led by a man who was obnoxious. I really thought if we went down there with some upstanding women in the community . . ." Effa let her words trail off. She knew better. Respectability did not guarantee respect. Men like Mr. Blumstein paid attention only when their money was at risk. "I hate to say it, but I think we are going to need some help to pull this campaign off."

"We already knew that."

"I know. But I didn't think we would have to call in the

big guns so soon. I wanted to get our group more established first. You know, make a little more headway. Heck, make any headway."

Avis took her hand and squeezed it gently. "You mean make enough of a name for ourselves, don't you?"

Effa grinned at her friend. "You know me so well."

If she was being honest, it was more like gaining enough headway to make a name for *her*self. She winced, hating the sound of that even if the words were only floating around in her head. But the truth was the truth. She wanted to make Mrs. Richards proud. She wanted to make so much noise that Cora Rollins would hear it all the way in Chicago.

Yes, the goal was to get more Harlem girls working respectable jobs on 125th Street. But her ambition was for everyone to know that Effa Manley was the one who had made it happen.

It was clear that her kitchen-table project was destined to become a full-blown campaign. Campaigns meant people in the streets. They would need the big churches for those kinds of numbers. Effa knew how it would go once they invited the large, established Harlem ministers into the fray.

The cab pulled over to let Avis out. "Don't let this setback get you down. We're on the right side of a good cause. They'll have to yield to our demands eventually."

Effa nodded and waved goodbye to her friend. The cab merged back into traffic to take her home. Effa caught movement in an alley. Movement that made her look twice. Effa blinked. A man was leaning against the wall. His head was thrown back and his face was contorted. In front of him, a woman in a ratty coat was performing a sex act on him.

Effa looked away. She wished she could be shocked. And she

would have been had she not known that some of her coworkers at the hat shop spent their nights doing the exact same thing. She shook her head. "The things women are forced to do for money," she muttered to herself.

Seeing that woman in the alley made it clear that reaching out to local clergy was necessary for her cause to be successful. Of course, the male leaders of those churches would take over, making themselves the mouthpieces of the whole thing. But she had no choice. The goal—decent wages with dignity for the women of Harlem—outweighed Effa's own ego.

EFFA SLAMMED THE front door closed when she came home that evening. She flung her portfolio onto the nearest flat surface.

"Babe, are you okay?" Abe emerged from their bedroom.

"No. I'm not."

Abe took a step toward her, his arms spread out to embrace her. Effa brushed past him, oblivious to his attempt to comfort her. Ideas and strategies for the Blumstein's campaign flooded her brain. She needed to write them down before she forgot them. She needed . . . to get out of these fancy clothes.

He followed her into the bedroom. Effa stood before the mirror, fumbling with the clasp on her pearl necklace. Abe lifted his hands to help. "Why don't you let me—"

Effa leaned away, still tugging at the clasp. "I don't want to talk about it. I need to think."

"Help you," he finished. This time, his hands touched her fingers. One set of fingers caressed the other. "I don't know what happened this afternoon, though it obviously wasn't good. But it doesn't make any sense to rip apart a perfectly good strand of pearls when I can take care of *this* problem at least."

Abe made quick work of opening the clasp, then cradled the pearls in his big, roughened palm. Effa took the strand from him and clutched them to her chest. The memory of his fingertips against her skin still warmed her neck. "Thank you."

"You're welcome." Abe cleared the cobweb of emotion from his throat as he stepped away. "I'm assuming that you're not in the mood to go out? Alex called. The Cubans and the Black Yankees have an exhibition game tonight at the Polo Grounds. He said he left a pair of tickets for us at the gate."

Alex Pompez owned the New York Cubans, a baseball team that had been part of the Eastern Colored League back in the 1920s. Pompez, the son of Cuban immigrants, recruited most of his players from Latin America. He was rumored to be one of the biggest numbers bankers in New York City, and Effa assumed that Abe had met him during his prior business dealings, although she knew better than to ask.

Effa took a minute to shift gears from the intimate moment they had been sharing back to her efficient-housewife mode. After today's unproductive meeting at the store, she wasn't in the mood for a night at the park with thousands of people. "Not really," she replied with an apologetic frown.

She felt terrible. She could see he was making an effort for them to spend more time together, but here she was making plans to impress some matrons she barely knew.

No, Effa wasn't interested in only that now. She wanted to make things better for that woman in the alley and for all the other girls around there desperate to make a living. But what good would she be able to do if she neglected her husband?

Effa played with the pearls in her hands. "But it would be rude to turn down those tickets. Would you give Alex a ring and let him know that we'll be arriving a bit late? I need to get out of these clothes and get my thoughts down on paper. I'm sure he'll understand."

"Of course." Abe paused for a moment as if he had more he wanted to say. Effa saw him wave off whatever it was before he left the room.

When he was gone, Effa finally felt safe to lose a little bit of her composure. She gripped the bedpost and breathed. Being married to a man like Abe was much harder than she had imagined. It was hard not to respond to intimate moments like the one they had just had in a way she would've liked. In a way that was normal for every other couple.

Effa and Abe were three months away from their first wedding anniversary. They had yet to come together as one like other married couples did. They came just close enough to ignite the flame of passion between them, and then . . . *phtt*. Abe would always back away.

Effa had told him many times that it was okay for them to go further, that she wanted him to go further. But damn it, Abe always pulled away. She was at her wit's end. She knew what was expected of her as a wife. She was more than ready to fulfill her marital duty. When she complained, he would bring up the fact that they had agreed not to have children or he made up an excuse about how tired he was. Or, worse, he would start an argument with her.

She didn't understand it, and he refused to talk about why he wasn't interested in having sex with her.

At other times—the times when he wasn't physically close to her—Abe's actions indicated that he adored and cherished her. He would cook dinner for her. Buy her gifts. Take her out on the town. But even then, he would never dance with her. He'd even said that it was all right with him if she danced with someone else. Danced or maybe even more . . .

What made it worse was that Abe came home at a decent hour. Effa couldn't even blame his behavior on another woman. He'd made it clear so many times that she was the only woman for him. Abe Manley was the perfect man in every way except that he didn't desire her.

What kind of marriage was that? It wasn't what Effa had expected from this union. She might as well have continued being a single girl. True, she wouldn't have the hefty bank account she now shared with Abe. One thing this unusual situation had shown Effa was that money was and at the same time wasn't everything.

She reached around for the zipper on her dress and grasped the tab but couldn't pull it down.

"Abe, would you . . ." Her voice drifted off. She hated to feel like she was begging her husband to take off her clothes because she knew that it would lead to nothing more than her alone in her bedroom wearing only her slip once again.

"Yes, Effie?" Abe stood in the doorway.

"I need help with my dress."

"Of course." He easily pulled the zipper down from her neck to her waist. He did so with no skin-to-skin contact. "There you go."

"Thank you. But don't get too comfortable. I'll need help zipping up the dress I'm wearing to the game." Effa hoped the smile she gave him didn't appear too eager. But she felt as if the urge to throw herself into Abe's arms would consume her. She wanted her marriage to work. She didn't want to be the first one to cheat this time. She didn't want to cheat at all.

"Just call me when you're ready." And then he was gone.

AFTER THE GAME, Abe took Effa to dinner at Smalls Paradise. She sneaked glances at him whenever he wasn't looking in her direction. She let her gaze linger on him until he glanced at her. This happened time and again throughout the meal. She caught a few knowing smiles shot in their direction from diners at nearby tables. She felt her cheeks warm whenever they did and she just knew that her pale-complexioned face had bloomed into some shade of crimson or pink. Blast it.

Effa lost count of how many times she hid an embarrassed smile behind her napkin while she dabbed the corners of her mouth. She could only imagine what everyone was thinking about her and Abe and their . . . well, still *newlywed* life. They most likely assumed that she and Abe had carried on before their arrival here and would surely continue their amorous ways when they left.

But anyone who assumed that would have been horribly wrong.

When she and Abe got back home, Effa found herself once more undressing alone in their bedroom while Abe busied himself with the radio and newspaper in the living room.

He was still there when she finally drifted off to sleep with the other side of the sheets cold, also deprived of the warmth of Abe's body.

Effa had not gotten into this situation blindly. Not totally. When they returned from their honeymoon, Effa had put on a silk nightgown and attempted to seduce her husband. Abe had pushed her away. It was then that he told her that an injury from his younger days made it impossible for him to satisfy her in that way. Then he said that he understood if she needed to find that kind of comfort elsewhere, as long as she was discreet.

At the time, Effa had told herself that she was fine with this arrangement. That it was ideal, really, since she was more interested in becoming a businesswoman than a mother. But she had not anticipated how difficult and lonely the nights would be. Her body thrummed with desire, a desire that had no outlet. While she had strayed in her first marriage, she didn't want to deal with the hassles that came with having a secret lover. Also, what good was a secret lover when her desires flared up at the spur of the moment? And when she still cared for her husband?

Effa's last conscious thought before she fell asleep was that she would direct her unfulfilled desire into the campaign against Blumstein's. The busier she was, the easier it would be to ignore how lonely she was in her own home.

Effa couldn't be lonely if she was out in the streets forcing change for the better in her community. Effa would not be only a part of the coming fight to integrate the workforce on 125th Street; she would be the one to lead it.

"I don't understand, Reverend Johnson." Effa tried to tamp down the alarm in her voice. "Why would the ladies who started this campaign be excluded from leadership roles in the new coalition?"

A month had passed since Effa and the HWA had met with Mr. Blumstein. As expected, nothing had happened on his end following that meeting. The store's sales force remained 100 percent white. Effa insisted that it was time to get the local churches involved.

Which was why Effa found herself here in the office of the rector at St. Philip's Episcopal church. She had no quarrel with Reverend Johnson. He was the one who had encouraged her to go ahead with this project. But when she'd reached out to him again for direction and support after the failed meeting with the store's owner, she hadn't thought she would be politely pushed out of a seat at the table with all the other decision-makers.

"Mrs. Manley, I assure you, you have nothing to worry about." He smiled at her gently. If he hadn't been a man of the cloth, Effa would have liked to grab him by his collar and give him a good shake.

The only thing she wound up shaking was her own head. "I wish I could believe you. I organized the women to get things moving. This campaign was my idea, remember? So I don't understand why I can't present the community-coalition phase of our plan to your clergy group. Who better to explain our cause but me?"

Effa hit his desk with her open hand. Reverend Johnson patted it with his own. "I understand your frustration. I would invite you to come speak for yourself, but as I've told you before, it's our weekly clergy-*only* luncheon. Spare yourself the embarrassment of being turned away at the door. I will advocate for you and your cause. Have a little faith, Mrs. Manley."

Effa recognized that this wasn't a battle she was going to win. Definitely not by alienating Reverend Johnson and the rest of his clergy group. "Fine. Just don't leave us out."

She left that meeting feeling like a batter whose pop-up hit to center field had been snatched out of the sky right before it landed in the bleachers.

By the end of the week, Effa found herself on the executive board of the newly formed CLFP—the Citizens' League for Fair Play.

As the secretary, she stood before the group to close out their organizational meeting. "We want to thank Reverend Johnson for agreeing to serve as the president of our new organization," she said.

Effa's hands shook as she gathered her things to go.

"Good job, Mrs. Manley." A minister from a nearby church patted her shoulder. "I like the way you took notes today. You were serious and no-nonsense. Keep it up."

She struggled to keep her mouth curved into a smile. Throughout the meeting, what she'd really wanted to do was scream. But she was just their good little secretary; Reverend Johnson had been appointed the president and spokesperson of the campaign *she* had started. To make matters worse, the Harlem Women's Association, the organization that had been born in Effa's living room, was dissolved and incorporated into the clergy-dominated Citizens' League.

This new group's leadership had decided that the next step was to boycott Blumstein's department store. Everything Effa had built had been snatched away the moment these men had been invited into the campaign.

She felt sick. She vowed that this was the last time she

would allow herself to be robbed of her rightful place at the table. Never again would she be silenced for the greater good of the cause.

"WHO LET THIS white woman in here and told her she was running things?" A man in a dark kufi hat stood up and waved his hands as if to shoo Effa off the dais. "I'm sure you mean well, white lady, but I led a picket of that store way before you found the nerve to trek this far uptown by yourself in broad daylight."

Effa had not expected to have her resolve tested so soon. It was the first public meeting of the Citizens' League for Fair Play, and Effa had just finished reading the minutes from the organizational meeting, which outlined their immediate goals and strategies. Since the first course of action was to organize a boycott of Blumstein's store, Effa had stressed in her report that they needed all hands on deck, even if some of those hands were not so desirable. The man in the kufi was there to represent the more radical social-reform community groups.

Effa cursed the flush she felt beginning to creep up her neck. In her mind, she thought of a string of colorful and not so respectful responses. The fact that they were inside of the church right now was the only thing restraining her from uttering them. She narrowed her eyes at this man, whom she recognized as one of the soapbox preachers who shouted about their distrust of the white man on the corner of 135th Street and Lenox Avenue.

She took a moment to compose herself before turning to face him. He knew good and well that she wouldn't give him the tongue-lashing he deserved—not in front of this audience.

"There is no need for name-calling. No one is denying your efforts in the past, nor are we indicating that they were not appreciated. I was talking about the current campaign. The one that is a result of the Harlem Women's Association's data collection and meeting with Mr. Blumstein himself. From what I recall, these ladies"—Effa gestured toward the women seated in the front row—"were in that meeting along with myself. You were not."

She wanted to add that attacking her appearance was low-hanging fruit and that she had heard better insults when she was a child. But there was a decorum to maintain. Instead, she said, "Respect our efforts as you would have us respect yours, sir."

Reverend Johnson cleared his throat. "Thank you, Mrs. Manley. Moving on . . ."

Effa sat back down. She scribbled notes to record the rest of the meeting. The only thing that kept her from stewing over that foul man's interruption was the fact that her name would be printed in the next edition of the *New York Age,* and his would not. His outbursts would not garner a single mention.

Chapter 7

D on't buy where you can't work!"

BY NOW, THE boycott slogan had found its way into Effa's dreams. She had been chanting it every day on the picket line in front of Blumstein's for weeks.

"Don't buy where you can't work!"

Effa no longer felt the ache in her arms from holding up the sign during her hours-long shifts. Whenever she felt like her fingers were about to give out, she had only to look down the line to buoy her spirits. It looked like all of Harlem had joined the picket line: Old, young, rich, poor, leaning on canes or walkers, dressed in their Sunday best. All chanting in unison, "Don't buy where you can't work!"

Neither Effa nor the Citizens' League for Fair Play could take credit for creating the slogan. It had originated with the Housewives' League of Detroit. Founded in 1930, the Housewives' League was an outlet for activist Negro women, much like the Harlem Women's Association, to demand fair treatment and hiring practices in the stores they patronized. The

Housewives' League had incorporated itself into a national organization last year. Although not part of that organization, Effa was proud to carry on its work in her adopted hometown.

As Effa marched past the department store's entrance for the umpteenth time that day, she still couldn't believe how the community had turned out in support of the boycott. It would be one thing if this were the first attempt to call out Blumstein's, but two or three previous campaigns, most notably Sufi Abdul Hamid's last year, had come and gone without any lasting gains. Effa was determined to make it count this time, even if she had to go outside the prescribed duties of her role as the group's secretary.

When Effa got home after that day's picketing, she felt like she could conquer the world. Her feet ached, but her spirits were high. There had been a last-minute Citizens' League board meeting. The announcement was made there that the smaller department stores and shops on 125th Street had pledged to hire Negro clerks and salespeople, some for the very first time, within the month. While the league's boycott had targeted only Blumstein's, the rest of the merchants took a residual hit from the picketing and reduced retail traffic. A request came down from Blumstein's management asking to schedule another meeting to discuss the Citizens' League's demands.

Effa kicked off her shoes and threw herself on the bed. She flung out her arms and legs like she was trying to make a snow angel on the bedspread. She closed her eyes, grateful to finally have a moment to . . .

"You said it was going to be a quick meeting, Effa, and that you would come home in time to listen to the game with me."

Her eyes fluttered open and she sat bolt upright. Abe stood in the doorway. His arms were crossed over his chest. She could hear the radio in the living room. The announcer was saying that it was the bottom of the ninth inning in the New York Black Yankees game. That's when she remembered.

Effa's hand flew to her chest. "I am so sorry. Blumstein's wants to schedule another negotiating session with us. And we had to work out our strategy—"

"I made dinner." The way Abe spoke . . . it was devoid of anger. Effa's high was gone in a snap.

That's when the aroma of corn bread, collard greens, and barbecue hit her nose. That only made her feel worse. She stood and made her way to the dining room. A plate covered with a cloth had been set in front of the chair she normally occupied. Abe didn't join her. Instead, he sat in his easy chair next to the radio.

Until the boycott started, Effa and Abe had spent almost every evening together. Either she made dinner and they enjoyed a radio program, or he took her to a ball game and they stopped at a late-night spot for dinner afterward. The nights weren't as hot and sweaty as Effa had hoped, but they were warm and snuggly, and she was finding that she could learn to live with that.

But now that she was embarking on the social end of her plans, that special one-on-one time with Abe had been pushed to the side.

"It smells wonderful," Effa called out. "Again, I am so sorry."

She brought her plate to the living room, put it on the coffee table, and sat on the couch. She placed her hand on Abe's leg and gave it a light squeeze. "What can I do to make it up to you?"

She felt Abe's thigh tense. He brushed her hand away. "Dig in. I know you must be starving. That is, unless you already had dinner with . . . someone."

She flexed her hand. For a second, she considered touching him again. Then she thought better of it. The unspoken part of what he was alluding to sank like a rock into the pit of her stomach. She didn't know what felt worse, being ignored by her husband or having him assume that she had been with another man.

Effa picked up her plate. "Of course I haven't eaten yet. I said I would eat with you."

That I only want to eat with you . . . Effa hurried into the kitchen before either one of them could say anything they would regret. Yes, Abe had said that he'd understand if she wanted to "engage" with other men for her more carnal needs. He'd even said he'd understand if she wanted to be released from her marriage vows.

She had been a fool to think that the money that came with the man would ease the pain of not being physically desired by that man. It didn't.

She scraped the food from her plate into a cake pan, then put it in the oven. Noting how saucy the ribs were, she put on her kitchen apron while she waited for her food to heat up.

"It smells good, babe," she called into the living room. "You want me to warm some up for you too?"

Abe grunted in response. "I already ate."

That made Effa feel worse. He had gone through all the trouble of putting this meal together for the two of them only to wind up having to eat it alone. She scooped up a few stray leaves of collards from the counter and dropped them into the trash. That's when Effa noticed the discarded takeout container in the can.

A takeout container in the trash meant that Abe hadn't stood over a hot stove to cook a doggone thing. She looked toward the living room with her mind set on saying something. But she held back. Two wrongs didn't make a right, especially since she was still in the wrong for missing dinner. It didn't matter if Abe had stirred the pot himself or stood in line to buy food that someone else had prepared so he could pass it off as his own. That did not change the fact Effa had not come home when she'd promised to.

Effa used an oven mitt to remove her food from the oven. She scraped it back onto the plate and returned to the living room.

"I owe you one, big fella. How about I make you something sweet for dessert tomorrow."

"Shh." Abe waved her quiet as he continued to listen to the radio. He leaned in as the radio announcer described the final pitch of the game.

"Fast ball straight down the middle and . . . a swing and a miss. Ooh, that one had to sting. And it's another loss for the New York Black Yankees."

Abe slapped his thigh.

Effa shook her head as she settled into her chair. "That Rev Cannady is too eager. Always missing the easy ones." The second baseman had been struggling at the plate all summer. It sounded like tonight had been no different.

On the radio, a commercial started up for Dickens frozen custard and ice cream. Abe snapped it off before the announcer could finish reading the tagline. "I'm glad I didn't have any money riding on this game or I'd be on my way to Hinchliffe Stadium right now to give that Bill Bojangles a piece of my mind. I told him it was a mistake to sign that guy. He's always swinging for the bleachers when only a base hit is needed. The kids in the street have more patience."

"Maybe you should go down there anyway and tell him to make you one of his scouts. You have a knack for spotting talent, Abe."

"You have a point there, Effie. I sure can spot them. But I'd last only a week in a gig like that. I haven't worked under another man for at least a decade. And Bill and James are the last two men I'd want telling me what to do. I'd be waiting forever for them to cut me a paycheck."

"Still, I think it would be a good idea to talk to him. You love baseball as much as I do. And you know raw talent when you see it. I know you're into real estate investing right now. Maybe there's some way you can combine that with Negro baseball. Get together with some of the owners and start building our own stadiums across the country." Effa shrugged. "Just go down there and talk to him. You never know what opportunities are out there. If I were a man with the funds to invest, I know that's what I would do."

"Fine, fine, fine. I'll go see Bill tomorrow. It'll give me something to do while you're running around trying to save the world." Abe softened his gruff words with the boyish smile that always turned Effa's insides to mush.

"Not the entire world, dear. Just the neighborhood."

IT WAS STILL daylight when Effa left the picket line on 125th Street the next day. It took a bit of doing, but she was able to wrestle her picket sign into the cab without too much damage. She gave the cabbie her address on St. Nicholas Avenue and they were off.

The Citizens' League leadership had done its best to get the Blumstein's executives to meet with them at lunchtime, but they had come back with excuses about scheduling conflicts and concerns about their white staff and customers' complaints about picketers harassing them when they tried to enter the store. The boycott leader decided that they weren't going to get anywhere today and sent everyone home early.

She pulled the newspaper out of her handbag. She had been glancing at the day's headline all afternoon, but this was her first opportunity to read the article below it. She still couldn't believe it as she read the *New York Age*'s headline again: "Koch's Dept. Store New Owners Vow to Hire Negro Clerks."

"We did it!" she said. "I can't believe we did it. One down and soon the rest will fall."

Their picketing and boycott targeted Blumstein's and Woolworth's stores. But Blumstein's was the more important one. The logic was that if the largest department store on 125th Street yielded to the Citizens' League's demands, the smaller neighboring ones would follow. And that was almost what was happening, but in reverse. Effa didn't care. Progress was progress. Blumstein's management would have to talk to them now.

"This is only the beginning!"

EFFA ARRIVED HOME bone-tired despite how early it was. All she could think about was drawing herself a nice, warm bath and throwing in a handful of the perfumed foaming soap powder that she loved. Maybe follow it up with a glass of wine. Thank goodness that ridiculous Prohibition law had been repealed the previous December.

But as soon as she pushed the apartment door open, the hope for that bath and glass of wine floated away like the bubbles she had been dreaming about.

She found Abe sitting in his usual chair, dressed in a suit. His going-out suit. The one he saved for nights when they went someplace special, like to Connie's Inn or a prizefight.

"Oh, good, you're home early. The fight starts in two hours." Abe stood up. He gestured to their bedroom. "I picked out a dress for you so it shouldn't take you long to get changed."

"The fight?" Effa racked her brain to figure out what Abe was talking about but came up empty.

The glint of anticipation in Abe's eyes dimmed. "You remember, right? I told you one of my associates from back home was in town and got us tickets for the fights tonight. One of his guys from Detroit is on the card."

"That young hotshot that they've been writing about in the Negro papers?"

The glint came back full force. Abe nodded vigorously. "That's the one."

Now Effa remembered. Abe had looked like a little boy when he'd told her about it last week, he was so excited. His friends from the sporting world would be there, people in professional basketball, baseball, boxing . . . all of them. The ones Effa had encouraged Abe to reach out to about becoming a talent scout.

"I am so sorry. I'm sweaty. I smell like outside. I fear I might embarrass you by falling asleep in the middle of a bout. Is there any chance we can skip this one?"

"Not this time. You know what these guys are like. It'd be rude to pull a no-show at the last minute. Tonight's fight is a sellout. I don't even want to think about what Mikey had to do to get us seats."

Effa could guess what Abe's friend had done to secure their tickets, but, like Abe, she didn't want to think about it. Big-time favors were owed, that she knew. She hoped that Abe hadn't been tied up in those owed favors.

"Then maybe you should go on ahead without me. Send Mikey my apologies. Maybe if you ring him now, he'll have enough time to give my seat to someone else. Or you can sell it at the door." She felt terrible. Terrible and tired. She knew she was putting her husband in an awkward situation with a crowd one didn't want to get in awkward situations with.

"Mikey will be fine. The point is that I was looking forward to going out tonight with *you*, Ef. We never do anything together anymore. Not since you got involved with this protest. We haven't even been to a game together in weeks. This time last year, we would've gone to at least a handful of Sunday games by now. I know this Blumstein's protest is important, but it's like you've forgotten about us."

Her whole body felt like it had been encased in lead. The frustration in Abe's voice made Effa's guilt weigh even heavier on her. This wasn't a new conflict between them. It had been going on ever since she'd started the Harlem Women's Association.

She was too tired to defend her constant absence from home. Not if it would lead to another argument. She already had to live with the weight of knowing that she had disappointed another husband.

"I miss going to the games with you too," Effa said quietly. "I agree, everything was less complicated before I started this Blumstein's campaign. It's taken on a life of its own. I thought this would be a quick one-and-done thing—add up everyone's transactions and present the totals to management, and that would be it. I never imagined how stubborn those people could be about making a much-needed change."

"I don't get why you ladies are so pressed to spend your money in them white folks' stores anyway. Especially when there are so many Negro-owned stores around the corner that already have Negro employees and are struggling to stay afloat."

An image of Loreli Steele flashed in Effa's mind. Loreli, who was a talented seamstress and just wanted to make a decent living so she could afford to nurture her daughter's musical talent and keep her son away from the streets and focused on school. Loreli was supposed to be her friend. Shouldn't she be patronizing her friend's business instead of Blumstein's and encouraging her new society friends to do the same?

Effa shook her head. "While we need to do a better job supporting those small businesses, this isn't an either-or issue. It is the principle of the matter. If these large stores are going to take up space in our neighborhood and profit from our dollars, they should respect us while we are in their stores. And they should be proactive in supporting our community while it is struggling."

She felt Abe's eyes studying her. "Well, it couldn't be me. I worked too damn hard to save up what I have. I won't say that I've always gotten it the right way or with the right people, but I can say that I found my success through respecting my own people and that they've always looked me in the eye while conducting business, even when that business was dirty. You're my wife, Effa. I'm proud to say that I can buy you anything you want, and you never have to worry about money again for the rest of your life. But I do wish you'd spend more of *my* money with our own."

"Does that mean you'll finally buy me the mink coat I've been asking you for?" Effa was glad to have found a way to lighten the mood. It was an ongoing joke between them. When they'd met, Effa had a few fur garments given to her by previous beaux. Abe asked her to get rid of them. "How does it look if I parade you around in clothes you got from another man?" he'd said. He promised to replace them with the finest mink to be found.

He had yet to make good on that promise. The two of them sometimes ventured into furriers' salons, but Abe never saw any furs he considered good enough.

Abe also looked relieved that their tense conversation had turned a corner. "Only if you can buy it from a Negro man."

"Or a Negro woman." Effa smiled.

"Or a Negro woman," Abe agreed. He studied her for a moment. "Now, there's something I haven't seen in a while. I sure do like it when I make you smile, Mrs. Manley."

"I like it when you make me smile, Mr. Manley."

"Now that we've worked that out, you stay here and rest. I'll go to the fights by myself. But promise me one thing."

"What's that, Abe?"

"Next time I come up with something that's just for us, promise me that you'll go with it. Deal?" He reached out his hand.

Effa took it and they shook. "Deal."

Abe tipped his cap to her, then left.

After Effa took a bath to ease her nerves from the excitement of the day, she started writing a list of how she could get her name in the newspapers again. After all, she was a woman with ambition. Playing second fiddle to a bunch of loudmouthed preachers simply wasn't Effa Manley's style.

Harlem
August 1934

"Effa, you look like you're ready to tap out." Avis frowned with concern. She fished out a handkerchief and handed it to Effa. "No one would blame you if you did. It's blazing hot out here."

The picketing outside of Blumstein's had dragged on during the dog days of summer. The diehards had weathered everything Mother Nature hurled at them. But today, heat rose in waves from the pavement, and the humidity enveloped them like a wet blanket. It felt like the elements had a personal grudge against the protesters and would not be satisfied until they knocked every one of them out.

Sweat glued the delicate silk of Effa's blouse to her back. She wiped her face and the back of her neck with the handkerchief. She took another step and stumbled on a small rock. She waved away the arms that reached out to steady her.

Mrs. Foster, an older woman from one of the churches, called out, "I just got here. I can take your place." Effa shook her head no to the woman's offer and raised her placard even higher. But even the cardboard looked wilted in the oppressive humidity.

One of the college volunteers thrust a paper cone filled with water toward her. Avis took it and placed it in Effa's free hand. "Drink the water, at least."

This was not a request. Effa gulped it down. "Thank you."

"Good. All of your efforts would be wasted if you wound up in the hospital with heatstroke. Or worse. And I don't want to see what that husband of yours would do if I had to tell him that something had happened to you and why. Lord forbid."

Avis crossed herself as Effa got another cone of water. She sipped a little, then splashed the rest of it on her chest. She didn't care that doing so might make her look like a half-drowned water rat. It was so hot. Effa wouldn't be surprised if the Blumsteins had figured out how to control the weather so they could overpower the protesters outside their store.

"Those Blumsteins won't get the better of me. If their aim is to be the last ones standing, then I can be the last one too." Effa was referencing the fact that, since the boycott of Blumstein's had begun just over four weeks ago, all of the other major department stores on 125th Street had capitulated to the Citizens' League's demands and begun hiring Negro sales-clerks. Koch's had been first, then Strickler's, Busch's Kredit Jewelry, and others soon followed, all pledging to hire more Negro clerks and salespeople.

But Blumstein's, the largest of them all, continued to hold out. Effa was beginning to think that the top executives' stubborn-ness was personal. Mr. Blumstein had basically ignored her and the rest of her group when they had come to speak with him back in March.

"I just don't get it, Avis. Why doesn't he just give in? If his competitors can come around and see reason, then why can't he?" Effa trudged on with her picketing. She refused to take a break partly out of pure stubbornness but also because she was in awe of the sea of humanity that had shown up to join the boycott. It looked like all of Harlem was on the picket line. Typically, they would get the housewives and ministers. Since it was August, they had college students who hadn't been able to secure full-time jobs for the summer participating. Yet another reason for this campaign to be successful.

But the one group Effa hadn't expected was the masses of working-class folks. There were men and women in every uniform she could imagine—men who hauled ice, domestic staff, day laborers, and even city workers. She saw young girls in their best outfits, whether it was the latest fashions fresh off the rack or clothes visibly mended with loving care. It was the part of Harlem that she didn't see mentioned in the newspaper society pages every week. They were the loudest and most boisterous of the picketers. Which made sense, since they would be affected most by the outcome of this boycott. The current economy was tough on everybody in every profession. More jobs, better jobs, and better wages everywhere would be good for Harlem.

"I think the man is a fool. He thinks that by digging in his heels, he'll keep those white women from downtown who come here to shop happy. But the only thing he's doing is spitting in the faces of us Negroes who keep his business in the black each month." Avis looked up at the top floors of the store and shook her fist.

"At this point, it's just embarrassing." Nonetheless, Effa was almost impressed by how stubborn the general manager of

Blumstein's was. She crumpled the paper cone in her hand. "He has to give in soon or the store will miss out on the back-to-school sales."

Effa saw one of the league's college volunteers pull Reverend Johnson out of the picket line. She watched as the youth whispered into the reverend's ear with obvious excitement. His animated gestures and smiles made Effa think that he was on the verge of flying away with the pigeons. Reverend Johnson responded by giving the man a hearty slap on the back. That's when Effa knew that something big was happening. And if something big was about to go down, she needed to be a part of it.

Now, *that* was a reason for Effa to step out of the picket line. Behind her, she heard an exasperated Avis say, "It's about time."

Effa made a beeline for the two men before she lost sight of them. If any of the other men on the Citizens' League executive board got the news before she did, they would find yet another way to shut her out of the action.

"Reverend Johnson!" Effa caught his sleeve just as he was about to walk away. "What's going on? I'd like to help if I can."

"Mrs. Manley, I have wonderful news! Blumstein's management team said they're ready to meet for negotiations. I think we finally got 'em, Miss Effa."

"I don't believe it."

"If you'll excuse me, I need to find Fred," he said, referring to Fred Moore, publisher and editor of the *New York Age*. "It sounds like management is willing to come to the table in good faith. But I won't feel comfortable unless one of our own newsmen is there to give an accurate account to the press."

"I have a pen and pad right here in my purse. I'd be glad to go with you and take notes."

"That is a generous offer, Mrs. Manley. But I'm afraid these kinds of negotiations tend to get a bit intense. Coarse language gets thrown around."

"Coarse language doesn't bother me. I grew up with three brothers. We don't have time for delays, not while the iron is hot. I won't accept any more excuses. You were the one who appointed me secretary of the Citizens' League, after all. It's my job to take notes at every meeting."

Effa hoped that would trigger some guilt in Reverend Johnson.

"You're right." He sighed. "I see Moore over there with our lawyers. Perfect. Follow me. I have a feeling that today is our day!"

All of a sudden, she was very grateful to have been given the "woman's job" on the board.

EFFA WAS BACK in Mr. Blumstein's office for the first time since the spring meeting with her women's group. Only this time, she wasn't seated in front of Mr. Blumstein's desk. And she wasn't doing any of the talking. She was also the only woman there.

From the back of the room, Effa did her best to keep up with her note-taking duties. That task grew challenging, as the conversation escalated into tense exchanges as soon as the initial greetings were over.

Blumstein started it. "What's it going to take for you and your followers to stop interfering with my business?"

Effa had to hide her smile. It was a classic move—pretend

that you don't know what the other side wants. Luckily, the league's members had anticipated this tactic in their planning sessions. Reverend Johnson stuck to the agreed-upon script. "What we've been asking for since day one: Negro employees on the sales floor."

"Commissioned Negro salespeople," Effa corrected. She kept her head down under the guise of taking notes. She didn't have to glance up to know that her comment had earned her more than one annoyed, over-the-shoulder look.

"You know good and well I can't do that." Blumstein fidgeted in his seat. "The commissions of the salesgirls I already have would tank. Your people would make a point of buying only from the Colored ones. How about I promise to hire one Colored girl to assist the existing sales staff? She can earn a bonus if their department hits their sales goals for the week."

Blumstein had barely finished talking when Fred Moore boomed, "No, our girls won't take a whittled-down cut when they'd be the ones running around doing all the work."

Now it was Blumstein's turn to talk over him. "I'm offering your people a chance to earn an honest wage and you're making me sound like I'm trying to scam you?"

"That's exactly what he's saying," Effa chimed in. That earned her some more dirty looks, but she didn't care.

"Let's take a second to refocus on the end goal here." Reverend Johnson held out his hands and pushed them down in an effort to calm both sides. "Our community is full of talented, hardworking, educated young people looking for the opportunity to make a living with dignity. No one is asking for more than an honest wage. There's no need for an assistant position.

Our girls are ready to do the job as full-fledged commissioned employees at the same rate as everyone else."

Effa nodded while furiously taking notes. She liked that everyone on the Citizens' League's side was not backing down.

Blumstein waited a beat before saying, "Reverend Johnson, I like you. I like what you do for this community. But my family has worked hard to build this business. I will not let you dictate to me how it should be run, nor will I let you continue to damage it with your boycotts and your bullying of my customers."

Blumstein directed that last bit at Fred. Since the beginning of the boycott, Fred's newspaper had published the photos and names of every Negro customer seen leaving the department store. The majority of his front page every week was dedicated to coverage of the boycott.

Blumstein turned back to the reverend. "If I let a Colored girl on the sales floor, I'd lose twenty-five percent of my business on her first day. Let me speak plainly: My customers from the Upper East Side would never set foot in here again. I can't afford that kind of loss, you understand? So in the same way you don't see me down at your church telling you how to conduct your Sunday services, I need you to stop trying to tell me how to run my store. It comes down to respect in the long run. Respect and knowing your place."

"Respect is something you should start showing to the community that keeps your family's business afloat," Reverend Johnson shot back. "For the life of me, I can't understand why you're so willing to throw over your Harlemite patrons for those ladies downtown. If they did stop coming to your store, the loss of their sales would barely make a dent in your bottom line.

Now, if we decide never to darken your store's doors again, you'll be out of business before the end of the summer."

Mr. Blumstein stood up so fast, his chair flew into the wall. "Was that a threat, Reverend?"

"Only if you want it to be," Reverend Johnson said through gritted teeth.

Blumstein sat down again, and the two went back and forth like this for a good ten minutes. Mr. Blumstein had his executives lined up behind him like a wall of support. Reverend Johnson had done the same with the Citizens' League executive board. To Effa, they looked like two college football teams ready to battle it out on the gridiron. But this wasn't a gridiron. It was a place of business.

And they were getting nowhere.

Frustrated, Effa began bouncing her knee. The heel of her shoe made a loud tapping noise against the wooden floor. The men quieted and turned their attention to her.

"Do you have something to say, Mrs. Manley?" Mr. Blumstein's words dripped with condescension, or maybe it was amusement. Effa wasn't sure, but either way, she was ready to be done with this pissing contest.

"No, I . . ." Effa stopped. Her immediate reaction was to hunch her shoulders and apologize for the distraction. That might have been fine if the outcome of this meeting affected only her. She would have been content to have gotten their attention and she could have said her foot-tapping was part of her note-taking process. She had already earned enough clout by being present in the room. That fact alone would guarantee her name in the next edition of the newspaper.

But the outcome didn't affect Effa alone. It also affected her friends, the Avis Blakes and the Loreli Steeles of the world, the women who needed or wanted to live independent lives, the women looking to fund their dreams whether out of ambition or from a desire not to be indebted to any man. Most important, the outcome provided other avenues of work for women like the one Effa had seen in the alley. Whether or not that particular woman would, or even could, take advantage of the employment opportunity wasn't the point. The point was that the option should be available for her to take if she chose.

Effa straightened her shoulders. She would have gotten an earful from her mother for such poor posture. She had nothing to hide from or apologize for. Given how the men had been acting, she felt like the only adult in the room anyway. And Effa had been waiting all summer for a moment like this.

"Well . . ." Effa placed her notepad to the side and stood. "It seems like all of you have missed the point while you were throwing jabs at each other. The point is that our community is the lifeblood of your business. Your business needs workers to keep going, Mr. Blumstein. The young women in our community need work. If you don't do your part to invest in their professional development, you won't have them or their families as your customers in the future. And not because of scorn or bitterness, but because they simply won't have the money to spend in your store. They'll be too busy trying to scrape together a living on the streets because no other employment options will be available to them. Nothing but prostitution, or worse."

Each man's jaw fell. Mr. Blumstein turned an interesting shade of pink.

"Mrs. Manley, we might have a difference of opinion on

this matter, but there is no need to be vulgar." Mr. Blumstein pushed his seat back and stood up. "Perhaps you should leave. I'll have my secretary take the notes."

Effa glanced at the door but stood her ground. "If anyone is leaving, it should be you. And your store. Move your entire operation to Midtown, since you value those shoppers so much."

Aware that she now had the attention of every man in the room, she put her hands on her hips and carried on. "But you can't do that, can you? The rents down there would run you out of business before you reopened your doors. Meanwhile, we would forget you had ever been here. The other major retailers on One Twenty-Fifth Street have agreed to our demands. It's time to face the music, Mr. Blumstein. *You* need Harlem. Harlem doesn't need you."

"Please take it easy, Mrs. Manley. You shouldn't be getting yourself worked up like this. I know you've been outside all afternoon. You're obviously feeling the effects of heat exhaustion. I would feel terrible if you passed out because you overexerted yourself." Mr. Blumstein took a step forward. She could tell from his condescending tone that he was going to use his mock concern to push her right out of the room.

Not today, mister!

Effa shot him a look that she hoped would hit him like a line drive to the chest. "The only thing I find exerting is having to explain this to you over and over again. We all know that putting our girls on the sales floor is the right thing for you to do for your business and for this community."

Effa sat down. She had to admit, she was starting to feel

warm. She began fanning herself. Having to talk sense to a man without any was exhausting.

Blumstein gestured to one of his executives. "Benny, get Mrs. Manley a glass of water." The man rushed out of the room so fast that he forgot to close the door. Outside, she could hear him barking an order at the secretary to get the water.

Her supposed distress created a much-needed break in the tension that had been building in the room. It felt very much like a baseball game when the score is tied in the bottom of the ninth, and Effa was the one who had just hit the ball deep into center. It wasn't clear yet if the ball would be caught or go over the wall.

Benny returned with her drink. She accepted it. As she took a sip, she almost wished she had a straw to stir it with, like those Mob bosses in the movies when they had their enemies cornered. She leaned back and got comfortable so she could enjoy this sense of control.

By the time Effa and the rest of the League members left that meeting, Mr. Blumstein and his team had committed to hiring thirty-five Negro women and men as clerks and salespeople by September.

She emerged from the building with a "We did it!" The supporters who had been picketing on the sidewalk broke out into cheers. Effa was eager to share the news with Abe. But people surrounded her, asking questions and patting her on the back.

"Get away from her! Let the woman breathe!" Avis pushed her way through the joyous crowd closing in on Effa, grabbed Effa's hand, and pulled her out of there. "You look like you could use some fresh air."

When they were free of the picketers, Avis led Effa into a waiting cab. Once the car was moving, Effa didn't waste time catching her breath. "Thank you for getting me out of there. But honestly, I loved it. Did you see how excited they all were? How they were looking at me? It was like I was some kind of hero. Imagine that—Effa Manley, the shopping savior of One Twenty-Fifth Street!"

"I swear, you are good. You walk around here with this humble, hardworking persona, but you don't fool me. I know you, Effa. Not only do you love the attention—you live for it. I can see it clear as day."

Effa turned to watch the wide boulevards of Harlem whiz by. "Why, I don't know what you're referring to, Mrs. Blake."

"Of course you don't." Avis smiled.

Chapter 8

Effa had lost track of time after that last negotiation meeting at the store and the celebration on the street. She had no recollection of how she'd made it back home. For all she knew, she had floated up the stairs and into the apartment.

"Abe, we did it!" she announced upon opening the door. But there was no answer. "Abe? Are you here?"

Effa set her keys and purse down on the side table and entered their living room. The lamp was on, but there was no Abe. The radio was off. That was a sure sign that he was not home. The man threw a fit about wasting electricity if she left the radio on when she went to get a drink from the kitchen, but then he'd turn around and leave the light on without a second thought.

She made her way to the bedroom. With a huff, she sat on the bed and began pulling off her shoes. She rubbed her blistered foot. Yes, the promised employment gains were important. But for Effa, the real win was the fact that she no longer had to parade outside the store in the most sensible—yet still fashionable—shoes she owned, a pair of black T-strap low heels.

When both shoes had been removed and both of her soles had been rubbed, Effa slid her feet into her slippers and went about preparing dinner. She felt like it had been ages since she had been in her kitchen in the daytime. In reality, it had been less than a week since she'd prepared their Sunday dinner. Effa peeked into the icebox and let out a whoosh of relief. Thank goodness she had remembered to pick up some chicken breasts the day before.

She set up the dredging station on the counter. Today's victory called for fried chicken. And—she checked the contents of the icebox again—some coleslaw. It was a warm day, but a breeze was now coming through the cracked-open kitchen window. Yes, just enough to make the heat from the hot grease bearable.

It felt good to be able to cook like this in the middle of the week. Lately, she had been either too physically exhausted or too mentally drained after the picketing to think about cooking. It had been going on for so long without any signs of ending. But now that the boycott was truly over, she could assume the role of a proper housewife again.

When Abe came home, she had just finished dissolving the sugar in a pitcher of lemonade and had a pound cake cooling on the counter.

Abe stopped short when he saw Effa in the kitchen. "You're home?"

"Yes, and I have wonderful news. Blumstein finally agreed to hire Negro salesclerks at the store." Effa donned her oven mitts and held up the pound cake. "They've committed to bringing on fifteen by the end of this month and twenty more next month. I made dessert to celebrate!"

Abe broke out in a grin. "That's great, Effie. Then I guess it was a stroke of luck that I stopped to grab us some dinner."

He placed the brown paper bag he'd been carrying on the dining-room table. He started pulling out wrapped parcels of food. "I got mashed potatoes, and fried chicken, and some greens, and . . ."

He stopped abruptly when Effa started laughing. "It looks like we'll be celebrating for the rest of the week, because I have a serving platter full of fried chicken in the kitchen. I hope you didn't get any dessert."

"No." Abe grinned. He pulled two bottles out of the bag. "But I did grab us some soda pop!"

"You're the best. I'll get us some plates." Effa felt tears threatening to fall. She turned away from him just in time to keep him from seeing them and let out a sigh of relief. She had been fearing the worst for a while, but it seemed that they had finally found their way back to the same page. Throughout the boycott campaign, she had been so scared that they were drifting apart, spiraling down the same path that she and George had been on before her first marriage ended.

But she was happy to see that she had just been overthinking it. What she had with Abe might not be the stuff of a dime-store romance novel, but with him, she felt like they were on more solid ground. Even if they had yet to find a way to come together as man and wife. They would figure it out. What was more important was that they had forged a true partnership together.

Two months later

"We want to know when our darker-colored girls are going to get some of those Blumstein's jobs, Mrs. Manley. You light-brights weren't the only ones who spent the summer sweating on that picket line."

The Citizens' League had called this meeting to address community concerns about the department store's recent hires. The local papers had published the pictures of the new Negro sales employees, and everyone immediately noticed that the young women had one thing in common: they were all fair-skinned.

Effa kept the smile frozen on her face as she sat on the dais with the other Citizens' League leaders. But she wanted nothing more than to shout down the middle-aged brown-skinned woman in a domestic uniform who was currently raking her over the coals. How dare she insinuate that Effa was prejudiced against her own people?

"I appreciate your frustration, Mrs. Neville, but I assure you, there isn't a secret dark-versus-light conspiracy here. We can't handpick individuals and tell the stores that this is who they must hire. That's absurd." Effa hoped that she did not sound as irritated as she felt.

Ever since the negotiated Blumstein's deal had been announced, every member of the Citizens' League leadership team had been bombarded with requests for references or a "good word"; everyone wanted to secure one of those guaranteed salesclerk positions. In most cases, Effa had refused. The one exception was Loreli Steele. Effa had typed up a reference for her, but Loreli said the hiring manager had seemed less than enthusiastic the moment he looked at her lovely medium-brown face. Now Effa felt like she was damned if she did, damned if she didn't.

"Smile that fake smile at me all you want. But we are tired of people like you coming uptown and playing like you are one of us, that you're down for the cause, when you live Negro when it's convenient for you but have no qualms about running downtown to their shops and hotels and restaurants when you need a break from oppression. You throw your last damn penny at the white folks who'd spit in your face the second they found out who you really were but always have some excuse about why you can't spend that same money right here in Harlem!"

The rest of the audience roared its approval, its agreement with the woman's accusations. The louder they got, the more the vise around her chest squeezed. Because as much as those accusations stung, there was no way that Effa could deny the truth that lay behind them.

She toed the Bloomingdale's shopping bag that sat beside her under the makeshift meeting table. Effa had gone down there this afternoon looking for a new couture hat. Now that the boycott was over, she had more time to get back to her plan for creating her own millinery business—*in* Harlem. But she had been away from the business for over a year. So yes, she had been downtown shopping. And she didn't correct the salesgirl when she assumed she was white. She'd bought the hat not just for herself but as an *investment*, so she could do her part to bring luxury handmade accessories to Harlem. If all went well, she'd need salesgirls of her own to help make and sell her luxury goods.

That is, if she ever got her business off the ground.

Effa squirmed in her seat as it became obvious that the

crowds before her weren't buying her excuses, no matter how rational and true they were. The more Effa thought about it, the more her excuses sounded flat. Even to her.

The lady eyed her up and down like she was filth—lying filth.

Effa might have become a savior to the women in the upper echelons of society here, but to the everyday women on the street, she was just another social-climbing fraud and phony.

She felt like she was being called a hypocrite, and she didn't like it. But there was nothing she could say that wouldn't sink her deeper into the hole she had dug for herself.

"I'm sorry you feel that way about me and about the work we've done so far in the community. All I can say is that I will take your concerns to heart and will do better going forward."

The lady looked Effa dead in the eye and sucked her teeth before sitting back down.

Effa felt her face warm. No doubt her blasted pale skin had given her away once more. But again, what more could she say? All she could do was make good on her promise when she had the opportunity.

At the other end of the dais, Reverend Johnson cleared his throat. "Does anyone else have any concerns?"

"I do," a male voice said from the back of the sanctuary. The lighting wasn't that good, so it was hard to see who had spoken. Effa hadn't realized that anyone was sitting back there. There was a sound of rustling as whoever this was got to his feet. A figure began walking down the aisle and into the light. It was a clean-cut young man wearing a bow tie and a suit.

"I just wanted to know how the white lady got a seat at the table here tonight, and she will most likely be offered one of them jobs you all keep claiming that you 'won' for the community. But whenever a brother like me asks to be included in the leadership of organizations like these, I'm ignored. Why is that?"

Reverend Johnson banged his hand on the table. "I think that we've all had enough for the evening."

"Wait." Effa held up her hand to stop any adjournment motions from being put on the floor. "I'd like to answer that."

Reverend Johnson frowned. He opened his mouth as if to protest, but then, after a beat, he waved away whatever he had been about to say. "Fine. Go ahead."

"Sir, I don't need you to remind me what I look like. I've had to look at myself in the mirror each and every day of the last thirty-some years. I am a member of the race and grew up as such, despite what you think you see on the outside. And I have a seat at this table because I made one for myself. I was instrumental in creating the group that was predecessor to the Citizens' League for Fair Play. As a matter of fact, I hosted the organizational meeting in my own home. We might not have originated the Don't Buy movement in Harlem, but we— the now defunct Harlem Women's Association—did start this particular campaign back in February. So I'm going to challenge you just like Mr. Blumstein did us when we placed our initial complaints with him: Show me the receipts. Do something. Anything. Get something going and I'll be glad to scoot my chair over to make room for yours."

Her impromptu speech received sporadic applause from

people in the pews, mostly women. Effa did note that Reverend Johnson faked a cough to rein in his mirth. Once he had himself under control again, he banged his gavel on its block.

"And on that note, I call this meeting adjourned. All in favor?"

This was met by a thunderous roar of *ayes*.

Effa's hands shook as she put her notepad into her bag. Reverend Johnson stopped beside her. "Are you going to be okay getting home?"

Effa appreciated the note of concern. It took her a second to regain her voice. "I'll be fine."

He looked toward the back of the sanctuary, the houselights now turned to their full strength, but the man in the bow tie had already left. "Don't let what he said get to you. Those types always feel like they're entitled to everything for just showing up and throwing out inflammatory statements. They're always punching down with their insults. You stay the course. You've been doing good work. Essential work. People around here are starting to take notice."

"That's good of you to say. Unfortunately, I've been on the receiving end of those kinds of comments all my life. Tonight will not be the last time. I just wish . . ." Effa shook her head. "I just wish what I do shone brighter than what I look like. I had no control over that. If anything, it's just one of the tools I have to make things better for everyone else."

She stopped before she said anything that would sound like those blasted *Woe is me*, tragic-mulatto novels that were so in vogue with the literati right now. The heroines in those novels had nothing to do with her, her experiences, or how she felt about herself. Effa didn't think she was better than anyone else because of her skin color, and she definitely didn't think she was worse off than anyone else because of it either. She had no desire to beg or fool the white world into treating her like a fellow human being. And she wasn't going to bemoan the fact that there were Negroes who would never accept her because of the way she looked.

If Effa were to magically acquire a darker permanent skin tone, she wouldn't be surprised if those types tripped all over themselves to find something else about her not to like.

Effa gathered up the last of her things, gave a quick nod to the few stragglers still chatting among themselves, went outside, and stood under the building's portico. Long shadows had fallen in the valleys of the wide uptown boulevards. She sighed. It had been a perfect early autumn day. Had the meeting ended a little earlier, Effa would have tried to make the trek home on foot. But now it was starting to rain, so that option was out.

Resigned, she looked down Seventh Avenue in search of a cab. There was none when she needed one, of course. "Can't walk home because it's raining, and I can't get a cab home. Like I said, I'm damned if I do and damned if I don't. Just like the rest of my world." She laughed, but it sounded hollow to her own ears.

Effa dug in her bag for a rain cap to cover her head but found only paper, pens, and her wallet. "Shoot."

"Problem?" A man who'd been passing by stopped and held his umbrella over her head.

"I didn't know it was going to rain tonight," she said absently. She was still looking down. "I can take a cab, but I'll get soaked when I try to hail one. I hate being unprepared."

He gestured up at his umbrella. "May I walk with you?"

"You're so kind." Effa hurried toward the man and finally took a good look at him. It was . . .

"Henry?" she breathed.

A raindrop fell on her forehead. Her instincts were pushing her toward Henry and his umbrella. But she stood frozen in place. No, she couldn't. Not again. He was the man who had led her to stray from her first husband's bed.

Splat! Another raindrop landed on her shoulder. The sprinkle of a few seconds ago was transforming into bigger, more consistent drops.

Henry walked over to shield her from the rain with his umbrella. "C'mon, Ef."

"I can't."

"Don't be silly. You're going to get all wet." Henry frowned. He looked just as handsome as when she'd last seen him. When they were supposed to start their new life together. But he wound up breaking her heart.

"Maybe that would be for the best."

"I get that you're still mad at me. But I won't let you catch a chill on my account. The least I can do is keep you dry while you hail a cab."

There was now a steady patter of rain hitting the umbrella. "Okay, fine."

Together, they walked down the street to the corner. She was about to hold up her hand to hail an approaching cab, but he beat her to the punch. Henry moved with the grace of a center fielder reaching to keep a ball from going over the fence. The moment his arm cleared the cover of the umbrella, it was drenched; the cab slowed but as soon as the driver got a good look at them, he turned on his Off-Duty light and sped down the street. Effa rolled her eyes. The cabbies did the same thing when she was out with Abe. They'd gotten into the habit of having Effa flag down the cabs.

"I hate when they do that." Effa gave Henry an appreciative smile. "And now you're all wet. I'm so sorry. You didn't have to do that."

He shook the excess water off his arm. "What kind of gentleman would I be if I didn't?"

But you aren't a gentleman was on the tip of her tongue. She swallowed the words. "Again, thank you." Effa took that moment to assess him. Henry had on an overcoat, and from the looks of it, he had a very good tailor. The garment fit him to a T. She took in how it draped over his broad shoulders. His mustache had been groomed into the pencil-thin line that was the style nowadays. It suited him nicely. The years had been kind to her former lover. But she knew better than to tell him that.

And then there was his smile. It had a boyish quality to it that reminded Effa of . . . Abe.

She stepped as far away from him as the span of the umbrella would allow. She spied another cab waiting at a red light a block up.

"I should try this time. I tend to have better luck. You know how cabbies are."

"If you insist." He waved the arm that was still dripping wet.

As soon as the light turned green, Effa held up her hand. The warm early autumn rain had her clothes sticking to her skin. She waved her arm excitedly as the cab approached. Luckily, this time it stopped.

Henry, still playing the role of knight in shining armor,

walked her to the passenger door and opened it. "My lady, your carriage awaits."

"Thank you."

He held the door until she was safely tucked in the back seat. "Is it all right if I call on you sometime?"

"I don't think that would be a good idea. I've remarried." She held up her left hand and flashed her rings.

"Of course you did. You were always a good catch, Effa."

The compliment hurt her. If that's what he thought, then why had he broken her heart all those years ago?

The smile on his face fell. The hurt must have shown in her eyes. "Well, then, let's just call this my good deed for the night."

"Let's do that. It's good to see you again."

"It's good to see you too." Henry shut the cab door and walked away.

The cabbie turned around, annoyed. "Hey, lady, where ya headed?"

Effa gave him her address, then turned to get one last glimpse of Henry. But he was gone.

The phone was ringing when Effa arrived home. She pulled off her hat and placed the receiver to her ear. "Hello?"

"Good evening, Mrs. Manley." Effa caught her breath. It was Lucy Richards. She hadn't heard from her directly since that dinner party at the beginning of the year.

"Congratulations on the Blumstein's campaign. The work you did caught the attention of many eyes in town."

"Thank you." Effa shifted her weight from one foot to the other. She wasn't sure where Mrs. Richards was going with this, but Effa's feet were screaming for a soak in a footbath.

"I have a new opportunity for you if you're interested." Effa had a feeling saying no to this was not an option. Mrs. Richards continued, "We're putting together a women's group to support Eunice Carter's candidacy for the state assembly. If all goes well, we will have a hand in electing New York's first Negro assemblywoman."

Effa recognized Eunice Carter's name from the local newspapers. She had graduated from Fordham Law School not too long ago and was, if Effa recalled correctly, the first Negro woman to do so. She'd also read that Mrs. Carter had passed the New York State bar exam last year.

Effa smiled into the phone, her sore feet forgotten. "Count me in. I would absolutely love to help get Eunice Carter elected."

On the appointed afternoon, Effa was one of several women in Mrs. Richards's sitting room. The other ladies in attendance appeared to have been carefully selected to take part in this organizing meeting under the guise of afternoon tea.

"It is time, ladies!" Mrs. Richards declared. "Time for one of our own to represent us in the New York State Assembly. And that someone is Eunice Carter."

Effa was the first to jump to her feet and applaud when Mrs. Richards gestured to the elegantly dressed brown-skinned woman beside her.

Eunice smiled and waved, then thanked the attendees for their support. Afterward, Effa made a beeline for Eunice and shook her hand. "Congratulations, Mrs. Carter."

"Since we're going to be working together, please call me Eunice."

"I'm Effa Manley. And you must call me Effa." Effa beamed at Mrs. Richards and mouthed, *Thank you*. She couldn't believe that she had been invited further into the social mix. Soon she would be able to call a state assemblywoman her friend. And a Negro woman at that!

When Effa returned home, she found Abe pacing the living room in front of the radio. The big boyish smile he wore made him look twenty years younger. She greeted him with a grin of her own.

"You're never going to believe this—" they both said at the same time.

Effa laughed and took a step back. "Okay, you first. Because there's no way your news will top mine."

"That's what you think. Effie, baby, hold on to your hat. Because we're about to go on a wild ride. Guess what—I bought us a baseball team!"

Effa had been about to blurt out her own news, but the words got stuck in her throat as her mind processed what Abe had just told her.

"I'm sorry, you what?"

"I said I bought us a team. Our own baseball team. Isn't that great, Ef?" Abe picked her up and swung her around. Effa was caught off guard. She held on to his shoulders for dear life.

"I—I don't understand. How did you just up and *buy* a baseball team? You mean a team like the Yankees?"

Abe set her down. "More like the Black Yankees. Remember when you told me to go and talk to Bill?"

"Are you saying that you bought the New York Black Yankees team from Bill and James?"

Abe shook his head. "No, even better. I bought us an *expansion* franchise. We're starting a new team from scratch in Brooklyn. The Brooklyn Eagles, to be exact. Isn't that great?"

"Brooklyn?" Effa squeaked. Her heart sank. She had worked so hard to earn a place for herself in Harlem's social circles. Now, with one rash decision, Abe was going to make her start all over again in Brooklyn. She shivered. That was where old-money Negro families lived. Their roots in the city ran deeper than those of Mrs. Richards. Talk about snooty. She'd heard rumors that breaking into those social circles was unheard of. It didn't matter how much money you had. If you weren't born into that world, you didn't exist.

"Surely you can't expect me to pack up and leave Harlem? Why, I was about to tell you about the election campaign I've just joined. I've made commitments, Abe. People are depending on me. My friends—"

The smile fell from Abe's face. All the joy he had unleashed in the room evaporated as well. "What about me, your husband? I'm depending on you too."

Effa hesitated. He had a point. But she wasn't going to let that make her back down. "Yes, but you should have discussed this with me first. I mean, for goodness' sake, Abe. Who in his right mind would buy a baseball team on impulse?"

"You mean like you sprung the boycott of all of One Twenty-Fifth Street on me? I don't remember you asking me how I felt about that. You were supposed to be hosting a little party for a few hours. Instead, you wound up birthing a movement!"

"Yes, but that was an *important* moment. People got *jobs* because of me!" Effa blinked back the tears that had started to form in her eyes. This was just like that damn Citizens' League meeting all over again. But this hurt worse. She had never expected Abe to make her feel selfish for accomplishing something so important.

No, it wasn't Abe making her feel that way. It was her own conscience.

"Yes, that was important. But let's face it, you had to stand on the sidewalk and beg for those jobs. With this team, we run the show. We're the bosses—you and me. We say who gets hired, who gets fired, and how much they get paid. We'll be employing a lot more than thirty-five people. We don't have to beg a white man for nothing."

Effa turned that thought over in her mind. Abe had a point. They would be their own bosses. Together. It could be a dream fulfilled for Effa, although not in the way she had envisioned it. Even if she was able to get her millinery shop off the ground, there was no guarantee that it would be successful, no matter how good she was at manipulating a piece of felt around a hat block. There was no way that all of Harlem would take notice of a retail space on a busy street. She might not be able to afford even one employee.

But at the helm of a baseball team? They would need players, administrative staff, a bus driver, attorneys, popcorn sellers, ticket takers, and more. Most important, all of Negro America would know who she was.

Still, Effa wrung her hands. "But the political campaign. I've made commitments—"

"There's nothing like a sizable donation to smooth that over," Abe cut in. "Just tell me how much and where to drop off the check."

"I . . ." It amazed Effa how much her life had changed since marrying Abraham Manley. Not even two years ago, she was worrying if she would ever have enough money saved to make her dreams come true. Now, her husband could wipe away her every concern with a swipe of his pen. Not for the first time, she wondered about the exact dollar amount that Abe had at his disposal. But she'd never had the nerve to ask.

In fact, she didn't want to know. Because that would lead to questions about *how* he'd acquired all that money. That, she definitely did not want to know. At any rate, confirmation of his actual net worth was more than likely to make her faint dead away.

"Okay, that roadblock is out of the way." Effa didn't mention that money would go only so far in smoothing things over with the election committee. She would still have to make things right with Mrs. Richards. But she would deal with that later. "What is it you'd want me to do, exactly? I don't imagine that you want me crammed on a bus with a bunch of sweaty men for weeks at a time."

"You won't have to worry about any of that. I'll travel with the team and go around scouting for new talent. You stay here in New York and do all the secretary stuff in the office."

"Secretary stuff?" It was clear that Abe had no idea what secretaries did. She had half a mind to tell him so.

"You know, the easy stuff. Typing up contracts, answering the phones, sending the game stats to the papers, handing out paychecks." He added quickly, "And everything else that might come up on a day-to-day basis."

Effa stared at her husband. She couldn't believe it. He really wanted her to give up the campaign and the possibility of building political connections in Albany to play secretary for his new hobby.

"Well, I don't want to move to Brooklyn." She crossed her arms over her chest. "That's not negotiable."

"We won't have to. The season runs from May to September. That's only five months. We only have to go out there for home games. You can do everything else here in the apartment."

"I still can't believe you're asking me to give up politics for baseball." Maybe she wouldn't have to give up Eunice's campaign. If the season didn't start for another six months, she could stay on the committee through the primaries in the spring.

"Ef, look at it this way: Politics is boring and you'd be doing it for free. With this, other people will be paying us to live and breathe baseball. We can have it all. You can do your community work through outreach with the team. We'll be bringing good-paying jobs to the community. Jobs with dignity. Wasn't that what the boycott was about? But this time, we can do it together."

Again, he had her there. They hadn't spent much time together this past summer with her being so consumed by the boycott. This was an unexpected twist in the plan she had drawn up with Cora Rollins. But if it meant that she could work her plan without the guilt that had been consuming her, then she was all in. Effa gave Abe a thumbs-up.

"You're lucky I love baseball."

"That's my girl!"

She hugged Abe. Leave it to him to find an ingenious way to save their marriage.

"I knew you would come around. That's why I convinced

the other owners to hold the annual league meeting here in New York. And . . ." Abe looked at her sheepishly.

"And what?"

"And I told them that you would host the welcome party held the night before the big meeting. And that you could pull it all together by January."

"You told them I'd do what? It's November! There's no way I can organize a decent party—and right after the holidays I might add—with barely two months' notice. Are you out of your mind?"

"You just got that tightwad Blumstein to hire thirty-five Negroes on to work on his sales floor. Babe, if you can do that, you can do anything."

"How about you promise to get me that mink coat I've been asking for and I'll see what I can do."

"You have my word."

Chapter 9

Harlem
January 1935

A wave of relief washed over Effa as she and Abe walked past the shiny car with the license plate reading *ES* parked on Seventh Avenue to the entrance of Smalls Paradise. Somehow she had managed to throw together tonight's event for the Negro team owners and their special guests.

Ed Smalls, the owner of both the car and the club, greeted them at the door with his arms outstretched to embrace her. That made her smile even wider as she gave him a big squeeze.

"Ed, you have been a godsend. Thank you for helping me pull this off."

"Anything for a friend." A slight drawl gave away Ed Smalls's Charleston roots despite his living in New York for decades. "Don't worry about a thing, Effa. My people won't let you down."

Smalls Paradise was a popular nightclub just around the corner from St. Philip's Episcopal church. It was the only Negro-owned late-night spot in Harlem that welcomed a racially integrated clientele. While Effa and Abe were not a mixed couple, they could easily be mistaken for one, and it was nice to be able to socialize in a place where they did not look like an anomaly.

Effa patted Ed's arm. "You and your staff are the best of the best. Especially the kitchen staff." This was an understatement. The waiters at Smalls serviced customers on roller skates and were part of the musical floor shows. One thing she didn't have to worry about tonight was whether their guests would be entertained. "I'm more nervous about who will show up tonight. Let's hope they will be on their best behavior," she said.

"Can I have my wife back, please?" Abe pulled Effa away from Ed, the gesture more playful than possessive. Abe and Ed had been friends for decades before Effa came along.

"I suppose, but only because I have a club to run." Ed laughed.

This dinner reception was a chance for the Negro National League owners to relax before their league meeting the next day. The annual meetings were held every winter to hash out playing schedules, revenue splits from ticket sales, and the overall business matters of the league, and they almost always became tense at some point. Socializing first was one way to keep the inevitable disagreements from becoming physical.

Effa had not met most of the owners before, but Abe knew them, some of them pretty well. He had been regaling her with stories of their colorful personalities and exploits for as long as she'd known him. She'd balanced out the guest list with her society friends. Tonight's mix of new and old money could be interesting and entertaining, or it might go completely off the rails.

Ed held open the door, and she and Abe descended into

the basement where the club was located. White-linen-draped tables lined three sides of the dance floor in the middle of the room; a bandstand was set up along the fourth. The music was the main draw for first-time visitors, but it was the food and the singing waiters that kept them coming back. Abe and Effa had come here often early in their courtship. But Effa and Ed's friendship went back to when she modeled in fashion shows and other charity events.

Effa was relieved to see Vere Johns already there, sitting at the bar. "Great. You're here. Thank you again for doing this."

"Standing in as your master of ceremonies for something like this definitely beats picketing in the hot summer sun," Vere said, his Jamaican accent evident. "I haven't sweated so much since I was a boy in short pants back home."

Vere was an editor at the *New York Age* and hosted his own radio show. Effa had befriended him during their time together on the Citizens' League board.

"Yes, compared to that, this will definitely be a piece of cake." Effa pulled her typewritten schedule of events from her purse. "Look this over. Let me know if you have any questions."

"Stop worrying. I've got this under control. You go and enjoy your guests."

"Thank you," she said, relieved. "I owe you box seats when we have our opening day."

"I'll hold you to that."

Effa flitted around until their guests started trickling in. She greeted everyone she already knew with a hug. She would have known Bill "Bojangles" Robinson even if he weren't one of the owners of the New York Black Yankees. The talented tap-dancing singer owed his fame to years on the vaudeville circuit and, more recently, to starring in several films. He couldn't walk down the street without crowds flocking to him. Bill might as well have been the unofficial mayor of Harlem. Tonight was no different.

However, Effa wasn't prepared for the uproar from all the men when a young man—a boy, really—arrived, with a girl on his arm.

She grabbed an excited Abe before he joined the fray. "Who's that?"

"Joe Louis. A young boxer out of Detroit. He's supposed to be the next big thing. He's in town to train for his first professional fight."

"I see. Who's the girl? She looks familiar."

Abe shrugged. "Beats me. I think she's from Chicago. Maybe we saw her somewhere when we were there on our honeymoon."

"Perhaps you're right." Effa let go of Abe's sleeve. He stayed by her side but his pent-up energy was palpable. "You might as well get over there. Just don't forget to introduce me."

Abe did more than that. He made sure that the boxer and the woman—his fiancée, Marva Trotter—were seated beside Effa at the hosts' table. As it turned out, Ms. Trotter worked as a model. Effa was correct in thinking that she had seen the young woman before.

"I know where I know you from now. You were in a fashion show I attended in Chicago. What a fun coincidence to meet here today!"

Marva had looked a bit nervous when she entered the club, like a baby deer in the headlights. But Marva seemed relieved after making the connection with Effa, no matter how tenuous. When Effa learned that Marva was only eighteen, she made a point of keeping an eye on the young woman. Effa tried to draw out her fiancé as well. At only twenty years old, Joe had a shy air about him despite his boxer's bulk.

As the evening progressed, the two started to relax and enjoy themselves. That didn't stop Effa from appointing herself as their protective big sister. Whenever the grown men who were boxing fans started to overwhelm them, Effa would shoo the pair onto the dance floor or lead them on another trip to the dessert buffet.

Joe leaned over at one point and mouthed *Thank you* to Effa. When she gave him a questioning look, he nodded at Marva. Effa responded with an understanding smile. There was too much going on for her to explain that she too had once been a new girl in town at an event like this surrounded by strangers.

Gus Greenlee interrupted the moment by giving Joe a heavy slap on the back. Gus owned the Pittsburgh Crawfords and their home stadium, Greenlee Field. He was the only owner in the Negro National League who owned his stadium outright. Like his hands, Gus's personality was huge. "I expect to make a lot of money off you, young man. Which means you better be as good in the ring as they say you are."

"You don't have to worry about me, sir." Joe gave him a reassuring smile, then steadied himself by wrapping an arm around Marva.

"That's my boy!"

Joe went back to sharing shy smiles with Marva once Gus had moved on. Then he looked around at the grown men in the room, most of them former or current numbers bankers, talking and laughing.

Effa leaned over to catch both Joe's and Marva's eyes. "I wouldn't get too overwhelmed by all of this fancy stuff. They're just making each other laugh with stories of their past exploits. Most of them are lying."

"Which means that some of them are telling the truth." Marva looked like a child in the middle of a grown-ups' party.

"Yes. But even the parts that are truth are greatly exaggerated." Effa winked.

"Where I'm from, the numbers men and gangsters are nobody to play with. It seems like all of them have so much riding on my fists. I just hope I don't let them down," Joe said.

"You just stay focused and true to yourself, young man," Effa advised him. "Do your best. Don't do anything that'll cause you to hang your head in shame when you look in the mirror. That's all you can do."

"Thank you, ma'am."

"Please. It's Effa."

"Okay, Effa. I ain't never been to a party like this before. The food is good. But I never seen this many forks at once."

"Miss Effa," Marva said, "I keep telling him to use whichever one he feels like. I doubt any of his promoters know which one to use either."

Effa pushed back her seat and stood over the two young people. "It sounds like someone is in need of an etiquette lesson. I guess that's as good an excuse as any to extend you both an invitation to my place for a home-cooked meal."

Joe broke out into a boyish grin. "Thank you, Miss Effa. I can't wait." Effa knew that had she been about twenty years younger, she would've given Marva a run for her money over her fiancé. Instead, she saw in Marva something like the young woman she had been when she had come to New York and found herself caught up in the glamour and excitement of living on her own for the first time . . . and then married to a stranger less than six months later. If only she had had a big-sister type who had scooped her up under her wing and helped her get her priorities straight.

In that moment Effa knew that she could and would be the big sister to these young people. The big sister she herself had needed. She didn't have long to enjoy the good feelings that came from this resolve, though.

"Mrs. Manley," a voice behind her boomed. "At last. I've been looking forward to meeting you."

Effa turned around to find a tall, well-groomed, fair-skinned middle-aged man. She could tell by the way he carried himself that he had been an athlete at some point, even if he was past his prime now. He still had that something that made him easy on the eyes.

Effa smiled and extended her hand; her new admirer took it and gave it a firm shake. "You did a lot of good in the community around here this summer. It was my pleasure to cover your boycott in my newspaper."

"And which paper would that be?" She went down the list of invitees in her mind. Yes, a number of reporters had been invited, but she already knew them all.

"The *Pittsburgh Courier*, of course."

She recognized, not the man himself, but the name of the newspaper. "Then you must be Cum Posey?"

He grinned at her correct guess. "The one and only. How do you do?"

Effa felt a momentary twinge of embarrassment. Of course she should have recognized Cumberland Posey. Everyone knew who he was. But she didn't think of him as the publisher of the largest Negro newspaper in the country. In this context, he more readily came to mind as the owner of the Homestead Grays baseball team.

"Oh my, it's so good to finally meet you in the flesh! I can't believe it. A walking, talking living legend at my little ol' party."

"Stop. I put my coat on one sleeve at a time just like any other man. And there's nothing 'little' about this party and you know it."

"You have me there. I tried to have an intimate gathering with just the owners, but Abe wouldn't hear of it." That was a small fib. All of the non-baseball people on the guest list were Effa's entertainer friends and society acquaintances, people she'd insisted on inviting.

"Of course." The twinkle in Cum's eyes told her he didn't believe her little fib. In fact, he looked charmed by the way she tried to downplay her role in putting the whole thing together. "Everyone knows you have Abe wrapped around your pretty little finger. The man adores you."

"No, it is I who adore him. Now, you go mingle. Have a good time and save all the business talk for tomorrow." Effa watched as he walked off. Cum Posey had a different air than the other owners in the Negro National League. First off, the man reeked of old money, so much that he could've taken a bath in it. He possessed a polish that Gus Greenlee and Alex

Pompez and the other owners just didn't have. They were rougher around the edges. One could tell that they had spent some time in the streets.

When she shook Cum Posey's hand, it had felt slightly rough from playing ball but not worn, not like he'd had to work his fingers to the bone at any point. Abe was missing the top of his left thumb—an accident when he worked at a sawmill back in North Carolina—and his hands were smooth now but still calloused. In comparison, Cum Posey's hands felt like soft pillows.

"He's a fine-looking man, isn't he?" A tall, brown-skinned woman approached her. She had a timeless face, the kind that made it impossible to determine her age. The only hint was in the way she carried herself and that tired, almost weathered look in her eyes. Effa guessed that she was a few years older than herself. But the most distinctive thing about her was her Southern accent. It was more pronounced than Ed's, which meant that she had left Dixie recently.

"He is. I can introduce you to him if you're interested." Effa positioned herself so that her back was to Posey. There were too many reporters crawling around this place. The last thing she needed was to provide fuel for their society columns.

"No, I was married to baseball a long time ago. I have no desire to chain myself to that circus again."

Effa inclined her head, recognizing that this woman might be a kindred spirit. "How so, if you don't mind my asking?"

"I used to own the Indianapolis ABCs. I took over the club after my husband died."

Now she had Effa's full attention. Effa extended her hand.

"Then we need to become the best of friends tonight. I'm Effa Manley. My husband and I own the Brooklyn Eagles."

"Olivia Taylor." She took Effa's hand and shook it.

Effa led Olivia to one of the tables in the back of the club where it was a little bit quieter and would be easier to talk. "My husband sprung the baseball business on me out of nowhere. Please, tell me everything."

"Well, the first thing is don't get caught up with any of the other owners. No flirting. No smiling. Nothing. You can be social all you want at parties like this, but don't let that fool you when it comes to the business. They don't want us there."

Effa frowned. "I hadn't planned on stepping outside of my marriage. But thank you for the tip. As for the business, it's as much mine as it is my husband's. They'll just have to deal with me too and get used to it."

Olivia hid a chuckle behind her hand. "That's cute. But trust me, they will pull out all the stops to make you miserable so you'll go back home and play house like a good little wifey. It doesn't matter how business-minded you think you are. The Negro League is where grown men with a little extra money go to live out their childhood fantasies and play games."

"Okay." Effa wasn't sure how seriously to take this woman. She sounded extremely bitter. From what Effa could remember, the Indianapolis ABCs team folded years ago. "Could you tell me about the day-to-day operations? I'll be handling more of that anyway. My husband will be dealing with most of the league affairs. That and the scouting and traveling stuff."

"Oh, child." Olivia shook her head. "He dumped all the work on you and you don't even know it. Life on the road as a ballplayer is tough; I would never want to live that life. But the day-to-day ain't no picnic either."

Olivia began ticking off items on her fingers. "There's uniforms. You have to design and order and maintain them for both home and away games. Then there's public relations and community outreach. You don't have ticket sales without those. Then you have to make sure the venue owners and the ticket takers aren't robbing you at the game. And then there's stocking the concessions stands and hiring personnel for the stands. I almost forgot—there's player contracts and payroll . . . I could go on. It is a full-fledged multitiered business, my dear. And you're going to be at the helm running it all."

Effa was beginning to understand why Olivia had that exhausted, haunted look in her eye. "Wow, that does sound like a lot."

"Yes, it was. But take what I've said with a grain of salt. Well, except for that don't-sleep-with-the-other-owners part. Definitely don't do that. And who knows, you might have an easier time of it than I did. You'll have your husband as a buffer when the boys don't want to let the girls into their club."

"Yes, that's a relief." Effa suddenly felt bad for Olivia, realizing that she had had to juggle all the tasks she'd listed on her own. And while she was grieving the loss of her husband, who couldn't have been much older than her. Talk about a shock.

"The baseball business is not all bad," Olivia continued. "Your community is your strength. They're the ones buying the tickets. They need baseball as much as you need them in the stands. And hold your friends close. I can't emphasize that enough. When the season is going good, you will feel like you're on top of the world. But I promise you, nothing prepares you for how lonely it feels when you're on the top."

Effa nodded as she took it all in. "Thank you for talking with me. You've helped point me in the right direction."

"Girl, I wish what I just told you was enough." Olivia fished a calling card and a pen out of her bag. She scribbled a telephone number on the back. "Here's my phone number. I'm living in Alabama now. I'll be back home in a week. Call me when you need me."

Effa took the card and placed it in her pocket. She made a mental note to put it in a safe place as soon as she returned home.

"I'm afraid it's time for me to leave." Olivia stood up. "I have to catch the train back down south."

"Thank you for coming. Thank you for sharing. I will definitely call you if I have any questions."

Effa watched Olivia Taylor climb the stairs to street level and could not help noticing that the woman took each step like she carried the weight of the world on her shoulders.

I'd better enjoy this party while I still have the energy. But she couldn't help thinking that maybe she would be better off running after Olivia and escaping what awaited her tomorrow. Maybe it would be best if Effa took herself as far away from the sports world as possible.

With that thought in mind, she returned to her seat. There was a natural lull in the party. It was a good time for her to finally get a bite of her dinner. She sat down, picked up her fork, and turned to the bandstand. There was a familiar face in the band setting up with the rest of the musicians. Effa's fork fell from her fingers and clattered onto the porcelain plate in front of her.

Marva's brow creased with concern. "Are you all right, Mrs. Manley?"

"I . . . I'm fine," she lied. Effa covered her mouth with her hand to hide her smile. "Just a little clumsy. I have too many of tonight's details flying through my head. I'm lucky I have enough sense left to put one foot in front of the other without them stumbling over each other."

Effa picked up her fork and returned it to its proper place. She looked over at the bandstand again. No matter how much she wished he weren't, Henry Clinton was still there, setting up his saxophone.

"If you say so, ma'am. But you look like you've just seen a ghost." Marva followed Effa's gaze. "A mighty handsome one."

"No one in this room looks as good as your husband-to-be. It might be best to keep your eyes on him." Effa winced. Her words had come out harsher than she had intended. Marva responded with a knowing smile. "Mm-hmm. I may be young, Mrs. Manley, but I've been around long enough to have seen some things. And right now, I am definitely seeing a woman who has a thing for a man who isn't her husband."

Henry chose that moment to look over. When he caught her and Marva watching him, he smiled and nodded. But he kept his eyes on Effa. Even with the distance that separated them, she could feel the heat smoldering from them. She felt herself beginning to melt as the intimate memories they created together came back to her. She looked away and quickly found the plate in front of her to be the most interesting object in the room.

It had been years since their association had led to the final straw that broke up her first marriage. She was still fairly young at the time but thankfully had gained a thimbleful of sense. Henry had promised her the world while she was another man's wife, said he'd let her do whatever she wanted when they were married, but once she was free, he'd changed his tune. Suddenly, he wanted her to sit at home like a dutiful wife and trust that he would provide for her and be loyal to her while he spent the majority of the year on the road. Effa had been a fool for lust once; she would not repeat that mistake again. She had told him that she would make do for herself. That they could figure it out when he was back in town and ready to stay closer to home.

That had been in 1925.

A thought kept nagging at Effa no matter how much she wanted it to go away: *I wonder if Abe really meant it when he gave me the okay to step outside our marriage?*

"It looks like trouble is headed this way," Marva warned. "What do you want to do?"

"You know what? It's time for me to make another round and mingle with my guests."

Effa got up, but the stars must not have been aligned in her favor that night because the first person she ran into was Ben Taylor.

Abe had hired Ben Taylor as their team's manager because Ben was the very best there was. And he'd been more than eager to leave the barnstorming team he had been managing out in Staten Island to work for a bona fide Negro National League team. And get the increase in pay that came with it.

"Mr. Taylor, so glad to see you."

Ben nodded at her. "Mrs. Manley."

"I never received an RSVP from you so I wasn't sure if you were coming."

Ben looked away, nodding and waving to passersby. Effa got the distinct impression that he'd rather be doing anything other than talking to her. And she had no idea why. She had spoken to him once for no more than five minutes, and that conversation was mainly about business related to her role as secretary for the team's affairs.

"My apologies. I misplaced my invitation," he said. "But I am Abe's manager, so I figured you'd know that my attendance here tonight was pretty much a given."

"I suppose so," she said slowly. She was stuck on the fact that Ben had made a point of saying he was *Abe's* manager. He was technically Effa's manager too, but it was such a picky thing that she decided not to question him about it.

"I saw you talking to my former sister-in-law over there." Ben nodded to the corner where she and Olivia had been talking.

"You mean Olivia Taylor?"

"Yeah, her. I don't know what she told you, but I wouldn't take too much of it to heart. She hasn't been right since my brother died. And then she thought she could stick her nose into men's business and run a baseball team. My advice to you is not to repeat her mistakes. Women have no business in baseball."

"But—"

Ben cut her off with a wave of his hand. "If you'll excuse me, Mrs. Manley. I see some players here I'd like to introduce to Abe and talk him into signing them for the team."

"Yes, of course."

Effa looked around, feeling like the odd girl out at a high-school dance. All the other guests were engaged in their own conversations. They seemed to be enjoying themselves, so at least she had the satisfaction of claiming this event a success. She just wished . . . if only she didn't feel so lost. So out of place.

At the podium, Vere tapped the microphone to get everyone's attention. "I hope you all enjoyed your dinner. Thanks to Ed Smalls and his staff for yet another delicious meal. And a round of applause to our hosts, Mr. and Mrs. Abraham Manley, for inviting us here tonight."

The house spotlight found Effa. She nodded with a smile, then went back to her seat as applause thundered around her. The bright lights kept her from seeing most of the faces in front of her, but she could feel all their eyes on her. Especially the eyes that belonged to the one man she wished were anywhere but here.

Vere continued on with his hosting duties as Effa returned to her seat. As she sat down, she felt very heavy, very tired. Suddenly, she just wanted this whole affair—both the party and the next day's league meeting—to be over. As much as she craved the adulation that came with pulling off this successful party, now she wanted nothing more than to be an anonymous face in the crowd.

Maintaining her composure while this person fawned over her and put her on a pedestal and that person went out of his way to put her in her place was exhausting. Others sat around waiting for her to make a misstep so they could expose her as a fraud. And then that one person—the one who made her forget herself—was always there, lurking in the shadows, goading her to succumb to her most forbidden passions.

It all made Effa want to slap herself on the forehead. Her former simple life of pretending to be someone else at the millinery shop and watching baseball games from her roof hadn't been this hard.

After all the dignitaries in attendance had been acknowledged, the reboot of Negro National League baseball in New York applauded, and prayers extended for the success of the upcoming season, the band struck up a tune and the bandleader invited the guests to the dance floor. Abe approached Effa with his hand extended. "Would you have the first dance with me?"

Now, that was a surprise. Effa leaned back and arched an eyebrow. "I'm sorry, who are you?" She smiled. "You look like my husband, but he would never ask me to dance."

"You're right," he said. "But this isn't an ordinary night."

The music was a mid-tempo tune. They easily fell in step with each other. Which was a relief, since, again, all eyes were on them.

As they swirled around, Abe nudged her with his cheek. "You did an amazing job pulling all of this together. Thank you."

Abe's praise made her insides glow. Once again, she made a small wish that this new baseball venture would be the thing to add fuel to the flame of their unusual marriage. That they could find a way to be partners and be man and wife. That it would be worth the sacrifice of her own personal dreams. That the highs and lows of a baseball game would be enough to quell any temptations for Effa to stray from her vows.

Effa opened her eyes to find Henry Clinton's heated gaze

locked on her. So much was still there that drew her to him. This blasted man.

And then he mouthed the words *I still want you.*

Stunned, she stiffened in Abe's arms. Abe took that as a sign to snuggle closer. "There's nothing to be afraid of, babe. As long as it's you and me together, the world is our oyster."

Abe's assurances soothed her like her former lover's caresses had in the past. She relaxed and closed her eyes again. Henry Clinton had already ruined her life once. She would not let him do it a second time.

"WHAT DO YOU mean, I can't stay?" Effa's rage made her voice tremble. She was trying to make her way to the owners' meeting-room table but Gus Greenlee was blocking her path. "I'm an owner just as much as my husband is!"

"No one's disputing that, darling. But your ownership is only on paper. We don't need no ladies in here distracting us while we get down to real league business." Gus lifted his arms and laced his fingers behind his head. She wanted to smack the smug grin off his face. Gone was the charming man she had met the night before. Well, as charming as someone with all his rough edges could be. He nodded at the *New York Age* photographer standing at the back of the room. "We only asked you down here today for the photo op. No one here is interested in listening to your . . . opinions."

The room fell into an uncomfortable silence. The rest of the men looked away or stared down at the notepads in front of them. Someone nervously tapped a pen or pencil on the table. She felt the energy in the shift, and it was all pushing her toward the door.

Her stomach dropped, not completely from humiliation. It was also from her anger at the realization that, for all their notoriety in the streets, these men were nothing but cowards.

Cum Posey pushed back from his seat, breaking the tension. She thought he was walking toward her at first. To stand with her in solidarity, she hoped. But no, he continued walking to the coatrack that was behind her. He lifted her coat from the hook and held it out to her. "Mrs. Manley, may I help you with your coat?"

"She ain't going nowhere." Everybody's head swiveled to where Abe sat. His normally jolly brown face and ears had blossomed into a heated red. His nostrils flared; he looked like a bull being held back from the ring. "We discussed this, *gentlemen*, when you negotiated the terms of the franchise. My wife and I are partners, fifty-fifty. She has as much say in the league's business as I do. If you all insist on something other than what we agreed on back when you were begging me to seal this deal, then I'm gone. And the Eagles franchise goes with me."

Abe stood up and quietly gathered the documents and notepad that he had brought with him. Then he walked over and stood by Effa. She gasped softly when his fingers wrapped around her hand. He gave it a soft squeeze, but he did not look at her. And she didn't look at him. She recognized this as the game of chicken that it was. But more than anything, she was too shocked to make any type of response. This was the first time anyone had staged such an act of defiance in her defense. Effa felt her knees go a little wobbly.

She took that moment to pull herself together. To get her head back in the game. No matter what happened next, she knew that she would always be in her husband's debt. He was not just her marriage partner, but also her partner in business.

Greenlee sighed in defeat. "Fine. We need someone to take notes anyway. Your wife can stay."

Effa stepped forward, ready to protest the slight. She was an owner, damn it, the same as the rest of them. She had ideas. She wanted to contribute. She—

Abe squeezed her hand, holding her back. "Thank you," he said, revealing every one of his pearly whites in a fake smile. To her, he added in a low voice, "You're still in the room. That's what matters. Now, let's get you a seat."

She pulled a spare wooden chair up to the table. It did not have the plush padding that all the other owners' chairs did, but like Abe had said, she was still in the room. It was a start.

BY THE TIME the annual meeting ended, Effa had been appointed the league's treasurer. Well, appointed by default. In actuality, Abe had been selected for the role once she had assured them that she could advise him based on her experience as treasurer for the Citizens' League. But they all knew that she would be the one keeping the books. Fine. One thing she had learned was that these men were tightwads when it came to their business dealings. If they wanted to save even a nickel in this next year, they would have to listen to her going forward.

Effa stepped into the foyer and waited for Abe to say his goodbyes to the rest of the owners. She personally had had enough of all their chest puffing and self-congratulations. Cum Posey gave her a nod as he rearranged his scarf and overcoat before venturing outside.

Brutal ice-cold winds were on the loose in the valleys of

the city's tall buildings. Jack Frost took the liberty of inviting himself inside when Posey exited the building. Effa shivered despite the thick wool jacket she wore. Next year, she would make sure she wore a thicker pair of stockings. *However,* she thought, *I wouldn't feel a thing if I had that mink I wanted.*

Which reminded her that she had to move forward with her plans for her millinery shop once their opening day was over. Most of the work she needed to do for the Brooklyn Eagles would be done by then. Any lingering tasks could be taken care of in her workshop.

Yes, it was a perfect plan.

Chapter 10

Garment District
March 1935

I t was a busy Tuesday on 33rd Street when Effa finally saw
the Gimbels Easter window display. She'd been trying to
get down here for the past week, but what was supposed to
have been an easy job—a few secretarial tasks for Abe and
the baseball team—had begun to consume the majority of
her time. From typing up contracts to fielding and returning
phone calls to sending out invitations to their inaugural opening day, helping Abe run things was more than a part-time job.
What Olivia Taylor had told Effa was true. Abe had dumped all
of the thankless work on her.

The thing that hurt most was that Effa had been too busy
with her baseball-related responsibilities to focus on anything
else. She'd abandoned her role in the Eunice Carter campaign.
She'd had to call in Cora Rollins in Chicago to smooth things
over with Mrs. Richards. And Effa didn't know when she'd last
had time to work on a new hat. Even worse, she had yet to
draw a paycheck of her own from any of it.

The irony of being your own boss was that you worked yourself to the bone but you didn't get paid until you sold something.

In the baseball business, that meant you didn't make money unless you sold enough tickets. And they wouldn't be able to sell any tickets until opening day, which was two months from now. Some days, Effa felt like she had been scammed.

It was a shame she had misplaced Olivia Taylor's phone number.

Effa stopped at a display window decorated in white and pastel colors. It was the headwear that had caught her attention. The cream and lavender fascinators tilted over the mannequins' eyes at jaunty angles. The padded satin halo headbands were bejeweled with diamond and pearl embellishments. Effa's hands itched to feel the materials as her nimble fingers jabbed needle and thread into the straw and velvet hat bases to secure the decorative trims.

Effa moved on to the shop a few doors down. The sign overhead read: Uniforms, Professional Quality. She opened the door and entered. Inside, the store was a mess. Different types of knits had been thrown atop various piles without rhyme or reason. Lint fragments floated in the air, made visible by the streams of light coming through the window. She could see a woman in the back hand-stitching numbers onto navy-and-white pin-striped material.

This place had been recommended to Abe by James Semler, who co-owned the Black Yankees with Bill "Bojangles" Robinson. Abe was told that this was the same place that did the uniforms for the New York Yankees. Effa angled her head to get a better look. The woman was stitching the number four onto the fabric.

"Oh my God." Effa gasped into the palm of her hand. The woman was working on Lou Gehrig's home uniform!

"Can I help you?" A man's voice came out of nowhere, causing Effa to jump. He emerged from behind the mountains of fabric bolts and appliqué numbers. The man appeared pale and haunted. He must not have been outdoors in a while. That or he had inhaled a great deal of dust and lint in the place.

"I'm here to order baseball uniforms."

The man waved her away. "We don't do kid sizes here."

His dismissal threw Effa off. "What makes you think I want kid sizes?" It took her a second to realize what the man was talking about. "Oh, no, I'm not here for a recreational team. I need uniforms for the Brooklyn Eagles."

"The Eagles? I thought they were out of Philly, not Brooklyn."

Effa took a deep breath. It was the same every time she went to a place like this on behalf of the team. Yesterday, she'd gotten into an argument over the phone with the embroidery shop about which shade of golden yellow the *E* on the players' hats should be. She was pressed for time, and she had to drop off the check for the deposit today. And now it looked like she was going to have to get into an argument with this guy as well.

Effa frowned. When had her life detoured from creating fashionable, adorable outfits to arguing about the minute details of an ugly baseball cap?

"Let's try this again. Hello, I am the owner of a professional baseball team. Our opening day is in six weeks. We are the Brooklyn Eagles. Our colors are blue and yellow. I will need forty home and away uniforms to get us going by then. I know that's a short turnaround window. I'm willing to work with whatever you've got."

"Oh, you want them for a real baseball team. Why didn't you say so in the first place?"

They spent the next hour looking at cotton fabrics and checking their durability. Effa finally selected the same white material and blue lettering that the Brooklyn Dodgers used for their home uniforms. Unfortunately, she had placed her order too late to have them ready for their opening day.

"You know what, Mrs. Manley? I like you. I think I got a deal that will work for you."

She brightened at the word *deal*. As wealthy as Abe was, even he was beginning to grumble about the start-up expenses. "Show me what you got, Marty."

"It must be your lucky day. The Yankees didn't like the away uniforms we did for them. They said it's the wrong shade of gray. I don't know what that means. Gray is gray, you know? We already put the navy-colored numbers on the back, but not the *New York* on the front. So it's not the right colors for the Giants or the Dodgers. If you don't mind the navy blue, I'll give them to you half price. What do you say?"

Effa frowned. "That's kind of you, but I already ordered bright blue and gold caps for the guys. The navy would clash." She was going to get an earful from Abe for passing up a deal like this, and she would have liked to save a few dollars herself, but she wanted her team to look good on the field. Even if the fans way up in the nosebleed seats couldn't see the mismatched caps and uniforms, Effa would know.

Marty slapped his thigh with a laugh. "Then today definitely is your lucky day, Mrs. Manley. The Yankees didn't like their caps either. Something about the *N* and the *Y* blending into each other. How about I give them to you for free?"

Effa paused for a second and thought again about those fans

in the nosebleed seats. She didn't want them to see clashing colors on her players, but she didn't give a damn if they saw a tiny *NY* on the caps of the Brooklyn-based team. Brooklyn was still part of New York City.

Effa held out her hand. "I think you have a deal."

That was the closest Effa had come to making a decision about fashion in almost a year.

As soon as she left Marty's store, she found a phone booth, called the embroidery shop, and canceled the order for the golden *E* caps.

LATER THAT AFTERNOON, Effa returned to Harlem exhausted. Marty's shop was busy getting the uniforms ready, and she was looking forward to going home, having a bath, and eating a dinner she didn't have to prepare herself. And she planned to pretend that the pile of papers waiting for her in the living room didn't exist.

What she also wanted was to take a day for herself to see the new Easter fashions uninterrupted. To have a chance to think about and be surrounded by pretty things.

But she needed to check on her girls, so instead of going straight home, Effa got off the subway at 125th Street and headed to Blumstein's.

Blumstein's had promised to hire thirty-five Negro sales-clerks, but they had been slow in fulfilling that promise. To the management's credit, a handful of girls had been hired. Sadly, Loreli Steele, the one who had sparked Effa to take action in the first place, had not been one of them. But she was hearing reports that the working hours given to the new salesclerks were inadequate for them to earn any kind of decent sales commission. Effa wasn't happy about that. But she wanted to do her part and support *her* working girls on a slow sales day.

Once inside, Effa made a beeline for the first Negro girl she saw in the dress department.

"Hello." She smiled. The salesgirl's name tag said *Bernice*. "I'd like some help finding something to wear for Easter Sunday."

Bernice nodded at her with a tight smile. "I'll get someone to help you."

Effa put her hand on the woman's wrist to keep her from leaving. "I was hoping that that someone would be you, dear. Your name is Bernice, right?"

"Yes, ma'am."

"Mine is Mrs. Manley. Good to meet you." With her hand still on Bernice's wrist, Effa pointed to the closest mannequin on display. "Perhaps you could bring me that dress in my size to try on?"

A line of perspiration broke out on the salesgirl's brow. Effa could not for the life of her figure out why the girl was so nervous. It was almost like she was scared. Effa made a mental note to talk to Reverend Johnson about this. She could only imagine what kind of treatment management was doling out to these girls for her to act this way.

"Of course—I'll just be a minute." The girl scurried away before Effa had a chance to tell her what her size was. She lifted an eyebrow, impressed. "Well, I'll be. She took one look at me and just knew. I knew our girls would do well here."

As soon as Bernice was gone, another salesgirl swooped

down on her. A white salesgirl. "Hello, ma'am." She greeted Effa with an eager smile. "How may I help you?"

"I'm fine. Bernice is helping me."

The girl's smile fell away. "Oh. I'm sorry about that."

"You're sorry about what?"

Now, the girl looked downright uncomfortable. She lowered her voice to a whisper. "She's only supposed to be helping the Colored customers."

Effa was stunned. For a moment, she did not know how to respond. By the time she had regained her composure, Bernice was back with the dress she had requested.

"Ma'am, I found—" Bernice stopped in mid-sentence as she realized that her coworker had joined Effa. "Oh."

The salesgirl snatched the hanger from Bernice. "I told you that the white customers were mine," she hissed. "It's bad enough you people are taking all the jobs. I won't have you taking all the commissions too. Now go finish setting up that display over there."

Bernice dropped her head. "My apologies, Mrs. Manley."

The white girl looked at Effa. "Sorry about that. She's new."

"And that was rude." That's when it finally dawned on Effa what was going on here. What was really going on behind Bernice's initial fear. She returned her attention to the salesgirl. "Am I to understand that the Negro girls are only to wait upon Negro customers?"

"Yes, ma'am. I—"

"Then you need to give that back to Bernice. I am in fact a Negro."

The salesgirl's cheeks flushed a bright pink. "No, you're not. I mean . . . look at you!"

Behind her, Effa heard Bernice smother a snicker. Maybe in the future, Effa would look back and find this funny. But right now, she was too tired and irate that her one moment of fun had been ruined by this nonsense.

"I am very well aware of what I look like. Whatever assumption you made about who you thought I was is not my problem. Nor does it excuse your behavior toward your coworker."

BY THE TIME Effa left the store, she had spent way more than she had originally intended. But she made sure that Bernice received the credit for every one of those purchases. Now, Effa was caught between a rock and a hard place. She wanted today to be the last time she ever darkened the door of the Blumstein's department store. But that would only hurt the Negro girls they had worked so hard to get employed there in the first place. You were damned if you did and damned if you didn't.

It was moments like this that Effa wished she smoked. She made a mental note to pour herself a finger of whiskey when she got home. But first, she had one more stop.

EFFA WAS CRANKY and irritated when she stepped into the real estate office.

"Mr. Wilhelm, please," she told the receptionist.

"Just a moment. Have a seat."

Effa yawned as soon as her bottom hit the chair. The business of getting the Brooklyn Eagles baseball team up and running had been consuming all her waking hours. Their opening day was scheduled for May 18; they'd be playing against Cum Posey's Homestead Grays. With that date breathing down her neck, she really didn't have time to be here today. But dreams were funny that way. They didn't care about whatever your other pressing needs were. It was a great opportunity to give her original dream some love and attention for once.

The receptionist returned with Mr. Wilhelm following. "Effa, aren't you a sight for sore eyes? So good to see you again."

"Same," she said with a smile.

Mr. Wilhelm had been her landlord once upon a time in between her marriages. He and his wife had been gracious enough to rent out a room in their home to a single woman when she had left her first husband. She hoped he would be kind enough to do the same with a retail space now that she was a married woman.

"So, how can I help you?"

"I saw the For Rent posting about a storefront you have on One Twenty-Fifth Street. I'd be interested in renting it out if the terms are agreeable."

"So now you have your eyes set on opening a business, eh? I remember when all you did was run around the neighborhood from fashion show to fashion show. You had more feathers in your hair than one of those showgirls."

Effa laughed. "Yes, those were the days. But even then, I had a dream of opening my own business. Now, about those terms . . ."

Mr. Wilhelm put his hands behind his back. "I don't know, Miss Effa. Opening a business now, with the economy being what it is . . . it's tough enough when the economy is doing good. I see you have a wedding band on your finger there. Shouldn't you be concerning yourself with matters that are closer to home? I mean, what if you have a baby? The rent will still be due even if you have your hands full with diapers and bottles and such." His face creased in a look of disgust at the idea of soiled diapers. He waved his hand for extra emphasis.

Luckily, Effa had anticipated this kind of argument. "That won't be a problem. I have a copy of my bank account balance right here." She handed him a copy of the statement from the account where she'd been stashing her savings since she'd divorced her first husband. "I have more than enough to cover expenses for one year." As for whether or not she and Abe wanted or could even have babies together . . . well, that was none of his damn business.

Mr. Wilhelm pushed the document to the side without bothering to glance at it. "I'm sure you do. I remember you always paying your rent on time in the past. But things are different now. You're married. I wouldn't feel comfortable leasing the space to you without your husband's permission. Speaking of which, does your husband know where you are right now?"

"My husband has nothing to do with this. I'd be the one signing the lease, not him."

Mr. Wilhelm walked around and opened the door for her, inviting her out. "Maybe you should go home and talk to him about it. Make him a nice pot roast to butter him up. You were always such a good cook. You bring him back and we can square everything away then, yes?"

Effa knew that she would not be coming back. She held off her tears until she was outside and down the block a ways. It was times like this that she got to thinking that getting married had been a mistake. Fulfilling that dream had wound up killing another—bigger, more important—dream. She kicked a piece of trash on the sidewalk with her foot.

That damn baseball team. She'd practically had Abe wrapped

around her finger before he'd bought that doggone franchise. And then she'd opened her big mouth, encouraging him to seek out a scouting position so he'd have something to do. What a fool she had been!

Effa watched a line of cabs go by but didn't bother to hail any of them. She needed to walk off this anger for a little longer. She needed to—

She stopped in her tracks at the sound of glass breaking a few stores down. A crowd had formed in front of what looked like the five-and-ten. She made herself blink a few times because she couldn't believe what she saw. The store's glass window was gone. What was left of it around the edges was cracked and shattered. That didn't deter any of the people who were crawling in and out of the opening. Those coming out had their arms filled with merchandise.

She stopped a man who was running from the scene. "What's going on?"

"Those damn cops killed that kid. They're saying they caught him stealing a soda pop and they killed him." The man looked as dazed as she felt. But there were more people—angry people—that were joining the crowd. The siren attached to the police car parked in front of the store groaned in protest as a group of men pushed it over onto its side.

The air felt charged. The overturned squad car did little to quench the thirst the crowd—no, it was on the verge of becoming a mob now—seemed to have for blood and justice.

Effa turned around in a circle, looking for a way out. But she was surrounded by people. Some were still pouring out of the five-and-ten with more merchandise. Others had made their way next door and busted out that store's window. Whatever control they had was evaporating by the second. She had to get out of there.

Effa started pushing her way back toward the larger department store. Surely the crowd hadn't gotten there yet. If she could just make it to the end of the block and around the corner, surely she could flag a cab—

But there were too many people. And there was only so much she could do with her fisted hands that were trying to keep ahold of her purse and shopping bags. But she didn't have a choice. It was either fight against the tide or be crushed standing in place.

She closed her eyes and said a quick prayer. She'd been fighting against the will of the masses since the day she was born. She wasn't going to quit now.

Effa took a deep breath, got as much footing as she could get, and pushed again.

This time she managed to force a small break in the bodies. She took advantage of the opportunity and crawled her way out of the tight space that had threatened to squeeze her. Finally, she could breathe. Finally, she could move. Finally, she could . . .

"I gotcha," a male voice assured her. One hand gripped her shoulder while the other pushed out and parted the crowd like it was Moses's staff parting the Red Sea.

She could feel her temples pulsing as another wave of fear washed over her. She had averted one disaster only to get herself caught up in another. She had no idea who had grabbed her, but she knew that he could easily snatch her off the street and no one would be the wiser.

Her fear quickly morphed into an urge to fight again.

"Get off me!" Effa wriggled her shoulder free, but he stayed pressed against her back. She looked to the left and the right. There were still too many people. She yelled, "Help," but there were too many raised voices and they drowned out her cries.

"Stop fighting me, Effa. I'm trying to save you."

His use of her name made her freeze for a moment. Just enough time for him to get a grip on her again. It wasn't just the fact that he knew her name that gave her pause. It was the way he had said it.

He didn't just know who she was. She *knew* him as well.

"Henry?" She tried to turn around so her eyes could confirm what her ears already knew. "How did you find me?"

"Shh, Ef. Follow my lead. We can talk later." It *was* him. Her mind began its panic all over again but this time even worse than at the Smalls Paradise dinner. Despite all reason, she relaxed and leaned into him, letting him guide her toward safety. The way he held her, the way he guided her . . . it felt like a dance. An all-too-familiar dance. Her mind continued to scream *No!* But the rest of her? Well, that was the part that had gotten her into trouble with him in the past.

And that's why you shouldn't let him ruin your future. Again.

"Here we are. We'll be safe here."

Effa blinked to get her bearings. She couldn't tell where they were now. But they definitely weren't on 125th Street anymore. It looked like he had taken her to . . . a hotel. She gulped. A familiar scenario. One he had put her into almost ten years before.

"No. We're not doing this again. I will not let you ruin my life again, Henry!"

"Ruin your life? Woman, I'm trying to save it!"

Henry pulled Effa into the Hotel Theresa, away from the danger outside. When they made it into the elevator, the operator said, "Hello there, Mr. Clinton. Who's the pretty lady you've got with you?"

Effa lowered her chin. There was a downside to making a name for yourself in a close-knit community like Harlem. Mainly, it was that everyone knew who you were. Especially if you were the one who always stood out for looking like a white woman.

"Just an old friend I bumped into. A riot broke out on One Twenty-Fifth Street. She just needs a place to wait it out until it all blows over."

"A riot, you say?"

"Yeah, the word is that some kid got caught stealing candy at Krewe's there on the corner and that either the owner or the cops beat him to death for it."

"My word. God bless his soul. It's always something."

"Yes, it is. Yes, it is."

Effa studied her shoes during the exchange, grateful that Henry had managed to direct the man's attention away from her and to the chaos on the street. Which was where everybody should be focused, as far as Effa was concerned. No one needed to pay any attention to where she was or who she was with or the disheveled state she was in as she made her way to Henry's hotel room . . .

When the elevator stopped on Henry's floor, he got out of the car. Effa stayed behind. The elevator operator gave her an odd look at first, but the elevator buttons quickly drew his interest.

"Come on, Ef. I know you're tired. My room is only a few doors down." Henry held out his hand. And then he put on his most irresistible smile for good measure.

"We both know that isn't a good idea."

"Speak for yourself. I think it's the only idea. You could've been crushed to death back there. You need a safe place to sit for a moment."

Everything he said was true. Except for the part about his hotel room being a safe place for her. "But—"

"No buts. That crowd was furious. And I don't blame them. I don't think things are going to cool down anytime soon."

"Fine, then, speaking for myself, it's not a good idea for me. I'm married. Not that that mattered to either of us in the past. But I'm not that silly young girl anymore. And this marriage . . . well, this husband means a lot to me. He's been . . . very good to me."

Effa closed her eyes to keep the image of Abe Manley and the vows she had made to him in the forefront of her mind. Of course, he had withheld some vital information at the time she had made those vows. But that was beside the point. It was because of Abe that Effa was finally able to toe her way into the living rooms of Harlem's most important socialites. To be honest, he was the reason she could probably be called one of Harlem's most important socialites herself now.

The tension swirling between them was filled with the heat of past intimacies and the intensity of the near-death experience they had just shared. Good common sense would be to wait here for the trouble on the street to calm. But past experience also told her that getting off this elevator with him would blow up in her face.

"No, I think I'll go back downstairs and take my chances. But thank you, Henry. Thank you for saving my . . . just thank you."

"Going down?" The elevator operator had apparently finished his thorough inspection of the buttons.

"Yes, please. I think that would be best." Effa felt the heat rush to her face as she made eye contact with the uniformed man. Then, when the glimmer of recognition lit his eyes, she felt downright mortified.

"Yes, ma'am." The operator pulled the gate closed and pushed the down button. Henry stood there holding her gaze until the elevator car had descended far enough that she could see him no more.

She and the operator shared an uncomfortable silence. Finally, she exhaled with a sigh.

"Are you all right, ma'am?"

"Yes. I am." He continued to study her as if he wasn't buying it. "I mean, I will be. It's been a long day. I need to get home. Hopefully, everything will have died down by now."

Effa looked up and tapped her feet. "I just hope my husband was able to get home okay." Abe had left early that morning to meet with the Dodgers operations staff to work out the final preparations for the Eagles' opening day. Thankfully, they had agreed to let them use Ebbets Field whenever the Major League team was out of town. However, the Dodgers management insisted on taking a heavy cut of the ticket and concessions sales.

Since Abe had driven the car out to Brooklyn, Effa worried

that he might have trouble getting back to their apartment once he crossed the river into Harlem.

"I'm sure he was." The man stopped short. It was almost like he had wanted to say more but thought better of it. He sighed, then continued. "If you don't mind my saying so, I thought it was a mighty fine thing you did last summer with the department stores. My niece wound up getting a salesclerk job at Gimbels because of you. Those wages made a difference in keeping a roof over her and my baby sister's head. I know it's not the ideal circumstances to say anything to you, but on their behalf, I just had to say thank you."

Effa stared at him for a moment. She looked away when she could no longer hold back her tears. "I don't know what you're talking about."

"My apologies, ma'am. I must have you confused with someone else." He winked at her. "As far as I'm concerned, you were never here. This conversation never happened."

"Thank you. I really do appreciate that."

IT TOOK SOME doing, but the doorman at the Theresa was able to hail Effa a cab. It was not a short or smooth ride home. From what she could see, 125th Street was a mess. There were still large groups of people milling around everywhere, looking for other merchants on whom to take out their rage. She saw that some shops now had handwritten signs in their windows declaring Negro-Owned Business or Negroes Employed Here. Those storefronts appeared untouched for the most part.

Effa wondered how Blumstein's and Mr. Wilhelm's properties had fared. Based on what she saw from the cab, she doubted if

Blumstein's remained unscathed despite the handful of Negro salesclerks they'd hired. They had yet to hire the thirty-five Negroes that had been promised. She doubted management would even bother now. Effa wiped away a tear at this realization. All that hard work was going down the drain.

She did not have the same emotional response when she thought about Mr. Wilhelm's business. While she did not wish ill on anyone's livelihood, Effa was pretty sure his office would not be spared. She had not seen one dark-skinned or even a faintly light brown face in that office this afternoon. He could make no legitimate claims about Negroes being employed there. The thought made her neither happy nor sad. All Effa could muster on the man's behalf was a shake of her head. "Too bad."

Inevitably, her thoughts kept going back to Henry as much as she didn't want them to. She felt confident that she had done the right thing leaving him like that. She squeezed her thighs tighter together, as the heat that had flared between them had yet to dissipate. At least she had done it for the right reasons. But somehow her brain had failed to communicate that to the rest of her body. She wanted to know if he was still alone now. So what if he was? What he did and who he did it with was none of her concern. Not when she was on her way to the home she shared with her husband. Her new husband. One who, this time, was doing everything he could to make her dreams come true in his own way.

Well, even if he was unable to satisfy her in every way. Unlike Henry, who had left her spent and breathless each and every time.

Effa squeezed her thighs together again. She shouldn't—no, she couldn't—think about such things. Why did forbidden fruit have to be so tantalizing and . . . well, so darn forbidden?

WHEN SHE ARRIVED at their apartment building, Effa was surprised and relieved to see the light on in their window.

The cabbie turned and said, "You make sure you lock that door behind you. Those hooligans might not have made it this far yet, but I don't see them cooling down anytime soon."

"I will make sure to do that." She handed him her fare. "You stay safe too."

"You betcha. I think I'm gonna head out to the Bronx for the rest of my shift. You have a good night."

After making sure she had shut the door into the apartment building tight and secured it, Effa flew up the stairs. She fumbled with her keys to unlock the door.

"Abe! Abe, are you here? Are you all right?" she called out when she did not find him in his usual spot in the living room, next to the radio. Silence.

She felt her heart sink, right before it leaped into her throat. He had to be here.

"Abe?" she called louder.

Finally, she heard some movement in the bedroom. She made a beeline for it. "Abe!"

Abe was sitting on the side of the bed looking at his feet. The rumpled sheets indicated that he had been under the covers a few moments before.

"I'm right here. I was asleep."

"Asleep! How could you be asleep at a time like this? I thought you were stuck out in the streets somewhere. I thought you were . . ." A myriad of possible scenarios flashed before her: Abe unconscious or dead in a totaled car; Abe a bleeding heap in front of a looted store; Abe laid out in a morgue, his body beyond recognition. That was when the emotional dam that Effa had constructed for herself since the nightmare on 125th Street began cracked. She didn't just cry. She bawled. A deluge of tears rolled down her cheeks.

Abe lumbered toward her with the handkerchief that he always had on him outstretched. "What's gotten into you? Look, I'm here. I'm fine. They called me at the last minute to cancel so I took a nap while waiting for you."

He held her in his arms, which made her sob even harder. Abe cradled the back of her head. He dabbed away her tears with his handkerchief. "There, there. It's all right. It's all right."

"No, it's not. I was out shopping, and a riot broke out. There were so many people. So many angry people. They say the cops killed a kid. I have no idea what's true and what's not. I was caught up in the middle of it. I thought they would crush me to death. And . . . and then, he . . . he saved me." She hiccupped.

"It's okay. You're here now."

"I had no idea where you were. I had to go to the Hotel Theresa to catch a cab. That took forever. When I saw how bad the streets were on the way home, I feared the worst."

"I'm here. We're both safe."

He held her for a few more moments, letting her go only once the adrenaline rush wore off.

"So, a riot, you say?"

Effa nodded and whimpered an affirmative, her throat too raw for words.

"How about I go see what the radio's saying about it while you go throw together something from the icebox?" She nodded again but remained sitting on the bed a few more minutes after Abe had gone into the living room.

A wave of exhaustion hit her. Instead of getting up, she lay down. The thought of cooking something for dinner made her body sink even further into the mattress. All that worry. All that stress. And Abe had been here the entire time. She couldn't believe it.

It's almost like those days when I was in that cramped apartment with George and his mama. Couldn't neither of them figure out how to put together a meal for themselves. Back then, the only one who ever thought to make her a meal or take her out for one had been Henry.

No. She would not think about him. She was determined to avoid making comparisons between the two men. Not this time.

Effa pushed herself up into a sitting position. Her whole body screamed to lie back down. Her feet ached when she finally stood.

"Kick off the damn heels at least, Effa," she told herself. One pump went flying into the closet, followed by the other. She slid her feet into the fluffy pair of slippers she kept by the bed.

Better.

"Now, dinner." Effa padded out of the bedroom and into the kitchen.

The bath she had fantasized about would not be drawn until a few hours later.

EFFA WASN'T SURPRISED when Blumstein's announced mass lay-offs in the weeks that followed the riot. Or that the employees who were laid off were the recently hired Negro sales staff. Management told the newspapers that the cuts were necessary to offset losses suffered as a result of the looting.

She finished reading the article on her way to their temporary office at Ebbets Field. When she got there, Effa picked up the phone and gave the operator the number for St. Philip's.

After exchanging greetings with Reverend Johnson, she got down to business. "Do we know who the laid-off employees are? We'll need extra hands at our opening day next month."

"It'll take me a few days to get that for you. We're still recovering from yesterday's service at the church." Effa only then noticed the exhaustion in Reverend Johnson's voice. Then she remembered—yesterday was Easter Sunday. She regretted putting another demand on his time.

"I should have thought of that before I called you. My apologies. With opening day breathing down my neck, I've lost track of what day it is. Don't worry about it. I'll figure it out."

Effa was just about to say goodbye when he said, "You know, I bet Mrs. Richards could help you get that list together in a matter of hours."

"That's a great idea! I'll give her a call." But Effa's stomach turned at the thought of having to ask Mrs. Richards for anything. "I know you're busy, Reverend Johnson, so I'll let you go. Be on the lookout for your VIP invitation and opening-day tickets. I'll put them in the mail today."

Effa and Mrs. Richards had not been on good terms since she'd had to drop out of Eunice Carter's election campaign committee. Not even a goodwill telephone call from Cora Rollins in Chicago could smooth things over. As a result, the number of tea and luncheon invitations Effa received from Mrs. Richards and her social circle had dwindled down to nothing. Not that Effa could have attended them. The "secretary stuff" that the baseball team required had taken over all of Effa's free time.

Still, it wasn't those young people's fault that they had fallen victim to the "last hired, first fired" curse. Effa was in a position to soften the blow to their pocketbooks and wallets. They shouldn't have another opportunity snatched away from them because two ladies who didn't have to worry about money had fallen out with each other.

THE OPERATOR CONNECTED them and dropped off the line. Mrs. Richards's greeting was cool. "Mrs. Manley, how nice of you to call."

"Thank you for taking my call." Effa had hoped enough time had passed that the woman would no longer be cross with her. That greeting confirmed that she had set her hopes too high. "Yes, my husband's little project has turned into a full-time job, I'm afraid. Which is why I'm calling."

Mrs. Richards sniffed. "I'm not a big enough baseball fan to trek all the way out to Brooklyn to support your team, if that's what you're about to ask me. The Black Yankees are Harlem's home team anyway."

Effa had planned on sending Mrs. Richards an invitation to opening day as a courtesy, but with that remark, she was tempted to scratch the woman's name off her invitee list.

Effa pinched the bridge of her nose to refocus. Pettiness was not the purpose of this call.

"I understand, ma'am. The reason I'm calling is to ask for your help in getting the names of those young people who were let go by Blumstein's. Abe and I will need extra staff for the opening-day festivities. It's not much, but we'd like to offer them a day wage, subway fare, and an opportunity to watch the game if any of them are interested."

Mrs. Richards did not respond immediately. Effa's heart thumped in her chest. Effa knew that the grande dame of Harlem society was intentionally making her sweat it out. She closed her eyes and swung for the bleachers.

"Ma'am, with all due respect, I did not call you with this request in hopes of getting back into your good graces. I know that ship has sailed. But I am in a position to put a little money in those young people's pockets. We both know they lost their jobs through no fault of their own. Please"—Effa paused, hating the sound of herself begging—"help me do this for them."

Mrs. Richards sighed so hard into the receiver that Effa imagined she could feel it. "Fine. I'll have the list ready for you by the end of the day. You can come by and retrieve it from my housekeeper."

Effa smacked her leg in triumph. "Thank you." After she hung up, she let out a whoop. Talk about hitting a home run. At least she'd gotten that one thing right. She looked over the rest of her task list. Everything else . . . not so much. She still had to arrange delivery of their baseball supplies and finalize their team bus rental for the first road trip and . . .

"Where's Abe?" Ben Taylor slammed the office door open, letting it bang into the wall. Effa looked up.

And there were a few more contracts to finalize, starting with Ben's.

"Mr. Manley isn't here." She rifled through the contracts on her desk, pulled his out, and held it out to him. "But your contract is ready. We called you down here to sign it."

Ben yanked the contract out of her hand. She eyeballed the soon-to-be team manager as he flipped through the pages. Effa had the urge to lecture him about his manners, but she knew it would fall on deaf ears.

Olivia had told her that Ben was tolerable when her husband, CI, was alive, but the moment Olivia took over the team, Ben had tossed pretenses of civility aside. It had been an all-out tug-of-war between them over ownership and control of the team. "Ben will never let a woman be the boss of him," she'd said.

Having gotten that bit of intel, Effa found it best to just let Abe deal with Ben.

Ben threw the contract back at her. It landed on her desk with a thud. "I ain't signing it. Abe said he was paying me fifty-five hundred dollars, not five thousand. Don't you know how to type?"

"Then you need to take your quarrel back to my husband. Don't take your anger out on me."

Ben left, slamming the door behind him. Effa ran her fingers through her hair. It was going to be a long season if he was at the helm in the dugout.

She hated that he was one of the best managers in Negro baseball. In a perfect world, she wouldn't let that man anywhere near her team.

Effa got her purse and coat. She'd had enough of this place

for the day. She needed to head back to Harlem anyway to pick up Mrs. Richards's list. She made a mental note to track down Olivia Taylor and ask her how to deal with her brother-in-law.

SHE GOT BACK to Harlem just as the latest edition of the local papers hit the streets. One of the headlines made Effa stumble over her own feet. Olivia Harris Taylor—the first woman to own a professional baseball team—was dead at the age of fifty.

Effa read the article over and over for any sign that it was about another woman with the same name. But she found nothing that would change the truth. The one person in the world who could relate to the challenges Effa was about to face was gone.

Whenever Effa had dreamed about running her own business, she'd thought only about the glamour and the power she would wield. Olivia had tried to ease off her rose-colored glasses that night at Smalls, but Effa was still too new to the baseball business to understand.

But now, with Olivia gone, those rosy lenses had shattered. Effa now knew that it was lonely as hell at the top.

Chapter 11

New York City
Saturday, May 18, 1935

I t was unseasonably cool when Effa and Abe left their apartment that morning. Stray gusts of wind whipped at their faces. Effa looked at Abe as he helped her into the car. "That's not good, is it?"

"If the game were being held here in Harlem, no. But there's a chance weather conditions might be better in Brooklyn. Cross your fingers."

She might be new to the business side of baseball, but she had been a fan of the game long enough to know that cool temperatures were not good. Cool weather meant that fans were more likely to wait for the game recap on the radio at home instead of dropping a few quarters into the turnstile at the ballpark to watch the game in person. Which meant . . .

Effa's thoughts strayed to all the personal invitations she had sent out to high-profile guests. The ones she had sent to mentors Cora Rollins and Lucy Richards were at the forefront of her mind.

Cora had sent her regrets when she passed through town last week to board a transatlantic steamer out of New York.

She was headed to Europe for the summer. But Effa had yet to hear anything from Mrs. Richards.

Effa said a prayer on top of crossing her fingers as Abe drove them out of Harlem. But by the time she arrived in Brooklyn, her hopes—for the overall fan attendance and for seeing Mrs. Richards—were gone. An even stronger gust of wind slapped her in the face with reality as soon as she opened the car door.

Abe saw her expression. "Don't look like that, Effa. The Homestead Grays will have to hit against this wind too." Then he clapped his hand on his hat to keep it from blowing away.

She wasn't concerned about what the opposing team did. It was *their* opening day. She wanted to win, but she also wanted to make a good first impression. She had been busting her tail in the home stretch, inviting dignitaries, twisting their staffs' arms to ensure those dignitaries would actually show up; she had even orchestrated an on-field parade during the pregame ceremony. The feather in her cap was that New York City mayor Fiorello La Guardia had agreed to throw out the first pitch. All of it would be a waste if their team wound up losing its very first home game.

On top of that, the majority of fans would stay home if the temperature was too low. Everybody in sports knew that. Effa had tallied up their baseball-related business receipts last night. She and Abe had dropped a fortune on this day alone. They needed every seat filled. She hated to think of how embarrassed she'd be if no one bothered to show up to witness what they had created. What Effa had created.

"You're doing that thing with your face again, Ef," Abe warned. "Stop worrying. Everything is going to be fine."

Effa took a deep breath and forced herself to smile for Abe's sake. "Of course everything is going to be fine." It had to be or she would die of shame.

It didn't get any worse once they entered Ebbets Field, but it also didn't get any better. The field crew were in the process of setting up the appropriate flags and red, white, and blue buntings along the wall that separated the front row of seats from the playing field. The wind was giving them a run for their money; the breeze picked up speed as it swirled around the bowl of the stadium. It was just their luck that the wind wasn't blowing out along the first and third baselines but right down the middle of center field to home plate.

Not good at all.

She looked up at the box that had been set aside for the team owners and their guests. Her eyes landed on the seat she had designated for herself and the one beside it that she had designated for Mrs. Richards. It was still empty. As empty as her social calendar had become.

Fortunately, everything that Effa had direct control over went like clockwork. Their players' home uniforms had arrived in time. Each light gray uniform with *Eagles* written across the chest hung from the correct cubby in the locker room. The bands from the Brooklyn Colored Elks Lodge Number 32 and the American Legion Post 116 had arrived at the appointed hour. She could hear them tuning their instruments in the runway leading out to the field. One by one, she was able to check items off her list: baseballs—check; refreshments for her guests—check; bats in the dugout—check . . .

By EARLY AFTERNOON, the weather conditions had not changed, but Effa was feeling a little less tense. All her players had arrived on time. The visiting team was getting settled in their locker room. The invited dignitaries had begun to trickle in. Well, all of them except . . .

Effa tried not to think about whether Mrs. Richards would forgive her for following her husband into the baseball business. It was time to play hostess to the guests who had shown up. "It's okay," she assured herself. "I just wasn't meant to be a Harlem socialite."

She could say the words, but that didn't stop her from hurting like hell.

Effa made her way to the front-row box that had been set aside for the mayor and his party. She went over last-minute details with his assistant, then gave a gracious nod to Samuel Leibowitz. "It's an honor to have you here. I hope you enjoy the game."

She shook his hand and held on to it long after she should have released it. "I'm such an admirer of your work." She made herself stop talking before she looked even more like a babbling fool.

"Thank you, ma'am." He nodded back.

Effa waited until she had walked away before breaking out into a few dance steps. She couldn't believe the lawyer who had represented the Scottsboro boys down in Alabama was in *her* stadium! Further proof that her part in this project was a triumph!

The Scottsboro boys were nine teenage Negroes who had been accused of raping two white women while hoboing on a freight train down in Scottsboro, Alabama. All nine had been tried and convicted within one day. Each defendant was given a death sentence, despite the doctor who examined the women testifying that he had found no signs of forced sexual contact.

New York–based Leibowitz had represented the young men in their numerous subsequent appeals, two of which had gone before the U.S. Supreme Court. Just two weeks ago, Leibowitz had convinced that court that the systematic exclusion of Negroes from the jury pool violated the due-process clause in the Constitution. Alabama's governor was forced to announce that going forward, the state "must put Negroes in the jury boxes"—a win not just for the Scottsboro boys but for all Negroes living in the Jim Crow South.

Understandably, two New York National Guardsmen now hovered close by Leibowitz, protecting him.

The voice over the loudspeaker boomed, "Hello, ladies and gentlemen. Welcome to the first ever opening day for your Brooklyn Eagles!"

It was time to start the show. The two bands assembled on the field. Avis arrived just as both teams were lining up behind the bands. She and Effa hugged. "Sorry I'm late," Avis said. "Eubie just left to go on tour with his orchestra. I had to see him off."

The procession began to move. The fans who had braved the elements to witness this historic sight cheered as the teams paraded out to center field.

"You got here just in time," Effa said. She looked behind Avis to see if anyone else had come with her. "Mrs. Richards?" she asked.

"No." Avis shook her head. "She said she had to catch up on her correspondence but that she would try to listen to the recap on the radio."

"I guess that's better than nothing with her."

The two women returned their attention to the field. The teams stood at the center of the stadium as the bands played the national anthem, then the baseball players went into their respective dugouts, and the bands went to stow away their instruments. Ushers would lead the band members to their seats to watch the game.

Effa was glad that she had had the foresight to arrange for both bands to stay. She looked around the stands with a frown. There were significantly more empty seats than occupied ones. She wished she had more experience with estimating attendance.

She nudged one of the sports reporters seated nearby. "How many fans do you think are out there?"

The gruff newspaperman gave the stadium a once-over before returning to his notes. "Maybe three thousand, if you're lucky."

That made Effa's heart sink. Ebbets Field could hold thirty-five thousand spectators. "This darn weather," she grumbled.

Effa was back to being a bundle of nerves when Mayor La Guardia threw out the first pitch promptly at three o'clock.

"Let's play ball," the umpire yelled from behind home plate.

BEN TAYLOR HAD assigned Ted Radcliffe to be the starting pitcher. Effa had heard Abe rave about this kid. She was eager to see his arm. She had yet to see any of the team in action. Her administrative responsibilities kept her chained to her desk in New York, so she hadn't been able to attend any of their road games prior to their home-field opening day. And it would have been more trouble than it was worth to go down to Jacksonville, Florida, with Abe and the rest of the team for spring training. With the Jim Crow laws and attitudes down there, a white-looking lady traveling with Negro ballplayers would have been an all-around nightmare.

By the end of the top of the first inning, after Effa watched Radcliffe shut down the Grays with only one run scored, she was his biggest fan.

"Good job!" Effa roared. She hopped up from her seat with her fist in the air. This amused the newsmen seated near the owners' box. "Now, c'mon, Eagles. Let's go!"

To Effa's delight, their very first batter, left fielder Clarence "Fats" Jenkins, led off with a home run.

"Yes!" Effa screamed as Fats circled the bases. "That's how you say hello to Brooklyn!"

Those same newsmen chuckled again. Effa didn't care. Just because she was a pretty face in stylish clothes didn't mean that she was above being swept up in the magic of a baseball diamond. Besides, it was *her* team. She and her husband had put their fortune on the line to entertain these people. As far as she was concerned, each run scored was another dollar bill returned to their coffers.

The next two batters got on base.

"C'mon, c'mon," Effa called to center fielder Rap Dixon as he came up to the plate. "Keep the rally going!"

Dixon wound up hitting a home run too. Effa could not hear anyone else above her cheers. Now the Eagles were ahead four to one. It was working. This crazy scheme of Abe's was actually working!

Effa didn't have long to enjoy her euphoria. The Grays scored four runs on Radcliffe in the top of the second inning.

Luckily, her boys added another two runs in the bottom of the second to pull ahead. The Grays answered with four more runs in the top of the third to pull themselves back into the lead.

Effa threw herself down into her chair. She covered her face with her hands. "I don't know if I can watch any more of this."

Seeing this game go down the tubes made her feel like she had when her women's group was absorbed into the coalition that became the Citizens' League for Fair Play. In both cases, Effa had a seat at the leadership table but she didn't have control over the crafting and execution of the strategies needed to win.

On a normal day, she hated to lose. But today was *her* day. *Her* opening day. With all the dignitaries *she* had invited in attendance. Reverend Johnson was there. Mayor La Guardia was there. And now Effa was stuck on the sidelines watching her team give away their lead and there was nothing she could do about it. Nothing but yell.

She leaned over and screamed toward the Eagles dugout, "Do something, Ben! Get Radcliffe out of there!"

Ben Taylor must have decided to listen to her for once, because a few pitches later, he walked out to the mound, took the ball from Radcliffe, and gestured for the reliever Elbert Williams to come in from the bullpen.

By then Effa had had enough. She stormed over to Abe. "I want to go home."

Everyone stared at her. Abe removed the cigar from his mouth. "What are you talking about? It's only the third inning."

"I don't care. I can't watch any more of this bloodbath. That wind coming in from center field isn't letting up. Radcliffe is a mess. How do you blow a two-run lead like that? Ben should have taken him out at least five minutes ago. I'm not built for this, Abe. Losing is not in my blood. Are you going to take me home or not?"

"It's too early to leave. There's plenty of time for our boys to turn this thing around. They're down by only three runs."

"See, this is why dames don't belong in baseball," mumbled a nearby sportswriter just loud enough for them to hear. One of the mayor's aides looked at Effa, shook his head, and agreed.

Avis put her hand on Effa's shoulder. "It's all right, Abe. I'll take Effa home."

EFFA WAS STILL fuming when Avis drove them over the Brooklyn Bridge. "I don't know, Avis. I hate to lose." She punctuated the last few words with a punch to her seat.

Avis took her hand off the wheel to pat Effa's hand, still clenched into a fist. "You're a sore loser. Good to know. Just don't take it out on the car. Okay, honey?"

Effa uncurled her fingers, flexed them. "Sorry. And you were so kind to volunteer to get me out of there today. But I can't do this every day for the rest of the season. Not when I've put my own dreams on hold for this."

Avis sighed. "Don't say you can't do this. Because I watched you every day last summer, picketing in the hot sun when those stubborn Blumsteins refused to take us seriously. Talk about an uphill battle."

Effa smiled at the memory. "It was so hot too. What in the world were we thinking?"

"We were thinking that we could change the world. And we did. More specifically, you did. You told it like it was and made a spectacle of yourself. Next thing we knew, boom, the impossible happened and they caved."

"They might have caved for that moment. But they have yet to hire those thirty-five Negro clerks like they promised. And then the riot happened . . . last I heard, they'd let go of almost all of our girls that they hired for the sales floor." If Effa were made of softer stuff, that would've made her lose what was left of her spirit. But she wasn't. "Thinking about that makes me so mad, Av. On top of that doggone game."

"It's just a game, Effie."

"Maybe. It used to be. You see, that's the problem. Baseball has become my entire life. And not in a good way. I can't just shrug my shoulders and hope for better luck tomorrow. Their wins and losses affect my husband's bank account."

"I get it. Believe me, I get it." Effa nodded, glad to have Avis's support and understanding. She remembered those times when Avis's husband, Eubie, had his stage shows flop on Broadway. They never knew from year to year if they would be living on Easy Street or lined up at the soup kitchen with the rest of Harlem.

"But here's the thing, Ef. I think it's great that you have this fighting spirit. But you have got to figure out how to keep it under control. If you throw an ing-bing every time the team has a bad inning, you will be in the hospital or worse before you get halfway through this season."

"I know. I just need to have more control."

"No, you want total control, and that's never going to happen. There are nine grown men on that field, God help you. No matter what you say or do or how much you scream, they are going to have bad days on the field. Just accept it—you went from being childless to having thirty full-grown man-boys overnight."

"I never wanted this, Avis—"

"You keep saying that, but you forget that I know you, Effa. You might hate the day-to-day, but you love the power and the attention that comes with running the administrative side of the business. You're in a position that very few women, Negro or white, get to be in."

Effa took a minute to mull that over. "Of course I know you're right. But today, I need to be hopping mad. However, starting tomorrow, I promise I'll be the consummate professional."

"I'd prefer you to be consummately yourself, Effa."

"That's fair." They both laughed.

BY THE TIME Avis dropped Effa off in Harlem, the Eagles had lost, twenty-one to seven. All the calm Avis had coaxed out of Effa disappeared when she heard the final score announced on the radio recap. Effa snapped it off, made a beeline for Abe's liquor cabinet, poured herself a shot of whiskey, and drank it.

Abe was fit to be tied when he finally got home.

"Goddamn it!" He threw his keys onto the table next to the door. He called down the hall, "Effa, we lost."

"I know," she yelled back from the bedroom, where she was lying down with a cool washcloth across her eyes and forehead. She couldn't tell if her headache was from the whiskey or her nerves. "Is it too late to give the league their franchise back? I don't know if I can take any more of this," she told Abe when he made it into their bedroom.

"No. Listen, babe, you can't go storming out of the stadium

every time the team has a bad inning. Especially in front of those reporters. They're already on me about letting you get your hands too deep into the team's business affairs, so it makes me look bad. And then there were all those people you invited—"

Effa winced. "Oh no. I forgot all about them. The mayor—"

"Don't worry. I had that PR guy you hired see to them. But you can't do that anymore. Either you're all in or you're out. I'll understand if you're out. I'm just not too keen on shelling out even more money to get a decent secretary. It'll cost even more for someone we can trust. Hopefully, she'll be a pretty little thing—"

Effa shot up into a sitting position. Her damp rag fell to the floor, forgotten. "The hell you will. I'll be back tomorrow, raring to go. I'll pencil a smile on my face if I have to. But I can't promise that I won't go off the rails sometimes. I'm passionate in everything I do."

"I know that, Ef. That's one of the things that made me fall in love with you."

That made Effa smile. "That's nice. But you are right—my behavior today was completely over the top. I promise that, going forward, I won't be selfish like that again. It's not fair to you or the team. From now on, Effa Manley is the Brooklyn Eagles' number one fan."

THE NEXT DAY, the Eagles faced the Grays again in a double-header. It was another unseasonably cool day with about five thousand fans in the bleachers. Effa turned her eyes from the empty stands to the playing field. Abe gave her a worried glance, but she ignored it. "For better or worse, I will be here until the last fan and player leaves. I am not going to lose my cool today," she said.

Effa found herself screaming like a lovesick cheerleader when *her* guys came back to wallop the Grays. They gave them a taste of their own medicine and won the game, eighteen to nine.

"Yes!" Effa hollered when the last out was called in the ninth inning. "Yes! Yes! Yes!" She took a sip of lemonade to wet her throat. She was being a good girl today, although a nip of whiskey wouldn't have been a bad thing. *You know,* she told herself, *to celebrate our first win at home.*

The high of the first win carried over into the second game of the doubleheader. But soon both teams settled down, and the game felt like it was dragging on interminably. It didn't help that the Grays' pitcher was holding her Eagles hitless.

"No, no, no. You're not pulling a no-hitter on us today. No, sirree," Effa yelled down to the pitcher's mound. She started pacing around the owners' box, a flicker of the rage and disgust from that opening-day debacle beginning to take root in her belly. It didn't help that Avis wasn't there today. Avis always knew the right thing to say to keep Effa from doing something foolish. There would not be a car magically waiting for her if she ran out on the team again. She had ridden in from Harlem with Abe. She looked over at him. He had made himself quite comfortable in the corner; a few of his numbers-running cronies and some local reporters surrounded him.

Effa was definitely here for the long haul.

As it turned out, the long haul ended at six forty-five that evening; the game was called at the end of the sixth inning. The win went to the Grays, who had four runs to the Eagles' two. Effa hurried down to the locker room. She wasn't planning on going in there, naturally. She just wanted to be there to congratulate her guys for winning the first game when they left to go home. Everyone seemed to appreciate her gesture. They either thanked her or, at the very least, gave her a nod.

But she was not prepared for what happened when the team manager emerged.

"Good games, Ben," Effa called. Ben looked at her, grimaced, and kept walking. "I said good games!" she repeated, thinking maybe he hadn't recognized her. She had on a beret and an overcoat because of the cool weather. But the way he shoved his hands in his pockets and shook his head told her that he had.

"Okay, if that's how you want to play it," she said to herself. Olivia had warned Effa about this. When Olivia assumed ownership of the old Indianapolis team after her husband's death, Ben, her brother-in-law, fought her tooth and nail on everything, down to which brand of baseballs she bought. She said that he had not bothered to hide his views about a woman's place in baseball: none. Which was ludicrous, given the headlines a few years back when a woman minor leaguer had struck out both Babe Ruth and Lou Gehrig. If anything, it was to baseball's shame that there weren't more women like Olivia and herself owning and running teams and that there were none on the playing fields. Girls were just as hungry to prove their mettle in the sport as the male Negro players were.

Chapter 12

Effa and Abe gave themselves a day off from the Eagles and accepted an invitation from Alex Pompez, owner of the New York Cubans, to that team's opening-day game.

"It's weird," Effa said to Abe, "but I think I might be able to relax and actually enjoy this game. Because no matter who wins, it does not have a direct effect on my pocketbook."

Abe smiled at her. "If only it were that simple. The outcome of this game still affects the standings in our division. Let's just hope *our* team wins its games today."

Across town in Brooklyn, the Eagles were playing a double-header against the Chicago American Giants, but Effa found it refreshing that it felt like her guys were a million miles away and were none of her concern. Well, at least not for the rest of *this* day. Tomorrow was payday. She would give them hell come tomorrow if need be.

The Cubans' opening-day ceremony began similarly to the Eagles'. But it looked like they had failed to snag Mayor La Guardia, Effa thought smugly. Instead, it was the Manhattan borough president who stood on the mound poised to throw out the first pitch in Dyckman Oval.

But a face familiar to Effa led the procession of players onto the field. Effa nudged Abe. "Hey, is that the boxer kid from our party at Smalls?"

Abe peered through his binoculars for a better look. "Sure is. That's Joe Louis!"

Effa looked around. "I wonder if Marva is here."

They were seated in the stands along the first-base side. Effa did not see the beautiful young woman who had accompanied the boxer to the Smalls Paradise dinner back in January. But she knew she was likely somewhere in attendance. She settled back in her seat, making a mental note to keep an eye out for Marva.

While waiting for the game to start, Effa and Abe struck up a conversation with the gentlemen in the section next to theirs. She didn't catch their names, but it turned out that they were businessmen from Cuba, associates of Alex's, who were just as baseball-crazy as the Manleys were. The Cubans were playing the Grays, and after the trouncing the Grays had given her team on their opening day, Effa was happy that their neighbors were rooting against the Grays too.

Their conversation veered more than once to the topic of the Winter Leagues in the Caribbean and Latin America. "It's a great opportunity for you as owners, as well as for your players, to make some money in the offseason. A good number of players from Major League Baseball come down too. That's when we see who the greatest players in the game really are."

Effa was intrigued by this and made another mental note to look into the Winter Leagues when she had the chance.

But now was not the time. She heard the umpire behind home plate yell, "Play ball!"

Those two words were the incantation that pulled Effa into the magic that was baseball. The first Grays hitter stepped into the batter's box. Effa joined thousands of others in the stands in booing him. Effa could barely hear the stadium announcer say the man's name. It didn't matter that her team wasn't on the field. The hated Homestead Grays were in her adopted home city. On days like today, Effa Manley was a New Yorker through and through. New Yorkers did not take kindly to out-of-towners disrespecting them on their own turf.

This became apparent at the top of the fifth inning when the Grays runner on first stole a base, spiking the Cubans' second baseman in the process. The infielder got to his feet with fists raised. That was all it took to empty both dugouts. The battle on the field turned into a brawl. Loyal fans jumped out of their seats and ran onto the field to defend their team.

"They wouldn't have the nerve to try something like this with our guys," Abe grumbled. Effa nodded in agreement while silently egging on the Cubans' defenders. If you play dirty tricks on the field, you should be prepared to face the consequences—that was the way she saw it.

"Wait." Effa grabbed Abe's arm, her eyes glued to the melee. "Is that Gus?"

Sure enough, the heavyset owner of the Pittsburgh Crawfords and the president of their league had inserted himself into the fray. One look from Gus Greenlee was enough to get a few of the spectators to haul their tails back to their seats. Gus continued to yank players out of the scuffle.

Abe stood up, but Effa held him back with a gentle squeeze

of his wrist. "Honey, remember what the doctor said." Her voice was low so only he could hear. She was referring to his checkup a few weeks ago—Abe's doctor had expressed concern over the results of his bloodwork.

With a grunt, Abe sat down. "You're right. I'm too old for this kind of foolishness."

It wasn't until police officers arrived on the field that a semblance of order was established.

"What an embarrassment," spit one of the Cuban businessmen. "Why would I want to waste another dime on these Negro players? They're nothing but ladrones y perdedores. Not worth the expense of bringing them down to play on our teams. You want to know why Major League Baseball wants nothing to do with them? Because they behave like this, like a bunch of second-rate amateurs."

Effa was on her feet before she knew what she was doing. "And you should be ashamed of yourself, sir. We will never get anywhere as a people with attitudes like yours."

The man gestured toward the mess on the field. Bats, baseball gloves, and trash were strewn everywhere. Players and fans alike had been taken off the field in handcuffs. While the man's insult about the Negro players was uncalled for, the chaotic scene supported his point.

"*Your* people will never get anywhere because they keep doing things like this," he continued. "Fighting and acting like animals at a baseball game where women and children can see. It is not civilized. I don't know how you can claim to be one of these people and not feel ashamed."

She paused to decide whether she would address the dig at her appearance. Effa stared him down until his own not quite brown skin bloomed with a reddish undertone. "Of course *they* are my people. Aren't they yours too?"

He glared at her. He struck his puffed chest with an open palm. "Soy cubano, señora!"

Effa didn't speak Spanish fluently but she'd lived in New York long enough to pick up the gist of what the man said. "I'd like to know how well your Cuban passport has protected you from good old-fashioned American racism with your skin as dark as it is."

The man's complexion was just brown enough to fail the paper-bag test.

"That is why I come here only long enough to conduct my business and then I leave."

"That's what I thought. It wasn't but a few minutes ago that you were bragging about your baseball league down in the islands and how desperate you were to snag *our* boys for the winter. If that's what you really think about us and our players, why don't you do us all a favor and head back to Havana now?"

The fans in the sections surrounding them broke out in cheers. The chastised man's cheeks bloomed an even deeper shade of rose against his sun-kissed brown skin. "My apologies, señora." He tipped his cap to Effa in respect.

He turned to Abe. "I see why you let her handle your team's business, hombre. Tú mujer has the same fire in her belly as our mambisas had during our own wars for independence." He started to hand Abe his business card, thought better of it at the last second, and placed it in Effa's hand instead. "I'm in town for another week. Call me. I'd like to see your boys play in my league when this season is finished."

Harlem
September 1935

"You spent how much on baseballs this season?" Avis stared at Effa in disbelief. They were in the Manleys' living room, and Effa was catching up on her accounting for her end-of-month totals. Avis was keeping Effa company. Abe was somewhere in New Jersey, scouting out players for next year.

"Five hundred dollars." It made her feel faint to hear herself say the amount. Effa rifled through the stack of receipts that had accumulated over the course of the playing season. She had kept track of the numbers on a weekly and monthly basis, but this was her first time seeing the overall totals for the entire season.

"On actual baseballs? The ones you play catch with? How is that possible?"

"You know, the sight of foul balls and home runs going into the stands thrilled me as a fan. Now that I'm an owner, the one who has to pay for every single one of those balls, it makes me sick. Each ball that a fan caught had to be replaced to continue the game. The replacements that weren't hit into the stands were fit to be used for only a few innings and then they too had to be replaced. Abe and I might as well be throwing stacks of cash into the stands instead of balls."

Effa stopped herself short of saying that she could have paid for her millinery supplies and a storefront in a prime location in central Harlem with the amount they had dumped into their baseball franchise over the past year. And all they had to show for it so far was a team that hadn't even placed in the top three in its division.

"At least your season ended before it got cold, thank goodness." Avis looked out the window and shivered. "The Major League teams are going strong. But now that the leaves are changing colors, I don't know how they do it."

"It's because they make a helluva lot more money than we do. Both the players and the owners. It helps that they don't have to pay booking fees to use their stadiums. Instead, they make their profits from charging *us* an arm and a leg," Effa grumbled. She showed Avis a newspaper photo of Babe Ruth in a coat that went down to his ankles. "And this is what they do with all that extra cash. Buy fur coats."

"Oh, darling, Abe still hasn't bought you that mink?"

"No. Now he says it wouldn't be a good look to splurge on something like that, risk having the newspaper run a picture of me wearing it. Not with so many people out of work around here. Also, we would lose leverage when it's time to negotiate contracts with the players and vendors. We can't claim we're cash-strapped if I'm spotted around town in an expensive mink." Effa caught sight of their laundering bills to clean the team's uniforms. "That's it. I'm fining these guys a dollar for every stain they get on their playing pants. My goodness."

"Let me see." Avis reached out. Effa handed her the laundry totals. Avis whistled. "Oh, yeah, you're never getting that fur at this rate."

Effa sighed. "I don't think that coat is ever going to happen. I tried hinting to Abe about it for Christmas. He asked what I needed a mink for when we're sponsoring a team in Puerto Rico for the Winter Leagues."

"Wait—you're wintering in Puerto Rico this year?" Avis looked stunned. "And you aren't taking me?"

"Ha! I wish I were going. We're sponsoring a team to go down there. And Abe may go if we make it to the championship. I'm staying here. In the cold. But he's not thinking about that part."

Avis thought about it for a moment. "Well, maybe you can find something else to keep you warm while he's gone?"

Effa tossed a throw pillow at her friend. "Avis," she warned.

"That's what I do sometimes when Eubie's on the road. The whole world knows that's what he's doing while he's away."

"I don't know how you two do it."

"Do what?"

"Stay together. Tolerate each other. All while living separate lives."

"Easy. It works for us because it keeps us from killing each other. I could say the same for you and Abe. I could not work with my husband all day and then come home and deal with him at night."

"I don't. He's on the field or in the locker room, and I'm in the office. He has his friends in the owners' box with him during the home games. And I . . . stay away from them. And I have the house and office to myself when he's away on road trips with the team."

"That sounds perfect. Now all you need is a boyfriend. You know, I've had some men ask me about you."

"What men?"

Avis grinned. "Nice men. The kind who don't mind wining and dining you and then sending you back home to your husband."

LATER THAT NIGHT, Effa found a picture of herself and her first husband, George, tucked away in a corner of her jewelry box.

He had been so handsome back then. She imagined that he still was. And she . . . Effa turned the photo over and found *Atlantic City 1916* scrawled on the back of it. She had been so young and foolish. And somehow also ambitious yet clueless.

She had a good thing going now with Abe. She didn't want to screw it up. Even if he had basically given her permission to see other men.

Effa got into bed. She pulled the covers tight around her to block the draft coming from the vents. It was only early autumn so a true chill had yet to blanket the city. But the absence of Abe's warmth made her feel like it was freezing there in their room.

Yes, she had a good thing going—Abe's abundant bank accounts and a nice roof over her head, and she was her own boss for all intents and purposes. Still, she was lonely.

She longed for someone to hold on nights like this. Nights when Abe was so far away.

And she was cold. The coldest nights served as a harsh reminder of how long it had been since someone had snuggled with her beneath the covers. Snuggles that led to kisses, that led to touching, that led to . . .

THAT NIGHT WAS the last straw. The very next evening, Effa finally found the nerve to do something about it. She put on something nice and met up with Avis at one of the smaller nightclubs in the area. One that neither Abe nor his cronies nor any of her society or activist friends had ever been to. It was one thing to seek the affections of a man who wasn't her husband. It was another to do so indiscreetly. Discretion was the one thing Abe had asked of her. With that, she would comply.

They entered the club and were seated near the bandstand.

"This place looks cozy." Avis picked up the menu and scanned it. "How did you find it?"

Effa shrugged. "I saw a write-up in one of the papers. They said the food was to die for."

She began studying her own menu so she wouldn't have to look Avis in the face while she lied. Well, it was only a half lie because she *had* seen a write-up about this supper club in the paper. Only it wasn't about the food. It was about the house band. And there had been a picture. But Avis didn't need to know that.

Thankfully, Effa's little half-truth didn't come back to haunt her when their plates were cleared away at the end of their meal. The chicken fricassee had indeed been to die for.

"My goodness." Avis patted her belly. "I might be too stuffed to dance."

"Yes, that meal was . . ." Effa's voice tapered off as the house band took their places on the bandstand. Her eyes automatically went to the horn section. There he was, his fingers steady and sure on the valves of his trumpet as he brought the instrument to his lips. Lips that, once upon a time, she had known well.

Henry Clinton.

"Delicious," she finished.

Avis turned to see what—or who—had distracted her friend. She turned back to Effa, her eyebrows arched. "Well, well, well. I see you haven't lost your appetite after all."

"What are you talking about?" Effa made herself look at her friend. Her fingers fiddled with the linen napkin on her lap. She fought the urge to look down, to look away from Avis's scrutiny.

Avis jerked her chin in Henry's direction. "You know good

and well what I'm talking about. You forget that I was there when you wrecked your first marriage. And here you are ogling that trumpet player. I see you have a type."

"I don't know what you mean." Effa pretended to be confused by her friend's insinuation. "Unless you're talking about Abe. Kind, settled, and boyishly handsome."

"That might be your type for a husband. But you're not looking at *this* man like that because he's husband material. I've seen that gleam in your eyes before. You're on the prowl for ruin-my-life material. That means you're in the mood for a tall, milk-and-tea-tan musical fling."

Effa laughed, but neither woman was fooled. "We're here for the food, remember?"

"Sure, Effa." Avis patted her hand. "When I planted the idea in your head about finding a plaything, I meant someone passing through from out of town. Not someone in the house band at a club around the corner from your apartment. Have you learned nothing from last time?"

Effa sighed. "I've learned plenty since my first marriage. Love doesn't guarantee happiness. Marriage doesn't cure loneliness. Following the rules doesn't keep you warm at night."

She stopped herself from adding that Avis knew this as well as she did. It was a poorly kept Harlem secret that her husband, Eubie, had affairs with other women, one of whom he had put up in an apartment of her own since the early 1920s. Effa might be direct and to the point at times, but she wasn't cruel.

"Let's just listen to the music, okay?"

"Yeah, but will you be ready to face it when this all blows up? Effa, you are a beautiful woman. And now, because of baseball, everyone knows who you are. You can have whoever you want. But you cannot be indiscreet. I beg you, as a friend, pick anybody but him."

Effa took a long sip from her drink before answering Avis. "I'm not picking anyone. I'm just enjoying myself."

Avis leaned back and frowned but she didn't say anything else about the situation. For that, Effa was relieved. She knew coming here and playing with temptation was a bad idea for a variety of reasons. She looked over at Henry on the bandstand.

She couldn't help but compare him to her husband. Abe was fifteen years older than her. Henry was closer to her own age, maybe not quite forty. Abe had money and was settled. Henry was . . . well, he was a musician. Musicians had no trouble finding ladies willing to adore them each night, no matter what their marital status might be. She knew that from experience from her younger days. Effa glanced at Henry's left hand. He didn't wear a wedding band. But that didn't mean anything either. He *was* a musician, after all.

She assumed Henry lived on the road just like Abe. The big difference was Abe cared more about the camaraderie with his players than he did about chasing women.

"Besides," Effa said, "you don't know if that trumpet player would be interested in me."

No, Effa had come here tonight to play with a fantasy. She didn't need to pursue another man. She was just lonely. She probably wasn't even Henry's type anymore. She was older now. Her body was changing—some parts were starting to droop, and others were blooming.

She tapped her foot to the music, finally ready to believe the lies. Unfortunately, that was the moment Henry's eyes landed on her. The glint of recognition shone there.

Effa placed her hand on Avis's shoulder. "I think we should pay our bill and go."

"It's about time," Avis said, relieved. They had stayed out past her bedtime.

The musical number ended just as they settled their tabs with the waiter and stood up. Henry jogged over to them before they reached the exit.

"Effa? I thought that was you." He put his hand on her shoulder. "You weren't going to leave without saying hello, were you?"

Effa acknowledged him with a nod. "Henry. I was just saying to my girlfriend here that I thought you looked familiar."

"Well, you were right."

Effa patted him on the shoulder with a smile. "And so I was. It's good seeing you again."

"You can see me whenever you like. My band plays here every Wednesday night."

She eyed him carefully. "Maybe I will," Effa said.

"Good." Henry smiled. "And if you ever need my umbrella services again, just say the word."

Effa sucked in her breath so fast that she almost choked. "I'll keep that in mind." She turned to Avis. "We really should be leaving now."

Once they were back on the street, Avis nudged Effa. "Yeah, you're definitely about to make a big mistake. Oh, well—have fun."

ABE WAS THERE when Effa got home. He was sitting in his easy chair fiddling with the radio like he always did.

"You're back." She said it as both a statement and a question.

Effa had had to deal with too many emotions this evening. All she had left at this point was neutrality. She was spent.

Abe looked like a giddy little boy. His expression reminded her of the day he told her he'd bought the team franchise . . .

"Oh no. I know that look. What did you do this time, buy a basketball team?"

"No. Of course not."

"Then why do you look like you're ready to bounce out of that chair?"

"Well, you aren't that far off the mark. I didn't buy another team. Well, not exactly. You know that guy I went to see in New Jersey about a trade?"

"Yes . . ." Effa drew out the word.

"Well, I bought out his interest in the Newark Dodgers instead."

"Abe, you just said—" Whatever remained of Effa's high from her evening out was gone.

"Let me finish. Yes, I bought him out, but not to take on another team. I did it so we could move our franchise to Newark."

"Newark—as in the one in New Jersey?"

"Yes!"

Effa's heart sank as she plopped herself down on the couch. "Is there even anything in Newark?" To her, Newark was just a train stop on the way to and from her trips home to Philadelphia to visit her family. She had spent years here in Harlem starting a new life and making connections and working her plan to befriend the right people, and now she would have to give up another part of her dream because her husband had—once again—made an impulsive business move without consulting her.

"I . . . I don't want to move to New Jersey. Not just for a five-month baseball season."

"We don't have to move," Abe assured her. "Not yet, anyway. We stay here in New York. We do next season in Newark and get the lay of the land, and then . . ."

"And then what?"

"And then we'll go from there. But hear me out, Ef. This is an amazing opportunity. The Newark Negro community is small, but it's growing. It's just like here, with people hopping off the train from down south to settle. Plus, it's a less competitive market. Last season, we had to compete with two other Negro teams plus the Yankees, the Giants, and the Dodgers for fans in the seats. Newark's got nothing but Colonel Ruppert's Bears."

Effa opened her mouth to protest but nothing came out. She couldn't argue with Abe there. She had worked tirelessly to promote the team and put together special days to bring in more fans, but there were too many other distractions for baseball fans in New York. It might have been impulsive, but Abe had made a sound business move.

"Even better is that I still got those two pitchers I was initially after in the deal. You're gonna love this one kid, Terrance McDowell. His arm can throw some heat. The first thing I want you to do is to get him under contract as soon as possible."

"Fine."

Abe pulled Effa into his arms and swung her around once. He buried his face in her neck, then asked suspiciously, "Where are you coming in from anyway?"

Effa went still. Abe's face was right next to where Henry had touched her. He might as well have scrawled a big red letter *A* on her skin. Oh, what irony that she was suspected of being unfaithful the one time she had been innocent of infidelity. Well, sort of.

"You reek of smoke," Abe finished. He pulled back, his eyes filled with unspoken accusations.

Effa stepped away and laughed off her husband's observation. "Avis and I went out to a supper club. Some little place she found that you've probably never heard of." She winced at the high pitch of her voice. She hoped she didn't look as guilty as she sounded.

To her surprise, Abe broke out into his boyish grin. The one that had made her fall for him in the first place. "Great. I'm glad that you're not sitting around here alone in the apartment when I'm on the road. I like that Avis. She's a smart one. Now, she's one woman whose advice you should be following. She's a good friend for you."

Effa let out a short false giggle. "Of course. She's one of my oldest friends." *If only you knew the type of advice she's been giving me,* she thought.

"That's my girl."

"On that note, I think I'll go wash up before heading to bed. You know how much I hate it when the club smell gets into my hair." She reached up and self-consciously brushed a loose curl behind her ear. All of a sudden, she was feeling quite . . . unclean.

Chapter 13

Newark, New Jersey
Summer 1936

I can talk to the manager and see if he can free up one of the bellhops to drive you over in the Lincoln." Abe hovered over Effa as she sat in the lobby of the Grand Hotel. Just outside the doors, a shiny new state-of-the-art silver bus with *Newark Eagles* printed on both sides idled on Wickliffe Street. To anyone else, he looked like a doting husband. But Effa knew better.

"There's no need to go to the trouble of bringing another car when there are empty seats on our bus." She kept her voice bright, hoping a cheery tone would make Abe see her logic. "Besides, it'll be fun. I never get to go on any of the team's trips. We're not going far, and I want to make sure that the bus accommodations are up to par after we dropped a fortune to get it." Yes, she knew that her riding on the team bus would ruin the boys' club feel of the trip. But Effa had just finished going over the numbers for the first half of the season. They needed to cut corners wherever they could. Everyone would just have to make do this one time. They were only going to Trenton for this exhibition game, for goodness' sake. Not even sixty miles away.

Their players, many of them new to the squad this season, had gathered in the lobby with their luggage and equipment bags. The knobbed ends of baseball bats poked out of everything. The men might have been wearing suits and pageboy caps, but there was no denying who they were and what they meant to the local community. Hotel guests craned their necks—sometimes stumbling over each other—to get a better look at the ballplayers.

The Grand Hotel was one of the few places in the city that provided overnight accommodations for the Negro community. A number of their players stayed here long term during the season. The rest of the team joined them at the hotel bar as their designated hangout spot after games, so that made the Newark Eagles good for business, as that bar was one spot where fans could get up close and personal with their hometown heroes. For better or worse.

One of their players emerged from the elevator with a woman on his arm. She handed him his luggage, winked, and kissed him goodbye. Effa frowned. She looked up at Abe, who had stopped looming over her to watch the couple. As easygoing as Abe was, everyone in that hotel lobby knew Abe Manley's rule: No women during the playing season. And what had just happened in plain view was an absolute no-no. But that was Terrance McDowell for you.

Effa saw Abe's nostrils flare, making him look like a bull raring to fight. She reached out, placed her hand in his. "Abe, no. Not here in public where everyone can see. Look, the head of the local NAACP is coming out of the restaurant." Effa waved.

The man smiled at her and said, "I haven't forgotten you,

Mrs. Manley. I'll call you to finalize everything for the fund-raiser this week."

"Great. Looking forward to it," Effa said. She returned her attention to Abe. "See? The eyes of the most important people in town are everywhere. Save it for the bus."

"Fine." Abe stroked the back of her hand with his thumb. "Maybe it would be good to have you around. To help me not lose my head."

"McDowell is young and talented. I'm sure he just needs a good talking-to."

"Yeah, you're probably right." Abe helped Effa to her feet. "You're always right. That's why I married you."

Effa laughed. "You married me because I look good and I was the woman who was screaming the loudest at the World Series."

"That too." Abe kissed her on the cheek. All the players whooped and hollered.

One of them said, "Hey, Cap, I thought you said no women before the game."

Abe retorted, "Yeah, well, this woman signs your checks and pays the bills. I figured it would be in our best interests to keep her happy."

"Well, when you put it that way, carry on."

They started filing out onto the street. The bus driver opened up the hatches beneath the bus, and the men loaded in their luggage and equipment. Effa moved toward them to help, but Abe steered her onto the bus. "That's part of their jobs as baseball players. Let them do it."

"Fine." She sat in one of the front seats, right behind the driver. She expected Abe to sit down next to her. But he got back off the bus and joined in to help with the loading. When that was done, she watched as he took Terrance to the side. She couldn't hear what was said between the older man and the younger one, but she could see Abe's mouth form the words *Don't do it again*. The younger man laughed it off and went back to goofing around with his teammates.

Once the gear was stowed, the players started filing onto the bus. They tipped their caps with a "Ma'am" or a "Hello, Mrs. Manley" as they passed by. Again, Effa expected Abe to take a seat near her, but he opted for one in the back.

Terrance slid into the seat behind hers. He nodded back toward Abe. "It wasn't nothing personal. He just gets carsick from the scenery whizzing past in the windshield."

"I appreciate what you're doing, but that sounds like a bunch of hooey to me. Abe has a cast-iron stomach. I know because he does all the driving at home. He won't let me touch the steering wheel of his Lincoln."

Terrance nodded and mulled that over. "Yeah, I can't blame him for that. That Lincoln is a beautiful car. But if I had ol' Abe Manley's money and a woman like you on my arm, I'd be buying my lady a Lincoln of her own to drive around. I'm just saying."

"Yes, well . . . you keep pitching like you do and I'm sure you're bound to make some young lady a very happy woman someday." Effa could see why there were rumors floating around about Terrance McDowell being a ladies' man. The woman they'd seen him with proved them to be true. He definitely knew how to turn on the charm.

Terrance got up and dropped himself into the seat next to hers. "Who said I only liked them young?" he whispered.

The way he was staring at her left no question that he was flirting with her. And challenging her. Probably, in some twisted kind of way, he was trying to get back at Abe for checking him.

"You didn't say that. But that is your business, not mine. My apologies for making assumptions." Effa frowned. A man having too much beauty and charm at a young age made him a fool. Terrance proved that with every word that came out of his mouth.

"I can make it your business if you like. Ain't no way that old man is taking care of you properly. Not in all the ways that matter."

"I can quite assuredly tell you that *that* is none of your business." Too much beauty and charm also made a young man too bold for his own good. Effa decided she didn't like Terrance McDowell. But she also found that she was drawn to him nonetheless.

THE EAGLES LOST the game that day by a wide margin. The number of errors committed on the field was high, even for them. Abe was fuming when they got back on the bus to go home. He unloaded it all on Effa.

"I told you women on the bus were bad luck. But no, you just had to come along to save money. Next time you're going in a separate car, even if it costs me every penny in my pocket."

It was quiet on the bus ride home after Abe's outburst. Again, Effa sat by herself in the front seat behind the driver.

"Never again," she whispered. She had had no plans to travel with the team before today. And she definitely never would again after this humiliation. Attend home games, yes.

League meetings, fine. If it made sense for keeping up appearances, she would take the train on her own out to Chicago for the annual East-West game in the summer. And she would ride in first class—on Abe's dime—when she did. It would be easier to get the upgraded accommodations if she was traveling on her own. No one would take a second glance if it was just her. No one would try to make her feel like she didn't belong. There would be nothing to suggest that she wasn't who she was on a daily basis—a woman caught between worlds. A woman out of place. There'd be no reason for anyone to go out of their way to humiliate her.

She would play her part, just as she always had. Just like she did when circumstances warranted it.

With half the bus asleep, no one noticed when Terrance slipped back into the seat next to hers. "Don't pay ol' Cap any mind. He's just mad that we lost."

"I know."

"You okay?"

"Yes, I'm fine. Thank you for checking on me. You don't have to stay."

"I know. But I kinda got the sense that you might . . . that you needed a friend."

A *friend,* she repeated in her mind. But she heard the words in Avis's voice. How ironic. "You are too kind. But I'll be fine."

"I know you will be. I like you, Mrs. Manley. You might look all soft and pretty on the outside. But I've been watching you. Been watching you for a while. You're as tough as steel underneath all of that pretty. Folks don't show you enough respect. They need to show more appreciation for the amazing woman that you are."

"Thank you."

Terrance placed his hand on her wrist. He walked his finger-tips up the heel of her hand to caress her palm. "I'd like to be the man who shows you how appreciated you are. If you'll let me."

If there had been any doubt about what Terrance McDowell's intentions were, they were all gone now in Effa's mind. Proper decorum dictated that she should shut him down. He was her employee, after all. She was his boss. Hell, she was married.

But he also saw her for who she was, who she was trying to be. Even if his words were coming from the mouth of an over-confident, younger man, he was still a man in his prime. And it had been so long—too long, actually—since she had been in receipt of such an offer. Not since . . .

Henry Clinton.

No. She wouldn't think about him. The way he looked at her the last time she'd seen him. Before she rejected him in front of Avis.

No. This wasn't the same. Terrance could scratch the itch. He was a ladies' man. That meant no attachments. No complications with the season ending in a few weeks.

With Henry, she feared it would not be a onetime thing. She could do this. She could . . .

"All right. I'll bite. Exactly what did you have in mind?" Effa smiled when she saw that she had finally left Terrance at a loss for words. He hadn't been expecting her to accept his offer. But it took only the blink of an eye for him to recover.

"Well, I . . . damn. It's not like you can come see me at the Grand. Everyone will know—"

She cut him off. "Everyone knows that you haven't signed your contract for next season yet. I'll bring it to you."

"Oh, okay. Right, right. I guess then I'll see you in my room on . . ."

"Next Tuesday," she finished for him with a smile. "An off day when everyone else will still be recovering from the road trip."

"Okay, then. Next Tuesday it is." Terrance gave her a big toothy smile.

"You can go back to your seat now, Mr. McDowell."

"Okay." He looked around. Effa could tell that he wasn't used to being dismissed. "I guess I will."

She looked on with amusement as the pitcher fumbled his way in the dark back to his seat.

And to think, Effa had been mad at Abe for talking her into being the bad guy when it came to contract negotiations.

Chapter 14

Newark, New Jersey

There." Terrance finished scribbling his name on the dotted line. "Signed. I'm all yours for the next year. Or longer, if you want."

"First, let's see what you do next season." Effa gave him a stiff smile. He'd been flirting with her like this since she got there. It was nice to . . . have a man's attention. She checked the clock on the wall. It was almost two in the afternoon. She had to leave soon if she wanted to get back to the office before rush hour. Abe had been elected vice president of the Negro National League, which meant more league paperwork for *her* to handle on his behalf on top of what she already had to do for the Eagles' front office.

"Stay . . ." he purred. He placed his hand on top of hers when she tried to pick up the contract. He gave her hand a little squeeze, as if that would be persuasion enough.

Effa pulled her hand—and the contract—out of his grasp. "Newark is a big small town. The Negro community is even smaller. You know I can't be seen playing handsies with a player." She made a big show of stowing the contract with Terrance's signature away in her bag.

"You should stay here with me and celebrate. No one will see if you come upstairs with me."

"That would be nice . . . but no. I have to go." Besides the league work she had to do, she had to check in with her assistant, Carrie, about ticket sales totals, and the local NAACP had their monthly meeting tonight. The team and the organization were cosponsoring a Stop Lynching fundraiser at the ballpark, and . . .

Well, there was a lot to do while she was here in Newark. Then she had to go back to Harlem. That is, if she didn't check in to one of the white hotels here in Newark. The one good thing about being new in town was that the non-Negro part didn't know who she was . . . yet.

"Then when can I see you again?" asked Terrance a little bit louder than was necessary. The guests at the reception desk turned in their direction. Perry, the desk manager, frowned.

"Terrance, stop." Effa stood. She clutched her bag to her chest. "That is how rumors get started."

She felt every year of the decade that separated them in age. There was a vulnerability showing on his face that she could tell he worked hard to mask with his on-field antics and bravado. Terrance might be a grown man in his late twenties, but in some ways he was still just a kid. A kid who was well on his way to becoming a star in a job that most grown men—Negro or white—would kill for.

She didn't know what to do. She had to break this off—whatever it was—before it went any further. No matter what she said next, she knew she was going to hurt him.

And according to the contract she had just tucked into her

pocketbook, she would have to continue working with him through the next season.

"Let's just play it by ear, okay? I don't want to be a distraction for you during the season."

"I'm Terrance McDowell. The best pitcher on the team. Distract me all you want, and I'll still give you a winning record at season's end."

"Let's hope so." Effa secured her cloche hat on her head, angling it so over her eye to give her a little bit of anonymity along with an air of mystery. "Now, keep your voice down."

After Terrance left, Effa looked around the lobby. It was mostly empty, and for that Effa was relieved. This was a dangerous game she was playing. She'd had an itch that needed some scratching. Terrance wouldn't be the one to scratch it, however.

Effa looked at her watch again. She was just going to have to hold off on her other tasks. Now it was time for damage control. Unlike the white hotels in town, the staff here knew her. And they knew her husband. And they were all either at the front desk or milling around the entrance helping new arrivals with their luggage.

Effa went into the hotel's restaurant. The hostess at the door smiled at her. "Good afternoon, Mrs. Manley. So good to see you again. Just you?"

"Afternoon." Effa smiled. "Yes, just me. It's been a busy day. I could use some tea and a slice of that coconut cake." She pointed at the dessert case near the restaurant's entrance.

"Good choice. I'll let your server know." The hostess led her to a table that was right near the door; anyone walking by could see her. Effa hesitated a second before sitting down.

"Thank you." Well, if people saw her, all they could say was that they'd seen her taking afternoon tea alone!

When her tea was delivered, Effa wrapped her hands around the cup to steady herself. Despite that, her hands still shook as she brought the teacup to her mouth. She took a sip and let the chamomile work its magic on her nerves. Chamomile was an old remedy that her German grandmother had used whenever she or her siblings had upset stomachs or antsy nerves. Her hands were a little less jittery when she returned the cup to its saucer. Still, she managed to slosh some of the tea onto the table in the process.

"What the hell did you think you were doing?" she whispered. "You should have shut him down right from the beginning. Playing with that young man's emotions is playing with fire."

The sports columnists in the Negro press did a good enough job portraying her as a sexpot and a hell-raiser without Effa doing anything to justify their claims about her. She hated it. The worst thing was that she had to take what they dished out. Abe told her that making a stink would only add fuel to the fire.

All she needed was for one of those writers to have spotted her with Terrance carrying on in the lobby. That was all they needed to give themselves free rein to assume the worst about her and write even worse in their headlines.

Now, Effa would be the first to admit that she did not have the best track record when it came to making good decisions about men. The luck of the Bambino must have been with her the day she'd met Abe. Abe wasn't perfect, but his wealth and laid-back demeanor went far in making those imperfections tolerable.

"Effa! What are you doing here?"

She nearly jumped out of her chair at the sound of Abe's booming voice.

"Abe, I . . ." She fumbled for the words that would make what she had done, had almost done, sound vaguely excusable. Thankfully he cut her off before she could get out any more.

"Effie, we have hit the jackpot, I tell you. The jackpot! I just got through checking out this young guy at Orange High who is the total package. He's gonna be huge! You'll see."

"Huge, you say?" Abe was too excited to notice the relief in her voice and her posture. "If he's in high school, then he's still a kid."

"He is. But he said it was okay to talk to his mother about maybe joining the team for some home games over the summer. Here." Abe pulled a slip of paper out of his pocket and handed it to her. "Here's her number. It's a good thing I bumped into you. Knowing me, I would've lost it before I got home."

"That's doubtful." She almost added that a good numbers man wouldn't be that sloppy. Thankfully, she caught herself before she made the slip about his previous profession out loud. "Not when I tried to get lost when we first met and you still found me."

"You got that right, darling." Abe sat down in the seat opposite her, as giddy as a schoolboy. "Bringing the team to Newark was the right move, I'm telling ya. Things are only going to get better. I feel a pennant in my bones."

BUT A PENNANT was not meant to be for the new Newark Eagles that year. Effa did everything she could from the team's head office to make it happen. All of the player contracts were signed by the time they returned from spring training in Jacksonville, Florida. They had brand-new uniforms for their home and away games. They had that shiny new bus for more comfortable road trips. And she even got her friend Joe Louis to throw out the first pitch on opening day at Ruppert Stadium down in the Ironside section of the city.

She had followed up with the high-schooler's mother, but that didn't get very far. Both she and his mother agreed it would be best for Monte Irvin if he waited to go pro until he graduated from high school. But Effa was able to wrangle a verbal commitment from Mrs. Irvin that she would contact the Manleys first when Monte decided the time was right.

They had a pretty good season in 1936. But the Homestead Grays kept the Eagles out of first place in both halves of the season, thanks to Josh Gibson's bat and Satchel Paige's arm.

"You know, Abe, the only way we'll ever get the pennant is if we steal Paige away from Gus Greenlee somehow." Effa yawned on their way home from the Sunday doubleheader. They still lived out of their Harlem apartment. During the second half of the season, Effa had a change of heart. Commuting back and forth between Newark and Harlem had become too much. She never had time to see her friends there anymore. Like it or not, her life was in Newark now. As a result, Effa had been begging Abe to get them an apartment in Newark for half the year. Abe, ever the tightwad with money on the things that made the least sense, said that he'd look into it at the end of the baseball season. That irked Effa. The end of the season was too late!

"Heh, that'll never happen. Gus would never let him go."

"I know. Which is why I used the word *steal*."

Abe got quiet for a moment. "I like the way you think. I'll give Satch a call when they get back to Pittsburgh."

"Speaking of which, owners stealing players from one another is something that needs to be addressed at the next owners' meeting. When integration comes—if it ever comes—we can't expect the Major League to take our operations seriously if we're snatching players from each other like it's still the Wild West."

"You know how they are. They'll never listen, especially if it's coming from you. Even if they all know that you are right. We can't even get them to see how making one of the owners our league commissioner is a huge conflict of interest. They won't even stand with us to demand that the booking agents cut us some slack when we rent out the big-league parks."

Effa rubbed her temples, then leaned her head against the passenger-side window. "Just thinking about that meeting makes my head hurt. It would be so much easier if you all would just amuse each other in Gus Greenlee's Crawford Grill and let the wives hash out the league's business."

The 1936 season ended with the Eagles in fourth place in the Negro National League East. By the last game, Effa was exhausted.

"Abe, let's not do Puerto Rico this year."

"But we're the defending champions, Ef."

"We've been doing nothing but baseball for the past two years straight. I love the game. But even I need a break."

For the past month, her assistant's message pad had been full of calls from Avis. There were some from Cora too. Effa had not returned any of them. Not even the one from Lucy Richards.

Last week, a sportswriter had asked her what it felt like to be so "glamorous" and the "envy of other girls." Had she more energy, she would have laughed in the writer's face. Effa's life was glamorous only if one enjoyed arguing with sweaty players about their paychecks and league owners about their business practices, or lack thereof. The only woman she spent any time with was her assistant Carrie. She wished Abe would take on more of the business end of things. She wished she trusted him to keep things running in an orderly fashion if he did.

But most of all, she just wanted the space to fill her mind with her own dreams again.

Chapter 15

Philadelphia, Pennsylvania
January 1937

"This year I'm staying in the meeting room. I am going to speak. And you all are going to listen to me." Effa stood before the assembled owners of the Negro National League for their annual meeting.

Cum Posey pinched the bridge of his nose. "Effa, we go through this every time. We've already established that you have a right to be in this meeting as a co-owner. This year, you're lucky to have a seat at the table—"

Gus Greenlee broke in. "Whatever you've got to say, Abe can say on your behalf for your team and as the league's vice president."

Effa felt her cheeks flush with anger as she thought of the countless hours it had been left to her *to do* all of Abe's work as the league's vice president. "Who do you think handles all of the paperwork and day-to-day work of the league vice president? I know more about how our league runs than the rest of you put together." Effa saw so much red that if she had been a bull, Gus would have been torn to shreds by now.

"She's got all the numbers in her head. She's right. She knows them backwards and forwards," Abe chimed in. Effa should have felt grateful for her husband's support. If only he didn't always back her up too late in the conversation. Still, she nodded at him in acknowledgment.

"All I'm saying is that it's only a matter of time before the Major League tears down the color barrier. And when they do, they are going to run all of us out of business if we don't tighten up our act. We need systems in place for reporting our games more consistently, a method of maintaining our statistics across the board. We also need to stop poaching players from other teams and start honoring each other's contracts. Otherwise, we won't have a leg to stand on when the majors come to snatch the best players from us."

Effa swallowed. Yes, she had encouraged Abe to go behind Gus Greenlee's back to get Satchel Paige. That didn't make her a hypocrite, though. She would never have encouraged Abe to do it if the league had an established rule in place. The rest of them were naive if they thought white baseball would honor any form of a gentlemen's agreement with them.

Greenlee waved his arm in her direction. "You women are always getting all worked up and emotional over the silliest things. You've been around long enough to know that we have our way of doing things. We've got an understanding. And they need to respect that instead of us messing everything up to copy white folks' ways."

Effa retorted, "When have they ever cared to respect our way of doing things when the ultimate goal was to decimate what we built?"

"There you go, overreacting again." Gus threw up his hands like his point had been made.

"That's enough. We need to get started on this agenda if we have any chance of finishing this meeting on time." That was Ferdinand Morton, the commissioner of their league.

Effa nodded to him in respect to his position and his attempt to get the gathering in order. She sat down, still frustrated with the backward thinking of these men but also proud of herself for speaking up.

By the meeting's end, Effa was ready to tear out her hair. Abe had once again made his case about the booking agents and their ever-increasing fees cutting into everyone's already thin profit margins. But over half of those in attendance, inexplicably in Effa's eyes, refused to support the proposal that the owners push back and demand more reasonable rates. Their other proposal, the one addressing the need to crack down on players skipping out on their regular-season Negro League contracts in the States for more lucrative ones in the Latin American markets, met the same fate.

Once husband and wife were back in their hotel room, Abe threw his jacket onto a chair. "I just don't get it. Those guys are more interested in making this business a gentlemen's leisure club even if it means bleeding money everywhere. It doesn't make any sense!"

Effa rubbed his back. "They're not worth getting yourself this worked up over. Remember what the doctor said about your heart. Listen, sometimes the best you can do is handle what you have control over. That means we run our own organization as professionally as possible. You've just been elected league treasurer for the upcoming season, so we make sure the league's finances are in the best shape for when the majors do come knocking. And we keep up the fight. Those guys will come around eventually."

"You're right. As usual. Look at Gus. He took one look at that state-of-the-art team bus you insisted on getting and went right out and bought one for the Crawfords."

"Yes, he did." Effa smiled. "Because I'm always right."

THE NEXT MORNING, Effa bumped into Gus in the hotel lobby while Abe was settling their bill.

"I hope you put some thought into those ideas we presented about making things better around the league."

Gus lifted his cap and ran his hand over his head. "I'm not saying I disagree with you. I'm just saying that I don't see everybody else putting in the effort to follow through. No sense in rocking the boat and causing hard feelings when we already know how it's going to turn out."

That line of thinking didn't sit right with Effa. She hadn't gotten to where she was today by thinking the best course was to settle for any old thing. "How do you expect anything to ever change, then?"

"I don't. Because I know how much money I'll be making this year if we do nothing. I get to go to my bar, live like a king, and watch the best damn baseball players around for free. When you think of it, I get paid to watch the game I love. That's all I need."

"Humph. Speaking of the best players, I heard that you and Satch have been getting into it again."

Satchel Paige was the best pitcher in baseball. Period. No

one could say for sure how old he was. If Effa were to believe some of the old-timers' stories, Satch had been a veteran player back when they were rookies in the 1910s and 1920s. Some said Paige was in his forties. Others claimed he was still in his thirties. Either way, everybody who watched him pitch knew that he still had the arm of a high-school sensation.

"Yeah, you know how it is. The better they are, the more colorful the personality. In Satch's case, he also knows how good he is and how he affects ticket sales. And that any team he's on is guaranteed to make it to the championship."

Effa nodded. "How much do you want for his contract?"

Gus stared at her. Effa could almost see the gears turning in his head as he figured out what to make of her question. "A whole lot. Does Abe know you're over here spending his money on something that'll never happen?"

"Maybe. But what if I said that Abe might be willing to put up five thousand dollars to make Satchel Paige a Newark Eagle?"

The way Gus frowned at her made her feel like a naughty child. "Then I'd say that Abe needs to come talk to me about it."

"Why? I'm going to be the one to negotiate on behalf of the Eagles in the end."

"Why? Because Abe is the one who holds the purse strings." He smiled. "Not you."

Effa scowled at Gus because she had nothing to retort. He was right. It was Abe's money, not hers. No matter how much he insisted that everything in their marriage was "ours." "Fine. I'll make sure he follows up with you before we leave."

Effa didn't think the deal would get any further than that hypothetical conversation with Gus. Satchel Paige was too valuable a player to have on a team. Even if he never played, his presence on any roster was like magic in the league. If there was even the smallest chance the Manleys could snag him, they had to try. Having Satchel in the Eagles' pitching rotation guaranteed that they'd make it to the championship at the end of the season.

As promised, Effa directed Abe to speak with Gus about the potential deal. That night, when they were driving back to New York from Philadelphia, Effa was caught unawares when Abe said, "Call Gus next week. The Satchel Paige deal is a go."

Effa blinked, taken aback. "Wait—you convinced Gus to let him go?"

"No, you did. Now make sure the contract locks Paige in tight. I don't want him thinking he can get away with any of his shenanigans when he's on our payroll."

By the time the team bus left Newark for spring training in Jacksonville, Florida, Effa wished she had kept her mouth shut. The transactional part of the contract buyout between the Pittsburgh Crawfords and the Newark Eagles was done. But Satchel had yet to sign his contract with the Eagles. Even worse, no one had any idea where Satchel Paige was. One thing Abe and Effa knew for sure was that he was not on the Eagles' bus.

"He's probably holed up somewhere with a woman," Abe said before he left with the team.

"I hope he is holed up with some woman somewhere," Effa scoffed. "Then he can stop bothering me about becoming his girlfriend."

Prior to pulling his disappearing act, Satchel Paige had had a good time taunting the Manleys in the Negro newspapers.

Particularly with antics that were aimed directly at Effa. While on tour with his offseason all-star exhibition team, Paige was quoted as saying that he would join the Eagles only if "Mrs. Manley agreed to be my girlfriend."

Normally, Effa pasted any news clippings that mentioned her or Abe into her scrapbook, the one she'd begun when her name started appearing in the paper during the Blumstein's boycott. But that particular clipping, along with the rest of the newspaper that it came from, was crumpled into a ball and hurled into the trash.

"It's infuriating," Effa complained to Avis over the phone later that week. "I'm wearing myself out trying to get us ready for the season, trying to help put together the best team possible, and this is all they can find to say about me in the papers?"

"Darling," Avis said, sighing. "I suggest you take that paper and use it to clean the dog dung off your shoes. That's all it's fit for. But you can't blame them. Even I've heard the rumors about you flirting with your players and their locker-room talk about you."

"Locker-room talk about me? That's ridiculous. And Abe's usually in there with them."

Avis laughed. "Then ignore it. Juicy headlines sell papers."

Effa sighed in relief. "You're right. And if they do talk about me like that, I'd rather not hear the details."

"Fine. Then I'll spare you. But I will say that from what I'm hearing, most of that talk is coming from one person. That McDowell pitcher guy."

Effa, who had been flipping through her scrapbook, went still. "Oh, him. Everyone knows that he's the biggest blowhard on the team. He's young. He's handsome. And he knows he has the most reliable arm on our pitching staff." And he had the most charming smile. Not that Effa would say that. "He's also a big flirt. He probably has a little crush on me. I think that's all it is."

"Hmm. You want to know what I think? I think the lady doth protest too much."

Effa went back to flipping through her scrapbook. "And I think that you've probably added a little too much gin to your afternoon tea."

"I'm not trying to be funny, Effa. I'm serious. You forget that I know you. And I know that I'm the one who encouraged you to seek affection outside of your marriage. But even I thought you had enough smarts not to piss in the pot you eat out of."

"Avis, don't be crass."

"Clutch your pearls all you want, Effa, but I mean it." Avis paused as a coughing fit overtook her. "Don't be stupid. Whatever it is you're doing with that young man, stop. If it is true that he is running his mouth like that in the locker room, then he has no discretion. He sounds like a hothead, if you ask me. Which makes him unpredictable. And that's never good."

"Why not?" Effa had her own reasons for disagreeing with Avis's assessment. Terrance wasn't stupid enough to risk his job, for one. The Manleys were known as the only owners in Negro baseball who paid on time. You never heard an Eagles player complain about getting shorted. And everyone knew that as laid-back as Abe was, he had some bite to him. Terrance did not want to poke the sleeping bear. But she wasn't going to go into that with Avis right now.

"A, because it means he has no respect for boundaries," Avis said, "and B, because it means he has little respect for you."

AVIS'S WORDS CAME back to haunt Effa at the home opener at Ruppert Stadium later that spring. Once again, Effa had worked her tail off to make the event a spectacle that the fans had to experience in person or be filled with envy for missing it while they listened on the radio.

Joe Louis, her friend and now the heavyweight boxing champion of the world, came through for her again, making an appearance to throw out the opening pitch. But his presence proved to be both a blessing and a curse.

Having finished his ceremonial duties, Joe had handed the remaining ball over to their starting pitcher, who just happened to be Terrance McDowell. In the course of the exchange, Joe heard Terrance mumble something to the effect of "No wonder Mrs. Manley doesn't have time for me anymore—she's giving up my hits to the Brown Bomber." Joe related the comment to her along with an offer to "take care of that punk" himself. All she had to do was say the word.

Even though there wasn't truth to the barb, Effa was ticked off. There was absolutely nothing sexual about her friendship with Joe. They were like sister and brother.

The team had a day off the Monday after opening weekend. She sent Terrance a note that she wanted to see him. She made sure to specify that they were to meet in her office. She figured it was neutral territory in the sense that there was absolutely nothing about her office that would arouse either one of them.

Her desk had invoices for baseballs, uniforms, and red, white, and blue buntings, for goodness' sake.

From a business standpoint, the location worked in her favor in terms of the power balance. This was where she controlled their burgeoning baseball empire, where she signed the men's paychecks. It was where she ran the show. Within these four walls, Effa was the boss.

At the appointed time, Terrance strutted into Effa's office. "You wanted me?"

"Yes, have a seat." Effa looked at her assistant Carrie, who sat just outside her office. "Would you close the door, please?"

"Yes, Mrs. Manley."

Terrance sat himself down in one of the padded leather chairs before her desk. Once Carrie closed the door, he lifted his leg and dangled it over one of the armrests. "I'm here." He smiled at her. "Now, what do you want to do with me?"

"We need to talk."

Terrance tented his fingers over his chest. He lowered his chin just a bit to give her a seductive, hooded stare. "Okay. We can start with that."

"I'm serious, Terrance. No hanky-panky. And get your leg off my chair. The least you can do is show me a little bit of respect."

He returned his foot to the floor. "Aren't you the feisty one today? I think I like this side of you."

"Which side is that?"

"The one that orders me around. It's sexy."

"I have to order you around. I'm your boss."

Terrance faked a shiver, like she had run her fingertips along his most sensitive parts. "Like I said, sexy."

"Speaking of which, I'm not sure I like this side of you."

"Meaning?"

"The disrespect toward me—in private and especially in public—has got to stop."

"Ain't no disrespect here, baby. All I'm doing is expressing my appreciation of you with my words and my body."

Effa placed her hands on the desk and laced her fingers together. "Well, your mouth needs to do a better job of controlling the words that come out of it."

The smug expression on Terrance's face vanished. "What the hell are you talking about?"

The abrupt switch in his tone from seduction to venom made Effa recoil. Avis's warning about Terrance rang in her head. She took a deep breath and squared her shoulders. "I heard about the insinuations you've been making about me in the locker room and what we may or may not be doing together. Joe Louis also told me about the dig you made on the mound. If you had done that anywhere other than in the middle of a baseball game, he would have knocked you out on the spot. You're a very lucky man."

Terrance scoffed. "I'm not afraid of no Joe Louis. Why should he care what I say about you anyway? Unless what I said about you and him was true." Terrance eyed her suspiciously.

"It's not. Not that it would be any business of yours if it were."

"Not any of my business? You're *my* woman!"

"No, I am your employer and you are my employee, and as such, you will show me some respect! I might have led you to believe that there could be something between us. I apologize for leading you on in that way. But there will never be anything more between us."

Terrance stood. Effa stayed seated, willing herself to maintain her composure. She told herself that she would remain cool no matter what. He walked around to her side so that he towered over her. She simply looked at him, her face impassive. But on the inside, she was a mess. She had no idea what he would do next. But what Effa did know was that she would not let him use his size to intimidate her.

And if he did try something, Carrie was sitting just outside the door. And Abe . . . well, hopefully he had made it to the office already or would be arriving any moment.

Effa said, "Do you have a problem with that?"

"No."

"So what are you going to do?"

"This." Terrance took another step forward, reaching out to her with his hand. His fingertips caressed the line of her jaw. He lifted her chin, then leaned in to kiss her.

Effa's eyes widened and she gasped. She hadn't been expecting that. She went stiff in her chair, unsure of what to do next. Thoughts of both pushing him away and yanking him closer became a jumble in her mind. Meanwhile, he deepened their kiss. He moaned, the rumble of which reverberated into her body through the meeting of their lips.

He held her chair steady, pressing forward with his kiss. Finally, Effa let go of all the reservations holding her back, freeing herself to enjoy the moment. She forgot all about the daily slights from reporters and other owners because she was a woman who dared to speak her mind. Gone were her carefully laid plans to ingratiate herself with Newark's Negro society while maintaining her place in Harlem's.

For once, she let herself not be restrained by all of that. Effa felt like she was flying. Soaring right into the arms of a man who desired her and exhibited the virility to make her feel special. To make her feel seen. Even if whatever was going on between them could bloom into nothing more beyond this. This kiss. This moment. She knew that she was just a conquest for Terrance. And that she was crossing a line with him.

But she didn't care. She just wanted to be taken care of. Abe would be furious, of course. She would deal with that later. Right now, she wanted to think about nothing while feeling everything.

Terrance reached out to her with his other hand, grabbed hold of her blouse, and began to tug it out of her skirt. And she was going to let him . . .

Until there was a knock at her door.

"Effa, you in there?" Abe called.

Effa instinctively pushed against Terrance as he jumped back. She could hear Carrie attempt to hold off Abe. "Mr. Manley, she's in the middle of—"

Abe knocked on the door with what sounded like his fist. "Effa!"

Effa shoved her shirttail back into her skirt. Terrance hastily placed his fedora back on his head. She scurried around her desk, ran to the door, and yanked it open.

"Abe! Is there a fire? It sounded like you were about to beat the door off its hinges."

Abe was breathing heavily through his nostrils. His eyebrows were furrowed at an angry slant. He looked like a bull.

A bull that had been taunted and played with and was ready to strike. Effa had never seen him this mad before.

"No, it's that durn Satchel Paige. He—" Abe marched into Effa's office but stopped short at the sight of Terrance. "What're you doing in here?"

Effa stepped between Terrance and her husband. "We were going over the conduct clause in his contract. He was just leaving."

"Why? What did McDowell do? His arm has been on fire lately and I haven't heard any complaints."

Terrance looked like a deer caught in the headlights of a car Abe was driving. But when all eyes turned to him, he fell into his usual easy smile. "You know how it is, Cap. The ladies love me. Sometimes they go too far in trying to get my attention, and then someone comes running back here to Mrs. Manley to complain about it."

Effa felt a rush of relief because she had had no idea how to explain his presence in her office. She would deal with how easily Terrance had come up with such a plausible lie later. "Yes, we were just discussing how these types of . . . distractions are never to happen again." And to Terrance, "Isn't that right?"

"Yes, ma'am." Back was his smug grin. Nothing was amiss about his demeanor. But to Effa's eyes, he might as well have been rubbing it in Abe's face. "I guess I'll leave you two to get back to all of your owner stuff."

He tipped his hat to Effa, his gaze lingering on her just a second too long. "Mrs. Manley."

Abe called after him, "You remember the rules. While you're playing for me, it's no booze, no gambling, and no women."

"All right, Cap." Terrance didn't bother to turn around.

Abe leaned out of the door to make sure Terrance was gone. "Carrie, why don't you take lunch. Take your time."

"Yes, Mr. Manley."

Effa waited until Carrie was gone too. "Abe, was that necessary? She's my secretary. I don't appreciate you—"

Abe cut her off. "What was that about?"

"What was what about?"

Abe pointed at her door. "That. Since when do you need to have the door closed with a player in here? With *that* player in here?"

"I—I wanted to save the man's pride. I don't feel comfortable giving him a reprimand with an audience."

"What audience? Only person here was Carrie."

"Carrie is audience enough."

"Well, you don't have to worry about that anymore. Whatever happens on the ball field, that's my business. I'll handle it from now on. You deal with everything else."

That added fuel to the fire. "Everything else. Like how a player conducts himself doesn't affect the clauses in his contract. The contracts that you make me negotiate. Abe, I don't like the way you're talking to me right now."

"You don't like how I'm talking to you? Well, I don't like how you're looking right now with your shirt half hanging out and your lipstick smeared across your face. I'm not stupid, Effa. I'm not a fool, and I don't appreciate you making me look like one."

"I don't think you're a fool."

"You know, when we got married and I told you about my . . . my situation, I gave you the okay to step out of our marriage.

That's on me. But I thought you would have the sense . . . no, have the *class* not to carry on with one of our players right in my face."

"Abe, I'm not . . . we haven't. I didn't—"

"I'm not in the mood for excuses, Effa!"

She watched his normally cheerful face harden. It made her wish the earth would swallow her up. She hadn't just embarrassed him with her indiscretion; she'd hurt him.

Abe had showered her with almost everything she had ever desired. Since the day she had met him at that World Series game, Effa had not wanted for food, shelter, safety, security. All he had ever asked of her was that she make him proud to have her on his arm. That she spend time with him. That she make him the center of her world.

And almost from the beginning, all Effa had done was take him for granted. She had been so consumed with her plan to acquire status and social power and fulfill her own need to feel like somebody in this world. She'd achieved all those things, yes, through her own grit and determination. But it had been Abe who gave her that first boost up the ladder. When he married her, his wealth had opened the one door she'd never have successfully cracked open on her own.

"Abe, I—I'm sorry. I was out of line. Let me make it up to you. I'll make you dinner. Your favorite—"

Abe waved off her attempt to reach out to him. To embrace him. To let him know that she did in fact respect him and love him as her husband.

"No. We're going back out on the road tomorrow. I'm behind as it is. I'll just grab something while I'm out. I'll probably be home late, so don't wait up for me."

His words landed a blow, as he'd intended. They almost exactly mirrored every excuse she had thrown at him whenever he had wanted to spend time with her during the Blumstein's boycott. She stared off in Abe's wake long after he had left her office.

"What a fool I've been."

Chapter 16

Harlem
May 1937

I t was awful, Avis. I've never seen Abe get that mad. Not even when the police mistook him for my driver." Effa and Avis were attending a luncheon fundraiser for the Riverside Sanitarium, for which they were both on the organizing committee. "He hasn't spoken to me since. He didn't get home until late last night. Then he got up early to meet up with the team and get on the bus for their road trip."

"I hate to say I told you so—"

Effa cut her off. "Then don't."

Avis took a deep breath and started again. "What I was going to say was that maybe it's time to start backing away from baseball."

Effa shook her head. "That's impossible. Who would take my place? Abe only wants to do the fun stuff—scouting players and going on the road. We can barely afford the two people we have on the office staff now."

"It seems to me that you are being stretched too thin for something that isn't even your dream. It's Abe's dream. What happened to the millinery and interior-design business you wanted to start? Wasn't that part of your grand plan?"

"It was. But then I got sidetracked by the community work. The Blumstein's thing took over my life. And then baseball . . ."

Avis leaned back with a satisfied smile. "Yes, and then baseball."

"The funny thing is that I probably have more visibility and bargaining power as a baseball executive than I would ever have with my own shop. I just never figured that I'd be closer to Abe in one respect yet feel so alone."

"You're the only woman in a boys' club. And you're the smartest one in the club—"

Effa placed her hand on Avis's arm. "Stop, that's not true."

"Of course it's true," Avis continued. "Everyone knows. Even those men. That's why they let you stick around. Because you have good ideas. And you're not afraid to jump into the thick of the fight. They just feel the need to shove you back in your place from time to time to soothe their fragile egos."

"It feels like they do it every day. It's worse during the season. I can't believe some of the things they say about me in the papers."

"That's because they have nothing else to say about you. They're just reaching for low-hanging fruit when the only thing they can find wrong about you is that you're too feminine for the position you hold while being too mannish to be as effective as you are."

"If that's meant to be a compliment, then I wish it didn't come with the sting of an insult."

"Forget them." At least, that's how Effa chose to hear what

Avis said. She never did care for coarse language. "It's good for the world to see a woman be free and happy and successful outside the bonds of motherhood. Negro baseball needs you. Hell, *all* of baseball needs you. The whole lot of them would be making a heap more money if they would just listen to you for once without all the hooey-phooey you have to go through to make it look like Abe's doing all the work when it's really you making it happen all by your damn self."

This made Effa want to squirm in her seat. "You don't understand what it's like to sit at that table in those meetings. I already tried that. They won't listen to me. My ideas have to come from Abe directly or via me playing the dutiful-wife role for anyone to even consider them."

Avis took her cigarette out of her mouth and stubbed it out in a nearby ashtray. "Damn men. Doesn't matter if they are Negro or not. They make it impossible to live with them, and impossible to live without them."

"The only place I'm able to shine is socially or when Abe is out on the road with the team."

"At least the vendors know who runs the show."

"Yes, there's that."

"Now that I think of it, I have a feeling that, all your personal drama aside, the baseball business has been an unexpected dream come true for you. It's no secret that you've always been power-hungry. Well, sweetie, this country bleeds apple pie and baseball. You don't realize how much power you hold in your hands."

Effa might have the power Avis described, but it was starting to cost her too much to keep it. She had no control over her public image anymore. The sports press was relentless in its search for any imperfection of hers to spotlight. Her marriage had been reduced to a business partnership. She had no friends. She had almost no social life outside of baseball. She had been able to pull off this fundraiser only because the bulk of the planning had occurred during the offseason. But come tomorrow, it was back to baseball. No matter what she did, it always came back to baseball.

Effa leaned back in her seat and mulled over Avis's reflection. "I give up. You're right. I just wish there were a nicer way to say it than 'forget' them."

"A nicer way to say it? You mean a way not to make the men who run baseball look like the idiots that they are. Anyway, now what you have to do next is decide what you are going to do with that power—are you going to waste it romancing that little hothead or are you going to wield it for a greater purpose and change the world?"

Avis's words were still ringing in Effa's head when she returned home that evening. Thank goodness she had Avis in her life. Effa could always rely on her friend to cut through the walls she put up and see the real Effa. And tell her the truth unfiltered.

Effa could not deny that she had needed a talking-to. Had needed a hard-to-swallow dose of Avis's tough love.

She drifted off to sleep with a smile on her face. If not for Avis, Effa's life would be well on its way to a total disaster.

Newark, New Jersey
February 1939

Effa stumbled through the myriad of moving boxes that littered the living room of 19 Crawford Street looking for the ringing phone. Abe had finally had enough of the long commutes to and from their Harlem apartment. He'd bought this house not long after the last baseball season ended. But they were far from finished turning this house into their home.

The telephone continued its shrill ring.

"Hold on, hold on. I just gotta find you." She finally located it under a box that held her scrapbook and a stack of business files. She grabbed the receiver. "Hello?"

"Hello?" Avis said.

Effa braced her free hand against the box to maintain her balance. "Avis?" She tested the telephone's cord length before crossing the room to the padded easy chair that was free of stuff.

"Yes. Did I catch you at a bad time?"

"No. I was just . . ." Effa looked around at the chaos before her. "I'm just in the middle of unpacking while trying to get ready for the owners' meeting in Philadelphia."

"I'm so glad I caught you. I haven't spoken to you in ages." Avis began hacking a dry cough.

"Darling, are you all right? That cough doesn't sound so good," Effa said absently. It was hard for her to concentrate with her new living room in such a disarray.

"Oh, it's nothing but a nuisance. I had a little cold not too long ago. But this durn cough won't go away." Effa could hear a few wheezes through the static. It sounded like she was trying to muffle a new coughing fit.

"Now you have me worried. Please tell me you've made an appointment for a checkup."

"No, but I will. I promise. But enough about that. I was

calling to let you know I miss you terribly, Ef. Harlem just isn't the same since you and Abe moved."

"It's only been a few weeks. With the holidays, I'd think you would've been too busy socializing at all the usual events to miss me."

"No one fun ever shows up at those parties." Avis coughed again. When she recovered, she added, "Now, promise you'll come visit me just as soon as you come back from Philadelphia. I won't take no for an answer."

Effa sighed. "I don't know if I can, Avis. With the league meeting so late this year, I need to hit the ground running to prepare for the season when I get back."

"Oh, poo." Effa could almost see Avis poke her lip out. "Why don't you leave the meeting a day early? Or get there a day late? I just miss having you around." Avis fell into another coughing fit.

"I wish I could. I really do. Everything is a mess with the league." Gus Greenlee was threatening to resign his position as Negro National League commissioner and take his Pittsburgh Crawfords out of the league entirely because she and Abe had attempted to stage a coup to establish more sound business practices. Gus didn't want to listen. But Avis didn't want to hear about all that. The phone at the team headquarters had been ringing off the hook all day. In fact, Effa had gone home early to start packing for the trip and unpacking the house to clear her head. Let Abe handle that mess.

"You know what? We're staying at Mother's house while we are in town. Her chicken soup was like magic when I was growing up—how about I ask her to cook you up a batch? That'll give me an excuse to see you as soon as I come back!"

"That sounds like a lovely idea, darling. It's a date!"

IT WAS A date that never happened. The owners' meeting dragged on an extra day with all the turmoil from infighting. Gus made good on his threats. He announced his resignation as league commissioner the night before the meeting. Not only that but he'd sold his stadium, Greenlee Field. So that was one less venue where the owners would not be subjected to excessive booking-agent fees.

By the time Effa and Abe returned to Newark, Effa had forgotten the chicken soup and the date with Avis.

A week later, Effa's phone rang. "She's gone," said a man's voice as soon as the operator connected the call. Whoever the man was, he sounded like he was barely keeping it together.

"Who is this?" Effa frowned. She had been meaning to talk to Abe about getting them an unlisted phone number. Ever since the move, local kids had been making prank calls to them.

"Effa, it's me. Eubie."

"Eubie, I didn't recognize your voice!" Effa's heart was in her throat. For as long as she had known Avis and her husband, Eubie, she had never seen nor heard Eubie without a smile on his face or in his voice. But right now, he sounded like a man whose whole world had shattered.

"Avis is gone."

"What do you mean, she's gone? I just spoke to her. She was fine. She had that cough, but she was fine!" Effa was yelling into the phone as if raising her voice would contradict what

Eubie had just said. As if Eubie were prank-calling her with the cruelest possible joke.

"Wasn't just a cough. It was tuberculosis."

"Tuberculosis? What? How?"

"She'd been in the hospital for the last week and a half. She was in and out for a few months, to be honest. She was calling for you toward the end. Asking for you to bring her some tea."

"That's not what she told me!" Effa yelled into the receiver. "She said she would be fine."

Effa felt the bottom drop out of her world. All the distractions from the past week now felt like insignificant pebbles in her shoe: Gus Greenlee's juvenile antics. The damn booking agents. The endless negotiations to decrease the cost of each stupid baseball.

Baseball.

Stupid flipping baseball.

How had she let the blasted business of baseball keep her away from her dearest friend when she needed her most? Avis had been on her deathbed calling for Effa, and Effa had cared so much about this good-for-nothing game that she had forgotten what was important. *Who* was really important.

Eubie was able to calm down enough to give Effa the details of the funeral arrangements. Effa jotted them down and quickly got off the phone. Then she curled up into a ball in her chair and let out a howl that sounded like it had crawled out of hell itself.

She was still in that chair when Abe came home. He ran to her the moment he saw her.

"Effa, baby, what happened?"

"Avis came down with tuberculosis. She died."

Abe gathered her in his arms. "Oh, honey. You two were as thick as thieves. I am so sorry."

"I didn't get to say goodbye to my friend because of this stupid team. I . . . I don't think I want anything to do with this baseball team anymore." Effa sniffed into Abe's chest.

"I know. I know. I hate that this happened like this. I'm feeling like I'm starting to fall out of love with the baseball business myself lately. But now's not the time for that. I'll take care of everything. Tell me what you need."

Abe coaxed Effa to her feet. With his arm around her waist, he guided her to the master bathroom. There, he drew her a warm bath, sprinkled Epsom salts into the water. Then he undressed her with the care one would take with a helpless baby. Once she was in the water, he sat with her. He didn't say anything. Didn't try to make her say anything. Neither one was in the mood for pointless small talk. They just shared a comfortable silence. It would've been nice if not for Effa's heartbreak.

Chapter 17

The Bronx
March 1939

Henry Clinton showed up at Avis's funeral. He didn't see Effa at first, to Effa's relief. Her emotions were already a total mess. She didn't need him bothering her with old, unresolved feelings.

Abe wasn't there. She had given him an earful when he'd opted to stay in Newark and handle the team office in her absence. Effa had been beside herself with grief ever since Eubie's call. It was pointless to expect her to carry out her duties with the Eagles and oversee the preparations for the upcoming season. Abe quietly took over, enlisting her assistant Carrie to get everything done. Still, if ever she had needed Abe's arm around her shoulders, today was that day.

Now all Effa had to do was mourn. And figure out how not to beat herself up for letting her dear friend down in the end.

Effa still couldn't believe it. Avis had been in her forties, but she'd had the energy of a woman in her twenties. Every time she pictured Avis, Effa saw her laughing or dancing or telling a funny story about "Dummy," the nickname she'd given her husband.

Having to watch Eubie's grief at the funeral had been the worst part of the day. He hadn't just cried. He had broken down at one point, wailing his heart out, on his knees in front of Avis's casket. Effa felt her heart break all over again.

Finally, the grief in the sanctuary became too much. Effa ran out of there. Once on the curb, she let it all out. The tears rolled down her face in a stream that wouldn't stop. Sobs racked her body. The handkerchief in her bag was useless at this point. She cried into her hands until she began hiccupping.

"There you are."

Effa looked up. It was Henry. "Great. You're the last person I want to see. Especially when I look like this." Effa winced as soon as the words flew out of her mouth.

"I'm going to pretend that it was your grief insulting me and not you personally."

She gave him a weak smile. "Sorry. That was harsh. I did not mean it like that."

Henry wrapped her in his arms. "I know you didn't, beautiful."

"Beautiful. Ha. Look again. I'm a mess."

That made Henry laugh. The bass of his laugh reverberated through his body and into hers. "Then you're a beautiful mess."

She smiled into his chest. "Only you could manage to be charming at a time like this."

"It's at times like these that you have to make yourself find a reason to smile. Even if it is fishing for cheesy compliments. I'll take what I can get."

They quieted, soaking in the solace from their individual grief. Effa was the first to take a step back. "Thank you. But we probably shouldn't be doing that."

"Probably. But if we were in a perfect world, we wouldn't be at her funeral right now."

Effa dropped onto the concrete stairs leading up to the church. "I just can't believe it. I feel so guilty. The last time we spoke . . . she practically begged me to come visit her. And I forgot. I thought we'd have more time . . ."

Henry sat next to her. He took her hand in his. "We always think we'll have more time. I know I always thought we would."

Effa turned to him. "What do you mean?"

"You and me. Us. Back when we were together. Yes, I knew you were married. But I knew you weren't happy. I figured we would have all the time in the world to get it sorted out and live our own happily ever after."

"That sounds nice. Too bad you were spending all your free time sniffing after everything in a skirt."

"Ouch." Henry reached up to grab his heart. "Now, that hurt."

"It was supposed to." Effa grinned. "We had our time. It was fun. And then I moved on. I had dreams of my own that didn't align with yours. I have no regrets." She was done with this conversation, these emotions, with explaining to yet another man that she didn't need him complicating her life any further. Especially when Avis wasn't here to knock some sense into her.

Effa glanced at her watch. "Oh, dear. Look at the time. I need to head back to Jersey."

"Jersey. Is that where you are now? I was starting to wonder why I hadn't seen you around."

Effa scolded herself silently. She hadn't meant to tip him off to where she lived. "That fact is hard to miss. I'm in the Negro sports pages all the time."

"You know I'm not into sports like that."

"Ah, another reason why we were never meant to be."

"I remember now. You're a Yankees fan."

"I was a Babe Ruth fan."

"That's right. It must have hurt when the Yanks got rid of him." Even the most casual fans were still upset that the Yankees had released the Babe after the 1934 season.

"Yes. But I kind of got over it when the Colonel let us use his Newark stadium for our home games."

Henry studied her. "Nah. I'm not buying it. You Yankees fans don't let go of grudges that easily."

"Okay, fine. I *tolerate* the Colonel because he lets us use his stadium." She sniffed. "I don't know how to separate business from my fanaticism."

"Now, that, I believe."

"Good. Now that that's settled, it is time to get myself down to Penn Station." Effa made a show of standing up, smoothing the back of her skirt, and doing one last dab on the corners of her eyes with a tissue. "Thank you for checking on me, Henry. It was good to see you again."

As she began to walk away from the church, Henry stood up too. "I'll go with you. I wouldn't be a gentleman if I didn't make sure you got onto your train safely."

Effa stopped and turned. "You've done more than enough already. Don't act like I didn't live on my own in this city for all those years."

Henry jogged the few steps that separated them. "Oh, indulge me, Effa. I'm headed in the same direction anyway. Just think of me as a set of shoulders you have at your disposal in case you need to cry again on the way."

"Fine. But I was going to take a cab."

"Great." He smiled. "Then we can split it. That's less money out of my pocket."

"That's one way to look at it." Effa gave him a tight smile as if she hadn't already thought the same thing herself. The cab fare she'd save by Henry tagging along would be another deposit in her secret Get Out of Baseball fund.

The cab ride down from Harlem to Midtown Manhattan was quiet and uneventful. Henry sat on his side of the back seat. And Effa might as well have been hugging the window crank on hers. The sexual energy that had tethered her to him long ago no longer pulled on her. She was relieved, yet very much aware of its absence. Her attraction to Henry had been a part of her for almost all of her adult years. It was the loneliest she had ever felt in her life.

They reached Penn Station and settled the fare; Effa got out of the cab. Henry followed her.

"Again, I thank you, Henry. It was good seeing you again."

He tipped his fedora. "You made it here in one piece. My job is done."

He held his arms open. Effa stepped into them for one last friendly embrace. He planted a kiss on her cheek. It all felt very chaste. Almost too safe. Maybe he no longer felt a sexual attraction to her either. Maybe going forward, they really could be just friends.

She stepped back and looked up at him. "Goodbye, Henry."

"See you later, Ef."

She gave him one last small wave of her hand, then walked to the entrance.

The nightmare resumed the second she entered the train station.

Chapter 18

New York City
March 1939

A pair of hands yanked Effa as soon as she crossed the threshold into the station. They were big hands. Strong hands. But she was too stunned to make heads or tails of what was going on.

"I get it now. You threw me to the side like trash so you could sneak around with that stale crumb out there?"

"Terrance?" She couldn't believe it. She barely recognized the face contorted with rage as his. "What are you doing?"

"I thought I was enjoying a day in the city before I report to spring training. Instead, I see you hugged up with another man. Kissing and shit." He shoved her chest with both hands. She stumbled back. The kitten heels she was wearing did little to help her regain her balance. Effa landed on her bottom. The hard fall on the marble floor sent shots of pain up her back. She cried out. "Help!"

"I'll help you, all right. Help you learn what happens when a woman teases me." Terrance grabbed her hands, then slapped her across the face.

"Somebody help me!" Penn Station was always a hub of

activity. Unfortunately for Effa, that meant that most New Yorkers were used to seeing some kind of altercation or another on a daily basis. To Effa's horror, no one stepped in to intervene. The most passersby did was leave a wider berth around them as Terrance continued to abuse her.

"I tried to treat you nice. But you just wanted to play games with me. Boss me around." Now, Terrance yanked her across the floor. Her cries didn't faze him; he dragged her down the stairs to the main concourse.

"Hey, buddy, what's your problem? That's a lady!"

Terrance let her go abruptly. Effa was too stunned to make sense of the blur of people around her. She scrambled to her feet and moved far away from Terrance. A woman wrapped an arm around her shoulders.

"Ma'am, are you okay?"

"I think so." Effa started walking. She could hear sounds of an altercation behind her. Sounds that were still too close.

"Let me help you get your purse. You dropped it over there."

Effa let herself be guided where the woman steered her. All her energy was focused on controlling her breathing. She had started hiccupping at some point while Terrance was roughing her up. And now she felt like she couldn't get enough air. Her lungs felt like they were closing up. She shook the woman's arm off her shoulders. She needed air. She needed to go outside . . .

"Effa!" a man screamed. Effa winced. And then quickly relaxed. Well, as much as she could under the circumstances. The voice that had yelled her name was not Terrance's. It sounded more like . . .

"Henry?"

"Where is she?" Henry pushed through the crowd of people

who had gathered around her in the aftermath of the attack. Effa had never been so happy to see him in all her life.

"Henry! Where did you come from?" The woman who had helped her handed over her purse. "Thank you, ma'am."

Henry stood back just long enough for the two women to complete the exchange. Then he wrapped her in his arms. She sagged against his chest. "Did he hurt you?"

"I think I'll be fine. I'm just a bit stunned." That was a lie. Her ribs felt sore. And her face felt warm where Terrance's hand had struck it.

"Who was that guy? Did you know him?"

Effa felt shame flood her body. Henry was the last person she wanted to explain Terrance's behavior to. "Yes, he's one of my players."

It was the truth. She owed no further explanation to anyone. Well, except for Abe, maybe.

Effa groaned. *Abe.* There was no way she could get away with not telling him this. Her heart began to race again. Her husband might be a laid-back man for the most part, but he had a dark past that he didn't share the details of. One that she'd made a promise never to ask about. Her mind went wild with all of Abe's possible retaliations.

"That's it. I'm escorting you home. I'm not letting you out of my sight until I see you safely home to your—"

Effa nodded to cut him off. The crowd of people were still staring at her curiously. They had been exposed to too much of her personal life already, thank you very much.

"That's fine. Just get me out of here."

Chapter 19

Newark, New Jersey

Henry did not let Effa out of his sight until he delivered her to the Crawford Street home she shared with Abe.

"Don't worry." Henry finally let go of her arm. The spot felt cool at the absence of his touch. "I'll hang back down the block a little. I'll still have my eyes on you. I don't know what's going on with you and your old man in there, but I have no intention of making it worse. I just want you to be safe, Effa."

Effa nodded. She licked her bottom lip, but not out of desire. She was at a rare moment of not knowing what to say.

"Thanks again. For coming to my aid today, not once but twice. And now I've made you come all the way over to Jersey. I'm so embarrassed—"

Henry cut her off. "It's okay. Maybe fate had a hand in it in more ways than one. When all is said and done, I just want you to be safe and happy. Even if it's not with me."

Effa grinned at him one last time. "Again, thank you."

She waited until Henry was safely in the shadows of the trees a few houses away before walking up to her porch. She could feel his eyes on her back as she placed her key in the door. True to his word, he was making her feel safe one last time. And now she had to find the courage to step back into her life.

She looked behind her. She couldn't see Henry but she knew he was there. Then she turned her key in the lock and opened the door.

"Abe? I'm home," she called, louder than she normally would have. She had to make sure Henry heard her. Satisfied, she closed the door behind her.

Effa knew good and well that Abe was not there. At this time of day, he would be at the team's office in Newark. But Henry didn't know that. And she had to make Henry believe that she was inside safe and sound and under the protection of her husband. Otherwise, Effa had a feeling that Henry would stand guard outside all night. That was not an option. She needed him to go home and live the rest of his life.

She would deal with Abe and the repercussions of what happened at the train station when the time came. Effa hoped that the time would never come.

Once she was in her dressing room upstairs, Effa sat at her vanity and got her first good look at herself since Terrance had hit her. Her cheek was pink and puffy. A dark purple spot was beginning to form in the middle of it. The rest of her face was pale in contrast—paler than usual.

Effa rifled through her cosmetics until she found a compact and a powder brush. She began applying the powder to her face, knowing that it would take a miracle to conceal the mark.

That damn Terrance. What had she been thinking? She knew better than to start a flirtation with one of the players! Her own gut had warned her. Hell, Avis had warned her time and again that she was a grown woman playing little-girl games.

Avis . . . even when she'd had Avis in her life steering her to make better decisions, Effa had still found a way to mess things up. What was she going to do now that Avis was gone forever? God help her.

THE BRUISE HAD begun to turn into an ugly mix of purple, green, and yellow by the time Abe returned home that night. Effa had spent the evening wondering how she was going to explain the state of her face to him.

She hadn't expected that he would know everything before she opened her mouth.

Abe might as well have kicked the door down, he opened it with such force. "Effa!"

Effa sat up in bed, disoriented. "Abe?"

Abe burst into their bedroom and flipped on the light. "Let me see your face!"

"My face?" Memories from that afternoon flooded back. She held her hand to her cheek. "Now, don't get all riled up. It's really not that bad."

"I heard that bastard punched you and dragged you all over the floor!"

"It was a slap, not a punch. But how on earth did you find out?"

He came around and pulled her hand away from her face. His bottom lip began to shake with rage as he took in the extent of her injury.

"I'm sure it looks worse than it is."

Abe balled his hands into fists. "I'll kill him."

"Abe! That's taking it a bit too far."

"A bit too far? It's bad enough he tried to make a fool of me in front of the team. Him bragging about his conquests. Him bragging about you. I told you, Effa! I told you to stay away from him."

"And you were right. I promise you, I didn't go near him again. I didn't lead him on in any way. I swear."

"I don't care how good a pitcher he is. I'll show that son of a bitch." Abe stormed out of the house. He got back into his Lincoln and drove off with a screech.

Effa once again was left alone. She got up and took a look at herself in the mirror. Her reflection made her flinch. She couldn't blame Abe for his reaction. And she'd thought she looked like a mess back at the funeral!

She just hoped her husband didn't do anything to Terrance that would get either of them in a heap of trouble.

BY THE END of the next week, Abe had traded Terrance, who was the best pitcher on their roster, to one of the New York Negro teams in exchange for a rookie, who would go on to have a losing season for the Eagles, and a plate of fried chicken and waffles from the Wells Supper Club in Harlem.

Chapter 20

Newark, New Jersey
May 1945

Effa was elbow-deep in contracts when she heard a commotion on the street. Car horns honked. A woman screamed. People were singing the national anthem. She pushed aside the quote for her next baseball order, stood up, and looked out the window. "What in the world is going on down there?"

Her assistant Carrie yanked open her office door. "Mrs. Manley, they're saying the war is over!"

"What?" Effa dropped into her chair, clutching her blouse. "Are you sure? Go find out."

Carrie ran out the door and came back with a copy of a special edition of the local paper. The headline read "Germany Surrenders!"

The two women screamed and hugged. Every last shred of tension left Effa's body. Tears streamed down her face, and she didn't care who saw. The war was over. Her players would be coming home.

Carrie left the office but knocked on the door a few minutes later. "You have a call, Mrs. Manley. A woman from the Brooklyn Dodgers."

"The Brooklyn Dodgers? Did I hear you right?"

"Yes, Mrs. Manley. She's calling from Branch Rickey's office."

Effa felt her face light up at the mention of the general manager's name. Branch Rickey was her counterpart at the fabled big-league team. If his office was reaching out to hers, that could mean only one thing: The Major League was finally ready to play ball. It was turning out to be quite a day!

"Well, what are you doing still standing there? Tell me which line she's holding on."

"Line two." Carrie's face broke into a knowing grin. "And good luck," she whispered.

Effa gave Carrie a thumbs-up, then picked up the telephone receiver. "Hello, this is Mrs. Manley."

EFFA WALKED OUT of her office with a whoop a few minutes later. "He wants to meet with me. I need to speak with Abe. Carrie, can you get him on the line?"

"I'm on it."

When she finally heard Abe's voice on the phone and described the brief conversation, she felt like she was floating on air. "Yes, she said that he wants to meet with me in his office—"

"Who is she?"

"His secretary, silly. She said he wants to discuss the future of Major League Baseball now that the war is over." Effa felt breathless. This was it. The day that everyone in Negro baseball had talked about for years was finally here.

Effa and Abe had managed to hobble along in the baseball biz while war was raging in Europe and in the Pacific. At first, when the War Department started drafting the team's top talent into the U.S. military, Abe had been ready to throw in the towel. But Effa foresaw the opportunities that awaited them if they stayed in the game a little while longer.

Wartime industries sprouted up virtually overnight in New Jersey and just across the state's border in New York, and Effa was proven correct. It was not long before even the most impoverished members of the Negro community were lining their pockets with war-factory wages. And everybody turned to the local baseball teams—both white and Negro—to blow off steam while the clouds of war loomed overhead. As a result, the turnstiles at the gate were constantly spinning, and the sound was music to Effa's and Abe's ears. Each turn represented money in their pockets. They had seen record profits since the war began.

And now the war was over and the Major Leagues were calling.

"Well, that sounds good. But . . . I don't know. Doesn't it seem odd that Rickey is reaching out to you on the very day that the war ends?"

"I hear you, Abe. The call just came out of the blue. And it feels like the man is treating me like I'm at his beck and call. Have any of the other owners mentioned being contacted by Rickey?"

She tried to tamp down the nagging feeling that something was off. Rickey's office had asked for her specifically even though the baseball world knew that she and Abe almost always worked as a team, and when one of them did take the lead, it was usually Abe.

"No, they haven't said anything. But then again, who's thinking about baseball on a day like today?"

Effa laughed, in part to shoo away her own internal doubts. "Even if people are thinking about baseball, they'd be keeping their cards close to their chests. Speaking of which, we need to strategize before I go over there. Which players are we willing to part with and for how much?"

They spent the rest of the day hashing out the answers to these questions. Effa couldn't wait to meet with Branch Rickey. She just knew they could recoup all their losses from over the course of their years in baseball with just one deal!

EFFA ARRIVED AT Ebbets Field and walked into Branch Rickey's office expecting to have a one-on-one meeting with the Dodgers general manager. Instead, she found herself in the middle of a full-blown press conference.

That son of a—

Effa didn't let herself finish that thought. She was well aware of the looks thrown her way. The reporters were watching her like hawks, their eyes begging her to give them the kind of reaction that would make their news copy even juicier.

But by now, Effa was too practiced at this game to give them that satisfaction. She smiled and found a seat in the audience. She nodded at the sportswriters she recognized and introduced herself to the ones she did not. Her composure almost broke when the reporter from the *New York Times* handed her his card.

Whatever this is, it must be big. It had to be if the Dodgers' head office seriously thought they could grab headlines after yesterday's news. Effa leaned back in her seat, ready to enjoy the show.

Branch Rickey entered the office and took his place at the podium. And right behind him was Gus Greenlee, grinning like the cat that ate the canary.

Effa's stomach sank. She had seen that look on Gus's face numerous times in the past. It meant he was about to screw someone over. She had last seen it when Gus blindsided the Negro teams by resigning his post as president of the league, declaring his Pittsburgh Crawfords an independent team, and selling his stadium. Effa was pretty sure that the person who was about to be screwed over today was her.

She had been played for a fool. She just knew it.

Rickey began. "We are happy to announce the formation of the United States League, a premier minor-league system that will feed directly into the Major League. The USL will be the first step in identifying top Colored baseball talent with the ultimate goal of integrating them onto Major League teams." Rickey paused to let the implications of what he'd just said sink in.

Effa gasped, stunned. *That bastard.*

Reporters' hands immediately shot up into the air. The first person who asked a question didn't mince words. "Mr. Rickey, are you saying that the Dodgers are creating their own segregated minor-league system?"

"Yes and no. The USL will feed untapped talent into all of the Major League teams." He then proceeded to repeat every argument that she and Abe had made behind closed doors at their league meetings over the years: The Negro leagues weren't a legitimate business organization; they didn't enforce their own rules; they poached players from each other like it was the Wild West; their players weren't paid on time or sometimes at all; and so on. She would have slapped Gus Greenlee if he'd been any closer to her. He'd been playing them all along.

The next question was "What about the existing Negro baseball leagues? Do they support this?" Effa wanted to hug the reporter who'd asked that.

Branch Rickey's mouth curved into a wolfish smile. "Of course! As evidenced by the presence of Gus Greenlee, whose Pittsburgh Crawfords will be one of our inaugural teams." Rickey gestured at the grinning Gus.

Effa felt sick.

"And," Rickey continued, "Mrs. Manley from the Newark Eagles is also here to lend her support."

That rat bastard!

Effa jumped to her feet. "Then how do you explain the absence of the other Negro team owners today? Or maybe you would care to explain why your office personally invited me here for a meeting with you but neglected to mention that you planned to hold a press conference at the same time?"

Chaos erupted after Effa's questions. *Good,* she thought as she headed for the door. *It's what all of them deserve.*

Branch Rickey caught up to Effa as she pushed through the reporters and their microphones. He gently guided her into an empty office. She let him, but only because she knew he would find another way to talk to her if she didn't.

"What you did back there, Mr. Rickey, was low even for you," she said.

He closed the office door and shrugged. "I'm sorry you feel that way. It's just business. Now, how about we discuss how you can get a cut of the deal."

Effa yanked the door open. "I'll do you one better. How about you go to hell."

This time she left for real.

EFFA HELD HERSELF together long enough to make it to Newark and tell Abe about the knife Gus Greenlee had stuck in all of their backs.

"That's it, Abe. This is the beginning of the end. The Negro leagues are done."

Chapter 21

Ruppert Stadium hummed with anticipation as the first pitch was thrown out. The boys who had not donned the Eagles uniform for the past three years were back. Except now they were full-grown men, having survived a war in which so many others had perished. A few were still on their way. Second baseman Larry Doby was waiting for his military discharge papers so he could come back to his civilian life. Back to Newark Eagles baseball.

Effa sat in the owners' box, just as tense and grouchy as ever. She always got that way on opening day, the first game of the season, where all things were possible. But this year, there was an extra knot in her stomach. Not just because it was a new season or because the war was over, but because there was a new battle looming. One that in some ways had already begun. And her intuition had sounded the alarm that she would not come out as victorious as she had in the past.

"Play ball!" the umpire yelled from behind the plate. Leon Day settled himself into a crouch on the pitcher's mound before unleashing the first pitch.

The biggest surprise was waiting in the bullpen. Despite Abe's wrath driving him from the Eagles all those years ago, Terrance McDowell was back. Effa had no idea what had been said between her husband and Terrance before the pitcher returned to the team. But ever since the team came back from spring training, Terrance had steered clear of her, and she had made no attempts to speak to him. Abe had handled the contractual end of things. All Effa did was sign the man's paychecks.

She watched as Leon leaned forward with his hands on his knees, reading the catcher's signals. Behind him, the reassembled "Million-Dollar Infield" dug in the dirt and beat their fists against their gloves. Her Eagles were back. Now the only question was whether they still had the goods after three years away.

The next inning, the announcer called out Monte Irvin's name as the next hitter up to bat. Effa watched the young man walk toward the plate as the crowd cheered for him. She was grateful that Irvin was still with them on the team, taking a few practice swings before stepping into the batter's box.

Monte was no longer the teenager fresh out of high school who was still wet behind the ears with gangly arms and legs and an almost skeletal body. From the owners' box, Effa could see even better how he had filled out during his time away in the military. He was a man who couldn't be so easily swayed by the tough negotiating tactics she sometimes employed.

She'd been thinking about the anonymous phone call she had received with the tip that that damned Branch Rickey and the Brooklyn Dodgers had talked to Monte directly about signing with them to make his Major League Baseball debut. If it was true, then Rickey was not acting in good faith. Yes, finally integrating the Major League was a good thing. But deliberately going behind the backs of the Negro League owners to poach their talent was not.

Effa's eyes strayed to their bullpen and the empty seat next to Terrance where Don Newcombe should have been sitting. That no-good Rickey had already stolen one of the top players from her roster. She'd be damned if she'd let him have the satisfaction of snatching another one away. The weeks leading up to today's season opener had been a scramble to get everyone's contracts signed and a winning lineup secured, not just in time for the new season but also before white baseball general managers got their grubby little hands on the talented players who were still *her* property.

Branch Rickey had managed to seduce that Jackie Robinson fellow away from J. L. Wilkinson in Kansas City. Wilkinson was the first white team owner in Negro League baseball. Maybe he thought that he could get away with being sloppy. She and Abe didn't have that luxury. Even less so if Rickey wasn't interested in offering the courtesy of negotiation to a white Negro League owner.

They had already invested a few hundred thousand dollars of Abe's fortune into Negro baseball. And they would get back every penny of that one way or another. It was one thing to lose that money in the name of investing in the Negro community and providing good jobs for the Negroes they employed. It was another if that loss benefited only white baseball's arrogance and greed.

Thankfully, Monte had come back home to the Eagles in the end, but Effa had in no way felt relieved. Not when she had no assurances about how long the young man would stay. He was a good boy who had grown up to be a loyal man. But his loyalty to her and Abe would go only so far. Monte was married now, with a family. His first obligation would always be to earn as much as he could to support them and keep food on the table.

Effa couldn't fault him for that. She knew that the time would come when some Major League team would make him an offer that no sane person would be able to refuse. She just hoped that Monte would have a flicker of loyalty for her and Abe when it came time to negotiate the deal. They were the ones who'd plucked him from the obscurity of high school and Negro college baseball and made him a star. Well, enough of a star to pique the Major League's interest at least. And the deep pockets of Latin American baseball before that.

Yes, Monte Irvin had to feed his family. But show some damn appreciation. Even an ounce of loyalty would do.

Effa looked around. Her personal owners' box was filled with reporters and political dignitaries, including the Newark mayor and members of the city council. Those who weren't well known were the people who had proven their loyalty to her or Abe over the years. She imagined that they would call themselves her friends. But they weren't true friends in her book. Not the kind who were likely to stick up for her, to come to her aid if needed, had she not been Mrs. Abraham Manley, co-owner of a professional sports team.

They might call her by the more intimate nickname of Effie, but she doubted any of them knew that the name given to her at birth was actually Ethel.

The usual guests were also in the owners' box. Abe's associates from . . . wherever. They nodded at her, wide smiles on their faces. Their female companions waved at her. She didn't wave in return. Her nerves allowed only a small smile and a nod. They had a long road ahead of them this season. If Avis were here, she would've said something clever to get Effa out of her own head.

By now, everyone in that box was aware that Effa did not like to lose. At anything. She wasn't built for it. All she knew was that she was going to be a mess if they didn't have a winning season this year.

Chapter 22

Newark, New Jersey
July 1946

The season was halfway over and Effa's nerves were even worse now than when it had begun. It was their last game before the midseason East-West game, the Negro League version of the All-Star Game. The Eagles were in first place.

Effa was in her office finishing up the stats write-up before sending it off to the Negro News Press. But she found it hard to concentrate. The irony was that, as much as she nagged the other owners about the importance of getting accurate box scores out to the press *on time*, her mind kept drifting elsewhere.

The previous week, she had had a conversation with a Newark police detective that had left her unsettled ever since. One of the Little League players the Eagles sponsored had gotten himself into some trouble with his baseball uniform on, a direct violation of the agreement they all signed when they received their uniforms. So when the youngster refused to give his parents' names when asked, the only thing for the police to do was talk to Mrs. Manley.

Damn, those were the times that she wished she hadn't

done such a good job of public relations around town. When it was all fun and games, everyone's first instinct was to call Abe. But when there was trouble? They always called Mrs. Manley.

So that's just what Detective Alfonso Lee did when little Hank Miller got caught trying to pocket a stick of chewing gum at a corner store up on the Hill. When Effa rushed over from her office to collect the ten-year-old boy, she had not been prepared for the attractive pecan-colored man in a suit who greeted her at the station.

She had never seen him before then. But now, it was like she saw him everywhere. The problem was that she liked what she saw, and she had a pretty strong hunch that Detective Lee liked her too. She just had to figure out how to let him know she was interested.

Effa tapped her pen on her wooden desk to clear her head and redirect her mind back to where it needed to be. On her work. On the Eagles. On baseball and the fact that Branch Rickey and his Brooklyn Dodgers and their famous Negro minor leaguer Jackie Robinson were slowly but surely leeching away their fans. And not just from the Eagles but from the stands of all the Negro League teams.

Whenever the Dodgers farm team out of Montreal played in the States in a metropolitan area that also had a Negro team, the ticket sales for that Negro team would plummet. Given a choice, Negro baseball fans would rather support the white baseball team with one Negro ballplayer on it than the all-Negro baseball teams.

Effa quickly finished typing up the rest of the game's results. When she was finished, she pushed back from her desk with a sigh.

The day that she and all the other Negro team owners had been dreading for the past decade was hovering over them. No, it was already here. Yes, her team was winning, but she felt like she was clinging to the edge of the Palisades for dear life.

They had arrived at the beginning of the end of Negro League baseball. Her soul ached with certainty of this truth. Those damn men. If only they had listened to her. If only they had heeded the alarm that she had been fruitlessly ringing for years.

But they had been too proud to listen to a woman, even one who was trying to help them save their businesses. And now they all would lose everything.

Chicago, Illinois
August 18, 1946

Effa took great care in picking out her outfit for the day. Her standard modus operandi was to wear something stylish and in the latest fashion to the ballpark. But today was special, so what she wore needed to be as well.

"Effa, come on!" Abe yelled from the other room. "The car's waiting on us."

"Just another minute," she called as she rushed to the mirror to apply her lipstick. When she was finished, she stood tall and gave herself one last look. The ruching wrapped around her waist like a lover's embrace. The angle of her hat brim was haughty, just the way she liked it. Effa could almost imagine herself an on-screen femme fatale along the lines of Joan Crawford or Bette Davis.

Better yet, she looked like an idealized version of herself.

She gave herself a quick nod of approval before rushing out the door.

They arrived at Comiskey Park a few minutes later. The stadium's marquee announced *Negro League East-West Game Today!* She felt less nervous at this game than she had at any other so far this season. The stakes in today's game were both high and low. The outcome wouldn't have any effect on the Eagles' first-place standings in the Negro National League. And her and Abe's cut of the gate's proceeds as team owners would boost their net profit this year into the black. Talk about a win-win.

Once inside the ballpark, Abe gave Effa a peck on her cheek, and they parted ways.

"Enjoy the game!" Effa called out after him as he began climbing the inclined walkway to the box suites. She watched him go, tensing every muscle to keep her from rushing to his side and grabbing his arm. Abe stopped for a moment and looked around, then grabbed hold of the railing as he took another step. Effa noted that he was breathing hard. When had her husband gotten so old?

Effa stepped to the side and out of the way of a family with their boisterous son leading the way. "Oh, boy, Dad! My first real-life baseball game. I can't wait to see Josh Gibson!"

Effa felt her shoulders become heavier at the mention of the Pittsburgh Crawfords' catcher. Gibson rivaled her own Biz Mackey's skills behind the plate. As a batter, the man had no rival. Babe Ruth didn't even come close. Josh Gibson was the greatest player ever to swing the bat in any league.

But it was his off-the-field troubles in the past few years that made Effa's heart want to shatter into a million pieces. He had briefly fallen into a coma a few years ago and was rumored to have a brain tumor. Amazingly, Gibson had bounced back and returned to the game not long after. That kind of physical setback would break any other man, but Gibson had resumed playing at his top form.

Effa was still baffled by the fact that the Monarchs' Jackie Robinson had become the first Negro Leaguer to be signed by a Major League team. She had no doubt that, if not for his medical history, Josh Gibson would have been first.

Effa made her way into the stadium's business office. Since Abe was the Negro National League's elected treasurer, it fell to her to represent the NNL's interests as the gate proceeds for the East-West game were accounted for and tallied. If she was lucky, she might catch an inning or two of the game.

Effa sucked her teeth as she thought of her husband sitting around with his cronies enjoying the game while she did all the work. Abe didn't know how good he had it. It must be nice to have a wife.

Newark, New Jersey
Sunday, September 29, 1946

Unlike at the East-West game, during the Negro World Series, Effa was in her favorite seat in the press box. Her Eagles had risen to the challenge like she'd known they would and had gone on to capture the NNL pennant for the second half of the season as well.

And now, Effa found herself with her stomach all tied up in knots as Monte Irvin stepped up to the plate. Her nerves were more than justified, given that it was game seven of the Negro

World Series. She thought her nerves had been bad during the first game of the series. In that game, the opposing pitcher for the Monarchs was none other than her nemesis Satchel Paige. She had purposely avoided any nosy newspapermen and that morning's headlines on her way to the park because she didn't want to catch wind of any of Paige's quotable quips at her expense. She had not become his girlfriend as he had demanded back in '37, and he had not stopped being a perpetual pain in the rear for the owners of Negro baseball.

But now, it was the top of the ninth in the last game of the series. The Eagles had taken the lead early on and never let it go. They were one out away from everything that she and Abe had worked toward over the past decade. Even the day's weather had come through—warm and humid, but comfortable—to set the scene that settled in her bones like perfection. She took a big breath. She stopped herself just short of declaring, *It's a perfect day to win a World Series.*

Effa couldn't afford to take any of the next few moments for granted. She had been here on the precipice of victory too many times in her life and had still come home empty-handed.

Like when she had been a teenager who made it to New York, only to find out she had married the wrong man.

Or when she was a grown woman who had been so careful to hold out for the right man, then found out too late that you can't have it all, even with more money than you could dream of.

And then finally, when she had obtained the power and social status she craved, then had it all snatched away with the swipe of an unknown rookie's pen across the signature page of a big-league white baseball team's contract.

Yes, victory was close enough to grasp. But even when you do everything right, one careless error could end it all.

The drama in her head was just as over the top as the one that was playing out on the field as Eagles pitcher Rufus Lewis stared down the Monarchs' Herb Souell.

Her lungs burned like they had been pierced by knives from holding her breath. Souell hit a foul ball into the stands. Lewis's next pitch landed just outside the batter's box—a ball. The drawn-out tension had Effa on the verge of screaming.

"This next one is gonna be it," she muttered. She quickly added, "One way or another." Now was not the time to assume anything and tempt fate.

A hush fell over the grandstand as thirteen thousand baseball fans leaned in with bated breath.

Lewis wound up and hurled the ball. Effa closed her eyes. She couldn't watch. She felt her body tense to the point that it felt like she had squeezed herself into one molecule. She heard the crack of the wooden bat connecting with the baseball's leather.

Her eyes flew open. She searched the outfield for the traitorous ball. Was it a hit? A foul? Or, worse, a home run?

Effa breathed a quick prayer. More of a plea, really. "Please, God, no." She scanned the field frantically. Then she realized her outfielders were running toward the infield, not the far wall. Not a homer, then. "Thank God."

She followed the gaze of everyone else at the stadium as they zeroed in on her first baseman. Lennie Pearson held his glove up, positioned himself between the foul line and the stands, smiled at the descending ball, then snatched it out of the sky.

Effa gasped. She fell back in her seat. Despite the outspo-
kenness that had become her trademark over the years, in
this moment, she could find nothing to say. Her body buzzed
like she was in a hive with thousands of bees. And then,
nothing. All feeling was gone. Everything was numb.

For all she knew, she might have just died. And she wouldn't
have cared. They had won. Her Newark Eagles were the champions of the Negro leagues.

Chapter 23

Newark, New Jersey
June 1947

Back in April, Jackie Robinson had made the dreams of Negro America come true when he donned the Brooklyn Dodgers uniform for the first time. That was the beginning of the nightmare for Negro League baseball owners across the country. They were all losing money left and right.

As Effa recalled the empty stands from the past few games, she could already see the hit to their profits caused by Rickey's thievery. Her Eagles had won the Negro League championship last year, yet the stands were nowhere close to being as full today as they were at their home opener. Yes, the take from the turnstiles should cover all their operating expenses for the day. But whatever was left for her and Abe to take home would be painfully meager.

Effa was glad that the midseason East-West game was on the horizon. She needed a break from the daily heartbreak of dwindling ticket sales. Hell, she needed the money. Without the proceeds from last year's East-West game, they would not have broken even.

Effa was packing up for the day when Abe stuck his head in her office. She looked up and smiled at him. "I'll be ready in a minute."

At the height of the season, it was rare for Abe to be in the office. He still traveled with the team for their away trips. Even when the team had a home series, he didn't come in that often. Abe was either at the Grand Hotel holding court with his buddies or out at an area park scouting the up-and-coming high-school talent.

"Take your time. I'm heading over to the Grand. Gotta make sure the boys are following my 'no girls' rule tonight. Just wanted to let you know that you should expect a call from Bill Veeck tomorrow."

Effa went still at the mention of the man who owned the Cleveland Indians and the casual way the name rolled off Abe's tongue like it was no big deal. It was in fact a very big deal. It made her heart race with excitement. And at the same time, it made her stomach drop with dread.

Which one of her boys would be leaving them? So far, only the Brooklyn Dodgers had welcomed Negro players—Jackie Robinson, Roy Campanella, and Don Newcombe—onto their team. Effa felt the heat rise up the back of her neck every time she thought of how that blasted Branch Rickey has stolen away Newcombe, the star of their pitching rotation. For all his purported Methodist piety, he had not compensated the Manleys for the resulting broken contract. She had taken her very valid complaint to the Major League Baseball commissioner's office but had not yet received a response.

Effa knew better than to hold her breath.

But none of the American League teams had added a Negro

Leaguer to their rosters. If Bill Veeck was about to come sniffing, she planned on giving him hell. She wouldn't stand in the
way of any of her players' big break into the majors. But, damn
it, this time, she would make the majors pay.

"FINE. IF HE stays on for thirty days, I'll give you fifteen thousand for him."

Effa was beyond stunned. First, Bill Veeck had done her the
courtesy of coming to meet her in person on her home turf.
Now, she had talked him up from ten thousand for Larry Doby.
On the one hand, he had done her the courtesy of treating
her organization like the legitimate business operation it was,
respecting the existing contract they had with Doby. On the
other hand, the too-low dollar amount had Effa smarting like
she'd been slapped in the face.

She was stuck between a rock and a hard place. If she pro-
tested and blew the deal, she would ruin Larry's chance for
the big time and earn herself all of Negro America's ire for
standing in the way of racial progress. But if she said nothing,
she would lose another one of her star players for pennies and
she would be forced to grin and bear it.

"You know if Larry were white, you would have offered me
one hundred thousand, and that still would be a bargain."

Bill held her gaze. "Fifteen thousand after thirty days. That
is my final offer, Mrs. Manley."

The bastard. He was putting the screws to her, and she
had no choice but to be happy that she was getting even this
pittance.

"Fine. But you have to promise me one thing. We pay Larry
four thousand per season. He's earned it. I have no doubt that

he will earn that and more on the field for you. We've heard rumors that the Dodgers are paying their former Negro Leaguers next to nothing. You've got to promise me that you will pay Larry the same rate or better. Because we both know he's worth it."

Effa caught a gleam of respect shining from Veeck's eyes. He nodded. "Deal. You have my word, Mrs. Manley. As long as Doby plays for me, he will receive not less than five thousand dollars. You can take that to the bank."

Effa smiled at him. "I plan to."

"I know you do, Mrs. Manley. You've developed quite the reputation for being a pain in the tail when it comes to getting what you want."

"And that, *you* can take to the bank, Mr. Veeck."

"Now that that's settled, would you care to be my guest at Larry's first game as a Cleveland Indian?"

WHEN LARRY DOBY made his Major League Baseball debut, he became the first Negro to play for a team in the American League and the second, after Jackie Robinson, to play in the Major Leagues. The next day, Effa received a note from Lucy Richards. This was the first time she'd heard from the woman in years. Mrs. Richards's message contained only two words: *Well done.*

Chapter 24

Newark, New Jersey
Summer 1948

Looking back on that moment when the Eagles won the Negro World Series, Effa thought it might have been better if she had had a heart attack right as the championship trophy was put into her hands. It definitely would have made for a better story. One, Effa liked to think, that would have overshadowed the season that followed.

The box-office ticket sales during the 1947 season had been the worst she and Abe had ever seen despite the Eagles being the reigning league champions. Once Jackie Robinson made his rookie debut with the Brooklyn Dodgers, Negro League fans ran in droves to every game the Dodgers played, at home or away, to show their support. The losses were such that Abe had said, "Enough. That's it. I'm done."

And this time he meant it. By the time opening day of 1948 rolled around, she and Abe had sold the Newark Eagles to a Memphis dentist, who then moved the team to Houston. The players on the team still had jobs—for now, anyway. But the hardest part about walking away from the game Effa loved so much was knowing that their Newark-based Negro workers were now without the jobs that their organization had provided each game day.

That bittersweet reality did not take away from the thrill of the previous day's shopping spree. Monte Irvin, the local protégé she and Abe had molded into a baseball superstar, had made his Major League debut with the New York Giants. When they sold the Newark Eagles franchise, part of the deal was that the Manleys would get a cut of any proceeds if any of the players' contracts were sold to a Major League team. That's what happened in Monte's case.

When the Irvin check arrived, Abe agreed that Effa could spend it however she saw fit. Which was why she now had the long-desired full-length mink coat hanging in her closet. It was what she deserved after all she had sacrificed for this thing called baseball.

Effa's days now were no less busy. She still had her responsibilities with the local NAACP and other charity work. But her days felt less full. She couldn't help but feel aimless. She had exceeded her professional expectations by a mile before she had reached the age of fifty. But she had done it at the expense of her own dreams and without having built any close friendships. She felt like she didn't have anything to show for her life except a scrapbook full of newspaper articles and the silver trophy in her living room that she polished every week. What did a woman like her do now that she'd reached and passed her peak?

Effa suspected that the loss of baseball from their everyday lives affected Abe just as much as it did her. He still spent almost all his time at the Grand Hotel, but a regular afternoon there didn't have the same magic as it had right after a game with all the players and fans mingling.

When he came home from the Grand, Abe would just sit in the living room and look out the front window. The radio wasn't on most of the time when he did this. Abe had always been a quiet man. But now? He was . . . quieter.

"Abe, honey, are you okay?"

He took his time in responding, opting to shift around in his easy chair to get more comfortable first. "I'm fine. It just feels odd not to be at the ballpark on a day like this."

Effa glanced out the window in the direction Abe was looking. She saw a clear blue sky between the buildings and trees on their street. A gentle breeze made the leaves sway. She understood what Abe meant. It was a perfect day for a baseball game.

"You're right. Maybe we can go for a drive to some of the nearby parks after dinner. Maybe some of the kids around here will have put together a pickup game."

"Humph, maybe." Abe picked up the newspaper on the table and began to unfold it.

Effa went back to the kitchen and resumed busying herself with making a carrot raisin salad. It was much too hot outside to bother with a dish that required the oven. And quite frankly, she just didn't feel like it. Grating the carrots would keep her hands and her mind busy. Baking and broiling required too much waiting. She would go mad sitting around waiting for the timer to chime.

How about getting back to that hat-store dream of yours? she'd thought more than a few times of late. But it just didn't excite her as much. It felt too much like starting from scratch. And she didn't have that kind of patience anymore. She had had a taste of real power in an all-male empire via her role with the Eagles. How could making hats compete with that?

Abe rustled the pages of the newspaper as he turned them. After about fifteen minutes of this, she took her apron off and put the finished salad in the icebox. One thing she knew was that if she was stuck in the house with her husband much longer, she would kill him.

"Abe, please go find something to do. Outside of this house, please. You're driving me batty."

Abe smiled. "You do remember what happened the last time you told me that, right?"

"You went and bought a baseball team," Effa said. "On second thought, I'll go with you. Whatever our next adventure will be, this time we need to start it together."

Ashland, Kentucky
July 1980

Effa Manley had her mink coat draped around her shoulders as the hired car drove her to the second annual Negro Leagues Baseball Reunion. Despite the summer's heat, she had not hesitated to pack it in her suitcase. Effa had been asked to give the keynote speech tonight. Her boys would be there to see her. She had to look her best.

With that thought, she whipped out her pocket mirror to check her lipstick. The increased lines around her mouth created unwanted lanes for the red color to flow into. She dabbed at the corner of her mouth with a tissue.

How she looked had become more important to her now that her health had become a challenge. She cared not a whit about her doctor's appeals to bow out of this trip. How ridiculous! She was the last of the Negro League owners alive. Well, from the good old days, anyway. There was no one left who could tell Abe's story. "No, our story," she corrected herself.

"What was that, Mrs. Manley?" The limo driver's blue eyes checked on her in the rearview mirror.

"Nothing. Just freshening up."

"Very good. We'll be there in a moment."

Effa nodded. The driver returned his attention to the road. She leaned back into the buttery leather of the limousine's seat. The luxurious upholstery was nice, but it had nothing on Abe's old Lincoln. Sturdy, dependable, long-lasting, classy. Like her mink.

Feeling its weight around her shoulders made her feel like her old self again. Effa went back to checking herself in the mirror and dabbing at her lips one more time. There—she not only looked fabulous; she felt like she was in control of everything.

Control was a hot topic in baseball now that player free agency had taken root. Reggie Jackson, a Black player on the white Yankees team, caused a brouhaha by proclaiming himself the sole reason the team had had back-to-back World Series wins in '77 and '78. Effa had laughed when he'd said that he, not team owner George Steinbrenner, was the straw that stirred the drink in that clubhouse.

Effa fluffed her collar.

"Oh, honey," she murmured to her reflection. "I'm the

reason the majors let you even touch the straw, much less enjoy the drink."

THE HUMID KENTUCKY air enveloped Effa the moment she stepped out of the car. The event handler, a man named Stultz, was there to greet her. "It's an honor to have you here, Mrs. Manley. Let me help you with that." He reached out to ease the fur from her shoulders. She leaned just out of his reach, much to the dismay of her right hip.

"Thank you, but that won't be necessary." She shifted her weight off her hip and back onto her cane. The pain in her hip dissipated like a sigh of relief. She had had more than one health scare in the last year. No need to add unnecessary injuries to the list.

The space between the man's eyes wrinkled. "But, ma'am, aren't you hot?"

"Of course I'm hot. I look good, don't I?" Effa laughed. She imagined she looked ridiculous wearing such a heavy garment in the middle of the summer. Her sense of vanity required it. This mink represented her greatest accomplishment in professional baseball—the moment when she had triumphed against all odds in her personal showdown at the bottom of the ninth.

Effa spied a flash of gold on more than a few of the former players' fingers. No one was asking them to take off the mementos they earned from their greatest victories in the game. So why should she have to take off hers?

Once she was inside the Elks Lodge, the first familiar face she saw was Monte Irvin's. With the help of her cane, she picked up her pace. But she had to stop short when a salt-and-pepper-haired white man stepped in front of her, took Monte's hand into his own, and began to pump it furiously.

How rude, Effa thought. She was more than ready to lecture the man on how to conduct himself in the presence of an elderly lady. But the words stayed lodged in her throat.

The man's eyes went wide once he had captured Monte's attention. A flush spread across his face. He transformed from a middle-aged man to an awestruck schoolboy meeting his idol. Effa smiled at the sight, which instantly took her back forty years to the now demolished Ruppert Stadium in Newark.

"Oh, wow, Monte . . . I mean Mr. Irvin. I've been a fan of yours forever." The man spoke so fast that he had to gulp for air. "Can I please—if you don't mind—can I please have your autograph?"

Monte threw Effa an apologetic look. She nodded in understanding. It wasn't every day that the former young boys of Kentucky had the chance to see their baseball heroes in person.

That nod of understanding didn't mean that Effa's pride hadn't been bruised. There had been a time when sports reporters flocked to her side whenever she entered a room. A time when, if it looked like Effa Manley had something to say, people stopped to listen.

But today, it could have been that first Negro National League owners' meeting in 1935 all over again. No one seemed to care that she was there. The young people—and let's face it, she was eighty-three years old, so they were all young to her—rushed past her to get to the men whose recognizable faces adorned the trading cards in their hands.

Once again, Effa was made to feel out of place, and just like back then, she didn't like it.

Monte made a beeline for Effa as soon as he was finished scribbling his name on the man's baseball card.

"Hello there, Mr. Hall of Fame." Monte Irvin was the first of her boys to be inducted into Cooperstown. No doubt a result of her relentless letter-writing campaign for former Negro leagues to be considered.

"Sorry about that, Mrs. Manley." His voice was as apologetic as the expression on his face.

"It's all right. I imagine that fan will kick himself when he finds out who I am and realizes that I'm the reason you were on the Giants in the first place."

"Only a privileged few will ever know who the real boss behind the Negro leagues was and appreciate how much she's done for all of baseball, Black and white."

"Well, as long as you boys know." Effa patted Monte's arm as he guided her into the dining area. "That's what matters."

The words sounded nice coming out of her mouth, even if it was nothing but malarkey. Effa Manley wanted everyone to know who she was and what she had done. Unfortunately, she knew that most of the world would never care.

"That fur you have on is sharp. But isn't it kind of warm for a mink? It must be seventy-five degrees outside." Effa must not have done a good job of masking her true feelings. That was the only reason she could think of for Monte's obvious appeal to her vanity.

"You know me." She smiled. "It could've been one hundred seventy-five degrees today and I still would have worn it. I have to look good for my boys."

"Leave it to you, Mrs. Manley, to find a way to make every man here do a double take in your direction." Monte wasn't wrong. She had noticed more than a few men throwing long, lingering looks in her direction. And the few women who were there either rolled their eyes at her or frowned. Each time made Effa's insides warm. Not from the heat outside or from inside her coat, but from pride. Monte shook his head. They were exactly the reactions that Effa was going for. No one was ignoring her anymore. At least, not today.

When they reached the dais, Monte studied her for a moment. Finally, he asked, "Say, that wouldn't be the mink you bought when you sold my contract to the Giants back in '48?"

"Of course it is." Effa threw back her head and laughed. "It still looks good and it keeps me warm."

THE GATHERING QUICKLY took on the air of a good old-fashioned family reunion. Around fifty former Negro Leaguers were in attendance. She was happy to see that almost all of her Million-Dollar Infield was in attendance too. A wave of sadness washed over her as she took note of the ones who weren't there.

"It's a shame you didn't live to see this, Abe," she whispered. Images of Cum Posey, Alex Pompez, and even Gus Greenlee flashed before her eyes. None of them had wanted her to be a part of their boys' club at first. But all of them had come to respect her in the end. "All of you should be here to see this."

Monte stood and went to the podium. "I don't know why they asked me to introduce the lady being honored tonight. You all know who she is and what she's done for us. I'm just grateful that I get another chance to tell her thank you. Ladies and gentlemen, Mrs. Effa Manley."

Marrying Abe had been the smartest thing she'd ever done when it came to her interactions with men. That marriage had been the longest-lasting of her four trips to the altar. The two husbands she'd had after him hadn't stuck around long, each marriage lasting barely a year.

Henry Clinton had gotten her to say "I do" to him in 1953, almost a year to the day after Abe died. That should have been the first omen that she was back to making poor decisions again. But she hadn't learned her lesson. She divorced her fourth and final husband in 1957. He had run off with a right smart amount of the money Abe had left her.

In the end, Mother had been right. Marriage was best treated as a business transaction. To marry for love was foolish.

The applause that followed Monte's remarks brought Effa back to the present. She pushed those memories out of her mind. This wasn't a night to rehash all the things she had done wrong in her life but to reflect on what she had done right.

"Thank you. I see the lot of you flashing those fancy World Series rings on your fingers. Impressive." Effa stroked the fur pelt that hung around her shoulders. She buried her face in the collar for added effect. "But not as impressive as what Abe got me after I sold the first Negro League contract to the major leagues."

The audience—her boys—roared with laughter at that one. As she beamed, Effa could hear Abe's voice in her ear: *You still got it, Effie. You still got it!*

"Yes, I do," she whispered. Then to the Negro Leaguers before her: "But I'm still not satisfied. I won't be until each and every player in this room is recognized by the Baseball Hall of Fame for their contributions in the old Negro leagues and to the sport in general."

And then Effa Manley proceeded to give all of baseball— both Black and white—one last piece of her mind.

Author's Note

The real-life Effa Manley was a woman of color. Some people will argue that she was one hundred percent white biologically, based on her appearance and her reported parentage. Given that Mrs. Manley passed away before DNA testing for ancestry became commercially available and that she had no children, we will never know for sure. But I do know that census records have her maternal grandfather listed as either "mulatto" or Native American. At the very least, she was one-eighth non-white, and that was enough for her to be classified and treated as "other" during her lifetime. On top of that, she was raised in an African American household with African American siblings. On this basis, I chose to portray my fictionalized Effa as a fair-skinned woman who self-identified as African American or Negro.

Most of the published nonfiction material about Effa Manley focuses on her career as a baseball executive. However, Mrs. Manley led just as interesting a life outside the Eagles' front office as she did within it. I wanted to breathe more life into her experiences before and during that time. Thank goodness for the society pages in the Black newspapers during her active years. The *New York Age* and the *Chicago Defender* noted her social activities. I found a surprising amount of information about Mrs. Manley in the footnotes of works that had nothing to do with baseball, among them an academic text about African American retail-shopping experiences and a book chronicling the history of her first husband's family.

Speaking of unrelated subject matter . . . Effa Manley's scrapbook contains mementos from friends who were part of the Broadway theater community. Andy Razaf, who wrote the lyrics to "The Joint Is Jumpin'" and "Stompin' at the Savoy," was one. She was often associated with Avis Blake in the society pages, which is why I made Avis an important secondary character in the novel. Avis Blake was the first wife of composer Eubie Blake, cocreator of the first successful all-Black Broadway show, *Shuffle Along*.

I wound up reading the history of *Shuffle Along* and the history of Black Broadway to flesh out Mrs. Blake's character. I am so glad I did because I picked up something that previous Effa Manley researchers had missed or overlooked. There was a point in the late 1930s when she began acting out of character and making poor choices. In short, Effa was messy. It was rumored that she was having an affair with one of her players and there were whispers that this same player smacked her around in the train station. Another great Effa story was that she petitioned the State Department to revoke Satchel Paige's passport in an attempt to force him to report to the Eagles' spring-training camp.

Some of it is baseless gossip and some of it is documented. But all of the strange behavior, true or not, popped up around the same time that her friend Avis Blake died from tuberculosis in 1939.

If you believe the newspaper reports, Effa was a hot-to-trot interloper who needed to stay out of men's business. However, I believe that Effa Manley was spiraling as she grieved the death of a close friend who died too young.

This would be a good time to note that I watered down the "coarse" language that my fictionalized Avis Blake uses in the book. Evidently, when the real-life Avis Blake was with her friends behind closed doors, her language was as blunt as Lil' Kim's first album (and contained just as many N-bombs!).

I also want to address the liberties I took in telling Effa's story. Older Effa Manley biographies talk about an alleged affair she had with one of her players and suggest that her second husband, Abe Manley, had had an accident that affected their sexual relationship. I have no way of proving that she had an affair with the man in question. But what if she had? How would that have played out? And I won't ever know the intimate details of her marital relationship, but what if the speculation about Abe was true? How would that have played out between a wealthy Black couple in the 1930s?

I thought playing with these ideas made the story more interesting. To be fair to that real player's memory, I used a fictitious name for Effa's alleged love interest on the team. I also tried to portray the fictionalized Abe's condition in a way that maintained the dignity of the real-life Abe's memory.

If you'd like to learn more about Effa Manley's real life, I recommend starting with *Baseball's Leading Lady: Effa Manley and the Rise and Fall of the Negro Leagues* by Andrea Williams.

Acknowledgments

First of all, I'd like to thank Effa Manley. For existing. For her ambition. For her courage to be herself when the (male) world probably wanted her to shut up and go back into the kitchen. It has been an honor getting to know you. May you receive all the flowers your heart desires.

Thank you to my editors, Tessa and Madelyn, for putting up with me and my unpredictable life. One day, I will finish a book without the rest of the world imploding around me.

To the HarperCollins marketing, publicity, and production teams: Thank you for all that you do. You are the ones who make the magic happen.

Thank you to my agent, Kevan, for always having my back.

To the Divas and Lyonesses: Thank you for keeping me sane.

To Cassidy and the rest of the Baseball Hall of Fame staff, thank you for letting me (gasp!) touch—I mean review—Effa Manley's scrapbook. I hope my fangirling in your hallowed halls wasn't too disruptive.

To my Always in Style JJ peeps and my Spelman peeps: You make me strive to be a better me. Each and every one of you.

Shout-out to everyone who knew the die-hard Yankees fan

in the white Starter jacket, the tweenaged, mouthful-of-braces, tomboy me. OMG, they let me write a baseball book!

A special shout-out to Sis, who tweeted that she almost missed her flight because she was talking a stranger into buying a copy of *Sisters in Arms* off the rack at EWR. I think about you often. You are a real one.

Thank you to my friends and family for tolerating #DraftHell me, #RevisionHell me, and #CopyeditHell me.

To my daughter: Mommy can play with you now.

To D, thank you for holding it down while I'm off doing my author thing.

About the Author

KAIA ALDERSON is a women's historical fiction author with a passion for discovering "hidden figures" in African American women's history. Her specific areas of interest are women's military history, popular music, women in sports, upper-middle-class African American society, and women's international travel. She holds a sociology degree from Spelman College and a master's degree in education from the University of West Georgia. She honed her writing chops at the Hurston/Wright Foundation's and VONA's writing workshops.

DISCOVER MORE BY
KAIA ALDERSON

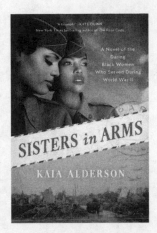

Kaia Alderson's debut historical fiction novel reveals the untold true story of the Six Triple Eight, the only all-Black battalion of the Women's Army Corps, who made the dangerous voyage to Europe to ensure American servicemen received word from their loved ones during World War II.

"Based on the true story of the 6888th Postal Battalion, *Sisters in Arms* gives readers an inside look at the racial injustices and rigors of wartime that the women battled. Alderson sweeps readers in with Grace's and Eliza's personal journeys through a little-known portion of our army's history. Themes of female friendship, bravery, and resilience radiate from the pages of this magnificent novel."

—*Booklist* (starred review)

"This is not just another World War II story; this is a stirring and timely novel about the only all-Black battalion of the Women's Army Auxiliary Corps, a group of women who had to fight resolutely against countless obstacles in order to be permitted to serve their country. Grace and Eliza stole my heart with their spirit and their resilience, and the ups and downs of their tumultuous friendship made me laugh and cry. Poignant and powerful—an untold story that you simply must read."

—Natasha Lester,
New York Times bestselling author of *The Paris Secret*

"A thrilling anthem to the courageous sisterhood of the Six Triple Eight as they faced down racism at home and war abroad. *Sisters in Arms* is a fresh look at the bold women who served America during World War II. A powerful debut!"

—Stephanie Marie Thornton,
USA Today bestselling author of *A Most Clever Girl*

DISCOVER GREAT AUTHORS, EXCLUSIVE OFFERS, AND MORE AT HC.COM.